ELLORA'S CAVEMEN

DREAMS OF THE OASIS

ELLORA'S CAVE
ROMANTICA PUBLISHING

An Ellora's Cave Romantica Publication

www.ellorascave.com

Ellora's Cavemen: Dreams of the Oasis I

ISBN # 1419955810
ALL RIGHTS RESERVED.

Edited by Raelene Gorlinsky.
Cover design by Darrell King. Photography by Dennis Roliff.

Electronic book Publication March 2006
Trade Paperback Publication April 2006

Warning:

The following material contains graphic sexual content meant for mature readers. *Ellora's Cavemen: Dreams of the Oasis I* has been rated E–rotic by a minimum of three independent reviewers.

Ellora's Cave Publishing offers three levels of Romantica™ reading entertainment: S (S-ensuous), E (E-rotic), and X (X-treme).

S-*ensuous* love scenes are explicit and leave nothing to the imagination.

E-*rotic* love scenes are explicit, leave nothing to the imagination, and are high in volume per the overall word count. In addition, some E-rated titles might contain fantasy material that some readers find objectionable, such as bondage, submission, same sex encounters, forced seductions, and so forth. E-rated titles are the most graphic titles we carry; it is common, for instance, for an author to use words such as "fucking", "cock", "pussy", and such within their work of literature.

X-*treme* titles differ from E-rated titles only in plot premise and storyline execution. Unlike E-rated titles, stories designated with the letter X tend to contain controversial subject matter not for the faint of heart.

Ellora's Cavemen: Dreams of the Oasis I

The Ambassador's Widow

By Myla Jackson

~9~

Call Me Barbarian

By Liddy Midnight

~57~

Spontaneous Combustion

By Nicole Austin

~103~

Dragonmagic

By Allyson James

~147~

Fallen For You

By Paige Cuccaro

~195~

The Joining

By Jory Strong

~237~

THE AMBASSADOR'S WIDOW

Myla Jackson

Trademarks Acknowledgement

~

Chapter One

ഇ

"Alone at last." Andre Batello leaned back on the canvas lounger, the hot, salty sea air washing over him. No other agent within miles, no boss, no mission to deal with. Blessed silence intermingled with the shoosh of waves shifting the sand along the shoreline.

He'd worked hard over the past eighteen months and deserved this vacation—no, needed this vacation—to replenish his strength, mind and soul. Working as a top-secret Chameleon agent had taken its toll. It was nice to lie back in his own skin, letting the world rush by while he relaxed at a beach bum pace. The cell phone and pager were off and he'd left no forwarding address when he'd checked out at the agency.

With one leg dangling over the side of the lounger, his toes dipping into the warm sands of the Koubes Beach in Crete, he couldn't remember a time he'd been more relaxed.

"Sir?"

Feigning sleep, Andre ignored the tentative feminine voice.

"Sir?"

Couldn't the woman take a hint? With a frown, Andre edged one eye open. "Yes?"

A young woman in the khaki shorts and loud Hawaiian shirt that was the uniform for the wait staff at the hotel leaned over his lounger, a pencil poised over a pad of paper. "Would you like a drink from the bar?" Her heavily accented

English was correct and attractive. At any other time he'd have considered it lovely, if he hadn't been craving silence.

"If I'd wanted a drink, I'd have ordered it before I lay down." He couldn't help the impatient sarcasm. All he wanted was to be left alone. A-L-O-N-E.

The woman's face flushed a mottled red and she backed up a step and gushed, "I'm sorry sir, today's my first day on the job and I was just trying to be helpful. Please accept my apology if I've disturbed you. I won't bother you again."

Guilt erased his impatience and Andre forced a smile to ease the woman's obvious discomfort. Just because he was tired didn't give him the right to browbeat the staff. "Thank you for asking. I'll take orange juice." He settled back, closing his eyes again. There, now that he'd done his good deed for the day maybe the girl would leave and let him get back to his nap.

"Sir? Would that be with or without ice?"

How difficult could a glass of orange juice be? Andre, his eyes determinedly closed, inhaled a slow, deep breath and blew it out before answering. "No ice."

Instead of relaxing, he strained to hear the sound of feet shifting through sand as the waitress scurried back to the bar to collect his drink. When he didn't hear the sand shushing, Andre peeped an eye open.

Fuck. She was still standing there, and now she was biting her lip.

"What?" he demanded.

"Did you want a large orange juice or a small one?"

The tenuous thread holding his control in check snapped. "I don't even want the damned orange juice, I just want peace and quiet!"

The lip she'd been biting trembled. Great, now she'd cry.

"Okay, okay." He sat up and fished in his pocket for a twenty-euro bill. "Make it a large orange juice, no ice, keep the change and don't bother me when you come back with the juice."

"Yes, sir." She snatched the twenty and ran for the bar.

Andre shook his head and breathed several calming breaths before he could lie back down to take his much-deserved nap. Just as his heart rate returned to normal and he'd allowed his eyes to resume the napping position, he heard the sound of sand shushing toward him.

"Sir?" The waitress voice was a mere whisper as if she were afraid.

"Give me back my twenty," he muttered.

"I'm sorry sir, but the telephone is for you."

He refused to open his eyes. "No one knows I'm here."

"You are Andre Batello, yes?"

"Yes." Okay, so he propped a single eye open.

"The woman insists on speaking with you." The waitress reached out as far as her arm could stretch without getting too close to him. What did she think he'd do, bite her?

Actually, at the rate his vacation was beginning, Andre might just consider biting the head off the next person who dared to wake him. "Give me the phone." He snatched the cordless telephone from the girl. "What?"

"Touchy, aren't we?" Melody Jones' amused voice sounded over the line.

On most occasions he wouldn't be bothered by the sound of one of his team but when he'd left the office, he'd left specific instructions not to be disturbed. "I'm on vacation."

"I know." Andre could almost see Melody's mouth twisting in a wry grin and a frown pushing her eyebrows to the center. "But this is an emergency."

"It's always an emergency."

"The boss says this could mean the difference between a thirty-year war going on for another thirty years and peace."

"Yeah, and if I don't get a vacation—an uninterrupted vacation—there could be a major meltdown on the island of Crete in the next twenty seconds."

"Come on, Andre. You can't be having that much fun. I hear there was a shark attack not five miles from your location. Killed a man. How much fun can it be with sharks swimming in the ocean?"

With a snort, Andre responded. "I should thank the shark. The beach is nearly empty, just the way I like it."

"Andre, William Payton died of a heart attack a little less than an hour ago. They need you to cover for him ASAP."

Andre draped an arm over his face and held the phone away from his ear for a moment before responding. He hated asking, but knew he had to. "And why should I care?"

"Payton is the ambassador to the former British colony of Tebakistan and the mediator between the three major southwest Asian nations, Kurkistan, Padel, and Tebakistan. After thirty years of incessant fighting, they're on the verge of signing a peace treaty."

"So, now they have a dead mediator. What's it to me?"

"The media hasn't gotten wind yet. We think we can fill in for him until the peace treaty can be signed."

"I feel the *If* coming."

"That's right. If you can get here in the next three hours. The talks resume at nine o'clock in the morning. The ambassador's staff sent word that the ambassador is not feeling well and decided to rest for a few hours. But he has to be in place by the morning. The sooner you get here, the quicker the transition."

"What part of 'I'm on vacation' did you not understand?"

"Andre…"

He hated when his partner used her "but please" wheedling voice. It crawled right under his skin and refused to be ignored. What was the old anti-drug commercial? Just say… "No."

"But the countries have been fighting for decades."

Her wheedling tone slid under the skin on his forehead and sent sharp needles of pain to his temples. He reached up to rub at the offensive stabs. "So what's a measly two more weeks?"

"If the negotiations stop now, they may never have peace." She sighed.

Uh-oh. Andre could picture Melody shifting in her chair, or rather shifting strategies. With a deep breath, Andre braced for her final assault, an appeal to his honor.

"Could you live with yourself knowing you might have helped the people of these countries to find happiness, but your vacation was more important?"

Zing. As true as any arrow could ever fly. She'd hit her target. Guilt was a powerful weapon. "That's dirty pool."

"Could you?" She didn't deny or acknowledge his accusation.

"I haven't had a vacation in over a year. I'm tired, I'm cranky and I haven't had sex in—"

"Okay, okay. I'll tell Tanner you're not interested in world peace. Forget I called. Go back to your vacation and I hope you get a suntan." She didn't have to add the words, *while people are dying in the fighting between Kurkistan, Padel, and Tebakistan.* The words hung in the subspace between Melody's mouth and Andre's conscience.

Andre sat straight in his chair. "I give up."

"Good," Melody's cheerful voice chirped over the line. "We'll be there, well, now, actually—"

Before she could finish her sentence, the roar of helicopter blades filled the sky as a helicopter blitzed in from over Andre's head and landed on the beach a few feet away. The spinning blades whipped the sand, creating a giant sand blaster for anything within fifty yards of the helicopter. Umbrellas toppled, people scattered and the towel draped over the top of Andre's lounge chair flipped up and slapped him in the face.

Fuck. Shielding his eyes from the blasting sand, Andre lurched to his feet, regret slicing through him for another vacation sacrificed to the good of mankind. Melody hopped out the side of the aircraft and waved Andre to hurry.

"I'll take my own sweet time," he muttered, his words whipped away by the beating rotor. The lounger seemed to hunch in the middle like a giant inchworm and then it folded and slammed into the ground, signaling the end of his dreams of an uninterrupted nap. A nap he'd hoped to be followed by reading the sports page—uninterrupted—and then canvassing the beach for the most beautiful babe in a bikini for a little physical recreation.

"Andre! We have to hurry!" Melody's voice vied with the roar of the helicopter.

Unfortunately Andre could hear her and he knew he had to go.

As he trudged forward, another voice called out behind him, "Sir!"

Andre turned to see the windblown waitress plowing through the sand, carrying a glass of orange juice.

A great start to a new day in the world of a Chameleon.

"Okay, give me everything you've got." Andre settled in his seat on the small Lear jet blasting through the sky en route to Padel. Having showered at the hangar, he wore sweats and a T-shirt, preferring to make the transformation in clothing that didn't bind and had a little give.

Sean O'Banion leaned over Andre and pressed a button on the panel above him. A computer screen dropped down and blinked to life. "Here's all the footage we could muster on the man and we provided notes from one of our operatives on the inside."

"What about DNA?"

Melody handed him a jacket with several brown hairs scattered across the shoulders. "Try this. It was the jacket they found on him when he died."

Andre turned the jacket over. Armani. The guy had taste.

"No one saw him croak but our operative. We think we got him out in time, the press didn't get wind."

Andre knew how the agency worked. The less the press knew, the more easily a Chameleon blended in.

"For now." Melody sat in the leather seat next to Andre and crossed one leg over the other. "But we can only hold them off so long. When the ambassador doesn't show up for the meeting tomorrow morning, the media will be all over it."

"So how much time does that really buy us?" Andre's gaze remained on the screen.

"Since only our operatives know he's dead, we have until he doesn't show up in his room tonight."

"Why should that matter?"

"His wife will worry."

"Wait a minute. You guys didn't say anything about a wife." Andre leaned back in his chair and held up his hands.

Melody laid a hand on his arm. "Keep your shirt on, big guy. They're somewhat estranged."

"Somewhat?" Andre's eyebrows rose. "Define 'somewhat'."

"Insiders say they sleep in separate rooms and as far as anyone knows, they haven't made love in months."

Muscles knotting in his belly, Andre had a sudden feeling of being trapped. "You know how I feel about widows. I don't do widows. You can turn this plane around right now. I'm not doing it."

"They're estranged, for Pete's sake." Melody leaned forward. "We need you in there, Andre. That treaty has to be signed and you're the best we've got."

"Why don't you get someone else?"

"You were the closest."

"Can't you do it yourself?" Andre pushed a hand through his hair and stared without seeing the man on the screen in front of him. The guy had a wife.

"I can't transform into a man and you know that. Even Chameleons have limitations. Sex changes aren't one of them."

"But you can fake the looks, even if not the sex."

"We can't risk it." Melody stood and paced the short aisle down the middle of the plane. "If someone discovers our deception, the entire negotiation process will become null and void. The Chameleon that goes in has to look exactly like Payton from the top of his head to…well, all the other necessary body parts."

Andre hunched down in the chair a frown settling between his eyes. "I don't like it when widows are involved."

"It can't be helped. Just stick to the estrangement and everything will be fine. No emotional entanglements, no unwanted sex — and I emphasize the unwanted part. If you find her attractive…"

Andre slammed his hand against the armrest. "I don't do widows."

"Not every widow is as weak as Patina Gorchev." Melody stopped next to his seat and rested her hand on his shoulder. "It wasn't your fault she committed suicide when she learned of her husband's death."

"No, but I could have prevented it."

"Patina had a history of attempted suicides." Sean fiddled with the keyboard on the tray table in front of Andre's seat. "Her husband's death just gave her another excuse. There." A picture of a woman appeared on the screen. "That's your wife, Briana Landers Payton."

A list of statistics scrolled down the screen. Age, thirty-eight. Height, five-foot-six. Natural blonde, blue eyes. Graduated magna cum laude from Princeton. Entered U.S. Foreign Service when she was only twenty-one. She met her husband, William Payton, then attaché to the British ambassador, while on assignment to Tebakistan. Married ten years, no children. Statistics aside, she had the most hauntingly beautiful face he'd ever seen on any woman. Even though he was staring at only a photograph, he couldn't look away. What was it about her — her upswept hair, the curve of her neck or those eyes a man could fall into? She had one of those faces that could sink a thousand ships, like Grace Kelly or Audrey Hepburn. Royalty by her carriage, if not by blood. Why then was she in an estranged relationship? Was her husband fucking mad?

"Earth to Andre, Earth to Andre." Melody waved her hand in front of his face.

Andre shook himself out of the trance. If Briana Payton had this effect on him through a computer screen, how would he react in person? "Take me back to the beach. I can't do this."

"You don't have a choice, buddy." Sean stared out the window of the aircraft. "We're here and the boss expects you to accept the assignment."

"Damn." He shoved his hand through his hair again. "You're sure they're estranged?"

"Yeah, they sleep in separate rooms and everything." Sean switched the computer back to film clips of William Payton. "You better study his mannerisms if you plan to pull this off. We can feed you the poop via the headset, but you have to know his moves."

"Separate rooms?"

Sean blew air out his nostrils. "Yeah, already."

Andre shook his head and settled in front of the video monitor. "I don't like it."

"So noted." The techie hit a button and started the video again. "Now are you going to study, or do I have to do everything for you?"

* * * * *

Briana Payton sat before the vanity mirror in her hotel room brushing her long blonde hair and wondering if she had the courage to go through with her plan. Another long, slow stroke with the silver-backed brush and she set it aside.

How long had she known she didn't love her husband? Five, six…eight years of the ten they'd been married? Or was it after her second miscarriage? However long, she knew she couldn't live like they had, apart in every sense of the word.

With a deep breath for courage she stood and walked to the bed, lifting the filmy black wisp of a nightgown from the cream duvet. Tonight would be her last attempt to breathe life back into their failed relationship. If she felt no spark, no returned affection, that was it. She'd leave. Destination? Who cared? Maybe one of the Virgin Islands in the Caribbean. Her husband thought them too provincial and perhaps his rejection made them more appealing to her. Briana found them welcoming, sunny and delightful.

Oh, she'd stay until the negotiations were complete, but after William signed his name to the peace treaty, she would leave Padel, William and life as the ambassador's wife. She might even go back to work, a job might make her feel better about herself. Being the wife of an important political figure had its own demands but she missed the excitement of meeting new people and using her mind for other than dry conversation with people she could barely understand. And the constant smiling she endured in the name of politeness. If she never smiled again, that would be fine with her.

Lace strafed her cheek, making her aware she was crushing the miniscule nightie in her fists. She should be thinking about a pleasant night ahead, a sexy interlude with her husband, not all the places she'd go when things didn't work out. Where had her optimism gone? Why had she already assumed this tactic would fail?

Because she'd tried before.

Briana sighed. One last time. Ten years of marriage shouldn't be thrown away because you run into a dry spell, should it? With a snort, she tossed her robe aside and slid the gown over her head. A dry spell was a week or two, not a year or two without any physical contact. She guessed

William had a secret bed partner. Most men couldn't last two weeks without sex. William couldn't be any different.

Yet it hurt to know he couldn't find in her what he found in another woman. A glimpse in the mirror reminded her she wasn't hideously ugly. Built much like the late Princess Grace of Monaco, Briana knew she could hold her own in the looks department. Yet William had chosen to sleep in separate rooms, sometimes not bothering to come home at night. Once she had questioned him on why he slept in a different room. He'd said because he didn't want to disturb her when he had late meetings with delegates.

But Briana knew he'd lost interest in her sexually. He probably thought she was frigid, lacking passion, basically a complete bore in bed. Because of his political career, she hadn't filed for a divorce, instead choosing to stick it out.

A smart and determined woman, Briana had done her research. Armed with X-rated videos she'd purloined from her hairdresser, she'd studied various techniques that seemed to work to turn a man on. In the process of viewing videos, she'd managed to masturbate herself into multiple orgasms. Wasn't that enough proof to herself she wasn't frigid?

Were mattress gymnastics all it took to be considered more passionate? If so, why hadn't she done this sooner? The past ten years of marriage could have been so much more...pleasant.

Where was he? Briana paced the plush carpeted floor, the sheer fabric of her gown swaying against the tops of her thighs, making her feel sexy and desirable.

William was already past the time he'd planned to retire for the evening. She'd left him at dinner to hurry up to her room and place her plan in motion. He'd promised only two more hours talking with the other ambassadors before he came up. Those two hours had stretched into three. Briana perched on the arm of a sofa, her bare foot tapping against the side. The lacy neckline of her gown was just beginning to itch. Lifting the edge, she blew gently on her skin to ease the scratchy feeling.

Was he really with other dignitaries? If she were him, that's where she'd be. The peace treaty was at the most critical point it had ever been and the closest to being a done deal.

Would William dare to sneak a little nookie from his lover at such a critical juncture in Tebakistan history? Briana sighed. Probably. Did that mean she should give up on her plan to seduce her husband knowing he might have just scored with another woman?

How icky was it to think of him sliding his dick into her after only a moment before screwing another woman?

Briana shrugged away her morose meanderings and trudged toward William's room. If she didn't try one last time, she'd never know if she'd done enough. If he found her in his bed, surely he wouldn't reject her. He'd have to sleep with her.

How she craved the feel of a strong masculine body next to her—to have warm hands smoothing over her breasts and down between her legs. Her own hands followed the path of her thoughts, cupping her breasts then slipping down her torso to delve into the mound at the apex of her thighs.

By viewing videos, she'd learned the art of masturbation, which she administered to herself standing beside the bed. But she'd always fallen short of absolute fulfillment, wanting more than her fingers inside her, more than a hard dildo. She wanted a man to fill her up, love her, and remind her that she was a desirable woman.

Her breath quickened as she crawled between the sheets and lay back against the pillows.

Tonight. She'd get laid, even if she had to throw herself at the man. How pathetic was she?

Chapter Two

ಐ

"William Payton died outside his assistant's hotel room door. Rumor has it his assistant, Tanya Bates, was also his lover. How convenient. Remember, you've been with your lover but your wife thinks you've been having after-dinner drinks with the other ambassadors." Melody walked backward in front of him tightening his tie.

Andre batted her hands away and loosened the knot. "Does my wife have a clue about my lover?"

"No. Here." Melody fell in step beside him and handed over a wallet and passport.

The more he learned about his look-alike, the less he liked him, but it wasn't his job to pass judgment on the people he proxied. His job was to play the part, accomplish the mission and get the hell out. Number one rule for all Chameleons was never get involved. Too often those who did lost focus and someone got hurt.

Like the woman who committed suicide upon his proxy's "death" — or rather, upon her real husband's death.

"If your wife asks about your job, what do you tell her?" Melody's words were short, clipped like a checklist for a NASA space launch.

"Negotiations are going well." Andre marked a mental check next to Melody's unwritten list item.

"Where have you been?"

"Drinking a glass of Scotch with ambassadors Abusaid and Nassar." Check.

"If cornered about your lover, what's your response?"

"I'm a dirty rotten bastard and I don't deserve you?"

Melody laid a hand on his arm and pulled him to a stop. "No fooling around. Payton rarely discussed business and never pleasure with his wife."

"No wonder they're estranged." He heaved a big sigh. "Okay, I tell her it's none of her business. I was feeling sorry for Mrs. Payton, but if she's willing to put up with a jerk for a husband, she probably deserves him."

"Well, you can make that call when you meet her. Here we are." Melody held up a photograph next to Andre's face. "You have him right on. Only I believe he had a bit of a sneer on the left side of his mouth."

Andre adjusted his lips. "Better?"

Melody smiled. "Yes."

"And you're sure they're estranged?"

"Absolutely." Melody touched her hand to his ear. "Do a mic check on your electronics."

With a tap to the tiny button behind his ear, Andre spoke quietly, "Sean, you playing video games?"

"Yes, sir! Just topped my highest score yet on Blastron. You hearing me clearly enough? No static on your end?"

"It wouldn't dare." Sean was the best techie Andre had ever worked with. If it had wires or circuits, he could make it hum. "Stick close, I might need information on the fly to fill the gaps on my orientation."

"Gotcha covered." The electronic gunfire of a video game found its way into Andre's headset.

Melody peeked out the service door to the hallway beyond. "Okay, lover boy, you're on."

"And to think I gave up the sand and sun of Crete for this." Andre sighed, tugged his tie and stepped into the corridor. Suite 3218 was the one he shared with his estranged wife, Briana. If he could convince her he was the real William Payton, he could convince the ambassadors who didn't know him any better. Hopefully, though, Mrs. Payton was safely tucked away in her own room in the spacious suite.

Andre pulled the plastic key from his inside jacket pocket and slid it into the door lock. "She better be estranged," he muttered softly.

"Don't worry, she is," Sean replied just as softly into his ear.

Senses at the alert, Andre nudged the door open and stepped into an empty sitting area. The door on the right was closed, the other wide open. He'd been told he had the room on the left. So far, so good.

He crossed the sitting area and headed for his room and quite possibly the first decent night's sleep he'd gotten in the past forty-eight hours. As soon as he stepped into his room, he yanked the tie from his neck and tossed it across a chair. Next came the jacket. God, he hated suits.

Perching on the edge of the bed, he slipped out of his shoes and socks.

He'd just unbuttoned his fly and was about to stand to shuck his trousers when the bed behind him moved.

"Ummm. I thought you'd never get here."

Andre froze when slim, manicured fingers slid around his ribs to connect with the buttons on his shirt.

"Want me to do that?" The voice was as smooth as the satin sheets rustling against his back and husky from sleep.

"Got company?" Sean whispered in Andre's ear.

"Yes."

The fingers flicked the buttons open one at a time. "Remember when we first met and you were just an aide at the embassy?"

"Er, yes."

"That was eleven years ago," Sean whispered into the wire in his ear. "Payton was a young social climber, full of high ideals and passionate about his work."

Obviously he was passionate about a lot more than just his work. "Remind me," Andre said, covering her hand more to hold it still than to encourage her to continue.

Once she'd completed unbuttoning his shirt, she rose on her knees and smoothed her hands over his shoulders, pushing the crisp white fabric of his shirt off his shoulders. Although he hadn't seen the woman's face, Andre was certain she had to be Payton's lover. After all, he was estranged, right? And a lover was easier to shove out the door than a wife.

"In a tight situation there, buddy?" Sean asked.

With a hand now sliding around his waist and an index finger finding its way into his belly button, Andre found it difficult to concentrate on the man in his ear. "Oh, yes," he managed to answer Sean in a way that wouldn't make the woman suspicious. Now to extricate himself. He lifted her hands from his waist and stood, his trousers still thankfully in the upright and fastened position. "If you'll wait just a moment, I'd like to wash up."

He turned, still holding her hands in his, and stared down into the haunting blue-green eyes he'd viewed an hour ago. The eyes didn't belong to Payton's lover but to his wife, Briana.

Andre's chest tightened until he felt he couldn't breathe.

Unlike the photograph, her hair was long and loose around her shoulders giving her the appearance of a much younger woman—a young and desirable woman.

Since he held her hands in his, the sheet slipped down revealing a sheer black nightgown that hid nothing of her exquisite form from his view.

Deep inside, he felt his body stir in reaction to the shadowy nipples peeking through the frothy black fabric. Instead of tearing his gaze away, he stared long and hard at those rosy brown tips until they hardened into turgid peaks. His cock rose in salute, pressing against the fly of his Armani suit trousers.

"You need help in there?" Melody's voice sounded over the microphone, jerking him back from his lustfest of the beautiful woman in front of him.

"Will you be long?" Briana stared up at him, her blue eyes filled with hope.

"No." He answered both women. Holy hell! How was he supposed to get out of this situation? With a forced smile, he more or less dashed for the bathroom, closing the door behind him. Andre turned the handle on the sink faucet until water sprayed loud enough to drown his voice. "Who the hell told you the Paytons were estranged?"

"Keep calm, Andre." Melody's tone was the same one she used when talking hostage negotiations, slow, cool and clear. "What's going on?"

"Don't give me any shit. You know good and well what's going on. Mrs. Payton is in Mr. Payton's bed waiting to do the nasty."

Melody laughed. "Is that all?"

"Is that all?" Andre paced across the tile floor and back to the sink. "She was supposed to be estranged, no longer in love with her husband."

"That's what several of our operatives reported. Look, maybe she's tired of being estranged. Maybe the estrangement was his idea, not hers, and she's trying to make it work."

"Great, the night she tries to fix her broken marriage I have to play the sorry son-of-a-bitch cheating husband."

"If you don't want to sleep with her, don't." Melody sighed. "Your choice."

"Damn right."

"So what are you going to do?"

Andre shoved a hand through his hair. "Hell if I know."

"Keep the mic tuned in, I could use a little X-rated entertainment," Sean cut in.

A tentative knock sounded on the bathroom door. "William? Are you all right?"

"Damn, it's showtime," Andre whispered. He turned toward the door and raised the volume of his voice to carry above the running water and through the wood paneling of the door. "I'm fine. I'll be out in a minute."

"Oh good." Sean laughed in his ear and Andre could picture him rubbing his hands together. "I can live vicariously while you're getting laid."

"The hell you are." Andre reached up to the tiny device behind his ear and yanked it out. Then he held it to his lips. "Tune in tomorrow." With a near soundless click, he switched the headset off and tucked it into his pants pocket.

"Did I hear voices?" Briana asked.

"I was just talking to myself, going over today's negotiations." Given the Paytons hadn't had much of a love life, William Payton probably preferred to review negotiations when he could be churning the bed sheets with a beautiful wife.

Andre splashed water over his face and neck to cool his burning skin. The thought of that beautiful, almost naked woman on the other side of the door made the water turn to steam.

How could he let her down easy when all he wanted was to climb between her legs and ride her through the night? A definite no-no in his book. Patting his face dry, he inhaled several deep breaths and then pulled the door open.

Where he expected to see Briana standing in front of him was only a wisp of a nightgown lying like a black cloud against the rich burgundy pattern of the Persian carpet.

Uh-oh. With his back teeth grinding against each other, Andre let his gaze lift to the king-sized bed covered in creamy satin and one long-legged naked woman.

Lying on her side, her nude body was a study in hills and valleys of silky white skin. Briana, with her hair draped across her breasts, was every bit a siren lying in wait of a careless sailor, luring him to his destruction.

And Andre was nothing but a sailor who longed for her destructive call. Moving forward as if drawn in on a long fishing line, he couldn't have stopped if he'd wanted to. Those curves, those breasts, the hair and the eyes had him hooked and there was no going back. He should have been lying on a beach in Crete, enjoying his solitude. Instead he was about to crash and burn in bed with the ambassador's widow.

Briana could have cried when William had practically run away from her and closed the bathroom door between them. Her plan had failed. Now she was destined to leave her husband of ten years and start a new and scary life on her own.

But if he thought he could hide from her until she gave up, bullshit!

She'd climbed from the bed and confronted the closed door. Landers women didn't give up without a decent fight.

Since subtle hadn't worked, she was forced to strip the kid gloves and go for blatant sexuality. She could do it— she'd watched the videos. All it took was a naked body, a bed and a come-hither look.

The jiggle of the door handle triggered her next move. A quick jerk and the miniscule gown flew over her head and drifted to the floor. With three giant steps, she lunged for the bed and landed among the cream satin sheets. The door was half open as she settled into what she remembered as a pose one of the porn stars had used to entice her man—on her side, one leg gracefully draped over the other, breasts and the curly hair of her mons exposed for William to see.

Maybe he needed a reminder of how good it had been between them.

As his eyes lifted from the gown on the floor, Briana put the final touch on her pose, curving her free hand around a breast and tweaking the tip. If that didn't turn him on, he had to be gay!

His gaze made a slow burn across the carpet, up the side of the bed to rest on her form stretched in what she felt was an increasingly more ridiculous look. If he didn't say something soon, she'd die of embarrassment.

But the look on his face didn't disappoint. His brown eyes burned a smoldering black as his gaze swept from the hair cascading over her shoulder down her flat belly to the pale brown curls between her legs. Her skin fairly twitched with the intensity of his stare.

She tried to laugh, the sound coming out as a cross between a nervous giggle and a choking cough. Briana resisted the sudden urge to cover her pussy. "Please tell me you like what you see."

Her words seemed to hit him like a sluice of cold water. His head jerked back and his gaze rose from her crotch to her eyes. "Like what I see? You doubt it?"

"Well, you're just standing there staring at me like this is the first time you've ever seen me."

"It is." He cleared his throat. "At least it feels like the first time I've ever seen you."

"I know. It's been a long time, hasn't it?" Her cheeks heated.

"Too damn long if you ask me," he muttered.

As she waited for him to make the next move, her body got fidgety and she sat up. What was he waiting for? She'd made the first move. If he wanted her, he had to come the rest of the way. But he stood so still. "So are you going to take me up on what I'm offering, or are you going to make me go to my own room?"

When William's gaze darted around the room to the door, Briana could feel tears stinging her eyes. He was going to send her away. Damn!

But his wandering glance circled around and returned, if somewhat reluctantly to her in the middle of the bed. She blinked back the errant tears and pushed her lips upward into a semblance of a sexy smile. "Don't you find me desirable, William? Even a little?"

Her tremulous voice must have hit a chord within him, because he crossed the room and grabbed her shoulders, staring down into her eyes. "You're the most beautiful and desirable woman I've ever met."

"Then why won't you make love to me?" The tears she'd been fighting tipped over the edge of her eyelids and tumbled down her cheeks. She rose up on her knees and ran her hands across his chest. "I need you."

Strong, sensitive hands claimed hers, stopping them from racing across his skin.

Briana's blood burned. She wanted to feel and be felt, to love and be loved. With their fingers clasped to his chest, she pressed her full breasts into their hands until they were rubbing against the curly coarse hairs on either side. Tugging one hand free, she reached up behind his head and pulled him down to kiss her, thrusting her tongue between his teeth like she wanted him to thrust his cock between her legs. A fleeting thought passed through her mind that he tasted different than the last time they'd kissed. More minty, no tobacco. Had he given up smoking for the evening? And his arms were stronger than she'd remembered. All those early mornings in the workout room had paid off. A thrill of excitement raced along her spine.

One of his hands slid free and circled around behind her, dropping low to her waist and even lower to cup her buttocks, pressing her against the hard ridge beneath the zipper of his trousers.

It was then she realized he was still wearing clothing and she couldn't wait to get him out of them. Breathing heavily, she pushed away, her hands diving for his button and zipper.

His hands stopped her when she had the button only halfway through the hole. Had he changed his mind? Would he once again reject her? Were the Virgin Islands becoming more of a reality? Her heart plummeted and her fingers shook in his.

"Let me," he said softly. "You're in such a hurry, you might damage the goods."

The look she gave him was his undoing. Her blue-green eyes turned up to him and a smile curved her lips. "Really? You're not going to stop?"

Andre's gut clenched. What had that bastard Payton done to his wife to make her so insecure about her desirability? The man must have been blind, deaf and incredibly stupid to miss the gem he had in his own house. The woman was beautiful and practically on fire with need. Any noble thoughts of backing out while the going was good were squelched with that one smile. Her face lit like the soft glow of morning light on dew. He couldn't say no to her, he'd rather lose a limb.

With deliberate movements, he flipped the button loose on his trousers and tugged the zipper downward. "I'll take these off, but I don't want you to touch me yet."

"But I have to, I can't help myself." As if to prove her point, she ran her hands up his chest, threading her fingers through the curly hairs until she found and rolled his hard brown nipples between her thumbs and forefingers.

Andre thanked God William Payton wasn't a slacker when it came to working out. At least when he went to bed with Payton's wife, Andre could feel confident in his body. And he *would* go to bed with Briana Payton. Nature wouldn't let him do otherwise. His balls would explode if he didn't find release inside her.

Once the zipper was down, Briana slipped from the bed, her hands smoothing over his stomach and beneath the waistband of his trousers and briefs to slide them from his hips and down to the floor. His penis sprang free and into her face as she bent to pull his pants from beneath his feet.

When she looked up from her kneeling position on the floor, she gasped.

The look of amazement for his size and length made Andre's cock jerk in appreciation and anticipation of future delights.

"I don't remember it being quite so big."

Andre reminded himself he was supposed to be William Payton whose DNA had blueprinted a smaller cock than Andre's real equipment. While he'd been lusting after Payton's beautiful wife, he'd loosened his hold on the shape of that particular body part. He'd have to be more careful, but for now, the enlarged cock would have to stay. He couldn't shrink it now. Not while it was engorged and aching for release. With a cough, he covered for his slip in his mission. "It's been a long time."

"Two years is certainly a very long time." Her fingers skimmed across the back of his calves and up behind his knees as she rose on her knees until she was facing his proudly protruding cock. "I've always wanted to suck your cock. Will you let me, William?"

Andre inhaled a slow steadying breath. Jeez, what red-blooded male could refuse? Had William? More fool him. In the meantime, what was he supposed to say? *No thanks, I'm on the job. I want you, but you can only be a one-night stand.* All the sensible responses to her titillating question fled his mind and he answered, "Uh, yes, please."

Even before he released the "s" in please, she had her fingers wrapped around the base of his penis.

As if in slow motion, her head moved toward his cock and it twitched in fervent greed for the warmth and wetness of her mouth. Her lips circled the head, her teeth catching on the swollen rim, lightly scraping the sensitive skin.

Andre's breath whooshed out of his lungs and he forgot to breathe to replenish his oxygen-starved brain.

She pulled back and laved the underside of his cock with her tongue from his balls to the very tip where a creamy drop of cum oozed from the hole.

Stop her, now. Stop her before you succumb to her witchery. Because she had to be a witch for Andre Batello to completely lose his sense of professionalism. He was there to sign a peace treaty, not to get a piece of widow ass.

Reluctantly, he laced his fingers through her hair, ready to pull her away from his straining, engorged cock. But before he could make that fateful move, she took him fully into her mouth, swallowing him until the tip of his prick bumped against the back of her throat. With strength he didn't know she had, she gripped his ass and pumped him in and out of her mouth until he teetered on the edge of orgasm. With only a thread of restraint remaining, Andre gripped her hair and tugged her off his cock. "Stop," he said through clenched teeth.

With a frown denting her smooth brow, she glanced up at him, her lips forming a rosy moue. "You didn't like that?"

His breath coming in shallow gasps, he couldn't stop the shaky laugh from emerging. "More than I should, darling. More than I should. But what about you?"

She shrugged. "We can make love now, if you like?"

Andre frowned and pulled her to her feet. With his cock poised to explode, he knew he couldn't just fuck her and call it a day. Reaching up, he smoothed a strand of hair from her face, tucking it behind her ear. "What do you want, Briana? How can I pleasure you?"

Her sharply indrawn breath was just one more clue her husband hadn't given a damn about her needs or desires. Any man who could go two years without making love to this beautiful woman was getting it elsewhere. And from the preliminary reports from inside operatives, William Payton had been doing his assistant, Tanya Bates.

Andre had seen pictures of Tanya and she didn't hold a candle to Briana. Not by a long shot.

Briana's brow knit in a delicate frown. "William, are you feeling all right?"

"Yes, of course. Why do you ask?" Damn Payton for his inattention to his wife. Perhaps he'd better back off and distance himself from the ambassador's widow. "If you're not in the mood, I quite understand." When he took a tentative step backward, she followed him.

"No, it's not that. I...want this, it's just that you've never asked me what I want before. Why now?"

Backed in a corner of his own making, Andre thought fast. "Can't a man make amends for lost time?" Could he be any lamer?

The frown slowly lifted from her forehead, replaced by a tentative smile. "I suppose." Her hand feathered over his naked chest, her fingers burning a path straight to his soul. Never before had he felt such a gut-wrenching jolt of guilt for doing his job. Something about Briana shook him to the tips of his toes and made him question his purpose in this charade.

Was his being there worth lying to this incredible woman? Was the fate of three warring nations worth the hurt she'd feel if she knew his role?

Andre argued with himself. Would she have known any more kindness, any loving tenderness from her dead husband had he lived? No. Why not give her one last night of passion and fool her into thinking her lousy husband really loved her? What would it hurt?

A vision of Patina emerged in his mind. The day after his proxy's death, she'd committed suicide. One day. And he could do nothing about it. He hadn't been there to stop her. Would she have taken her life if she'd learned of her husband's murder a week earlier in the natural course of events? Had Andre's interference pushed her that one step further?

Gazing down at the gentle determination and hope shining in Briana Payton's eyes, Andre knew he couldn't turn his back on her.

While he'd been ruminating over past mistakes, her hand had trailed lower to grasp his cock. "Do you want me to suck you again?"

"No, it's your turn." Before he could change his mind, he slid his hands behind her thighs and lifted her, wrapping her legs around his waist. Then he walked to the bed, easing her down his torso to rest on the edge.

"What makes you hot, Bree?" He dropped to one knee, his hand cupping the back of her neck. "What makes you want to scream with desire?"

"I don't know. Why don't you surprise me?" Her voice trembled, her tone a cross between excited and concerned.

His imagination launched into a dozen naughty visions of the things he'd like to do with this woman, but he'd take it slow, starting with…

The hand behind her neck circled around to cup her chin and he leaned in to claim her lips. With his tongue, he skimmed her ripe, full lower lip before he lightly penetrated the seam between her lips, bumping against her smooth, white teeth. When she opened her mouth wider, he dove in, tasting her like a bee drawn to nectar.

Briana moaned and leaned her breasts against his chest, lifting her legs to wrap around his waist again. Her cunt rested against his belly, her liquid warmth making him as hard as granite.

And that was just a kiss.

Forcing himself to move slowly, he worked his way over her jaw and down the tempting curve of her throat, stopping to nip at the thrumming vein beating erratically at the base.

Her fingers danced across his shoulders, alternately scraping and rubbing his skin in a frenzy of indecision. Was she afraid of the passion he was stirring in her? She was definitely stirred if the moist warmth of her pussy rubbing against his belly was any indication.

But he wanted more and he wanted to give her more.

He moved lower, sliding her legs up his waist to drape across his shoulders. With the tips of his fingers, he traced a line along her inner thigh until he reached the sexy swollen center of her, glistening with her juices. The tip of one finger delved into her, dipping in like a bear into a honeycomb. He brought his finger out and drew a line upward along her labia, sliding between the folds until he nudged against her clit. Briana jerked, her back arching, the legs draped over his shoulders stiffening. "Ohmigod, that feels so good."

"You like that?"

"Yes, oh yes." Her head dropped back, her hair swinging low to brush against her buttocks.

"If you think you like that, you'll like this even better." He replaced his finger with the sharpened tip of his tongue, flicking her nubbin until she grabbed his hair and pulled him back.

"I can't take it, it's so…"

"Intense?" He started up at her, a wicked smile curving his lips. "Baby, you haven't felt intensity."

"You mean there's more?" She fell back against the mattress, tossing her head from side to side. "I don't know, William. I don't think I can take it."

"Try." He didn't give her the opportunity to back out. He scooped his hands beneath her ass and pulled her into his mouth, his tongue diving into her vaginal entrance, lapping at the juice, tasting her desire. Circling her clit with his finger, he tapped the swollen tip gently, licking his way up to lavish his attention to that one erogenous zone he knew she couldn't resist.

With all the restraint he could muster, he gently sucked her clit into his mouth, tonguing the tip until she screamed out loud, her fingers laced through his hair, yanking until he thought she'd pull it out by the roots.

Then she collapsed against the sheets, her hands loosening their hold on his hair to slide beneath his arms. "I need you inside me now." Her legs slipped off his shoulders.

As he moved to climb to his feet, she pulled him up and over her body.

He leaned over the bed and took one of her plump, ripe nipples into his mouth while he guided his cock to the entrance to her mons. Poised on the edge, he hesitated.

"It's okay. I'm on the Pill," she whispered into his ear. Then with strength he didn't normally associate with a woman her size, she grasped his buttocks and slammed his cock into her all the way to his balls.

Her tightness engulfed him, squeezing his shaft, her moist walls lubricating his cock, allowing him to pull out smoothly before sliding back into her.

Good Lord, she felt like heaven, all silky skin and warm, wet desire. He could get used to filling her up and making her scream. But she wasn't his. He was only a stand-in for her lousy, no-good, cheating husband. A man better at negotiating with countries than with his own wife. Had he known what a lusty woman he had? Surely not.

Andre pumped in and out of Briana until his body hit that peak and exploded into a full array of the most intense orgasmic sensations he'd ever experienced.

With one final thrust, he collapsed against her, nestling his lips against the back of her ear. "You're incredible, Briana. Absolutely incredible."

"You've never said that to me before, nor have you ever lasted that long." She laughed unsteadily and stared up into his eyes. "Are you sure you're my husband?"

Chapter Three

ფ

For a moment, William grew still above her. Had she said something wrong? Would the sudden warmth he'd shown her disappear as easily as it had appeared? Briana could have stuffed her fist in her mouth for her faux pas. On what could be the eve of the end of her marriage or the beginning of a renewed relationship, she may have committed a huge blunder. Why did she have to be so critical of her husband?

Because he hadn't shown her any kindness or attention in the past two years. Because each time she tried to have a conversation he'd go to bed, claiming he was too tired to talk.

Oh, she had plenty of reasons to distrust his sudden turnaround. She might as well stick her foot in further and see if his recent passion was only lust.

Not sure how to phrase her thoughts, Briana threw caution to the winds. "I have to admit, I wasn't sure you'd want me." Now that sounded positively pathetic.

William rolled over to lie beside her.

Expecting him to climb out of the bed and retreat to her room, Briana was surprised when William settled in next to her and pulled her into his arms. "Not want you?" He rubbed his cock against her hip. "Even after spending myself, I'm still as hard as stone. Not want you?" With gentle tug, he pulled her more snugly against him and tucked her head beneath his chin. "I want you so badly, I can't think straight."

Her heart swelled into her throat. After two long years, those were exactly the words she wanted to hear. But why now? "Is this a trick?" She stared up into his face, her back arching her breasts into his chest. She liked the feel of his chest hairs against her naked nipples. If only he wasn't teasing her. If only their marriage could be like this all the time. "If you had rejected me tonight, I would have left you for the Virgin Islands."

"You would have left him—me?" He leaned up on an elbow and stared down into her face. "Why?"

Her chin dipped to her chest and she gazed across the room at a chair in the corner, not that she saw it or the pattern of paisleys in deep blues and greens. "I didn't think there was any love left between us. You had your interests," namely one slutty assistant, "and I had nothing. Other than to save face with your contemporaries, you didn't need me."

"And now?"

She shrugged and nestled into his arm. "I'm seriously reconsidering the Virgin Islands."

"Why the Virgin Islands?"

She squeezed her eyes shut and visualized the travel brochures from St. Thomas and St. Croix. "I like how sunny the skies are and the sugary sands I can dig my toes into." She wiggled her toes against his leg, liking the tickly feeling of his coarse hairs rubbing against the bottom of her feet.

William's hands slid around her waist and pulled her up close to him, snuggling his lips into the curve between her neck and shoulder. "I would like to be anywhere with a beautiful woman like you. Why don't we go together?"

With an unladylike snort, she rolled her eyes up at him. "You? Rolling around in the sand at a beach? I know better than to ask. You don't like the humid salty air, nor do you like the sand in your shoes or clothes."

"Can't a man change his mind?"

His low rumbling voice echoed in her ear, sending little tingles across her skin awakening her desire all over again. She turned toward him and draped her leg over his. "I don't know. You've never changed your mind before. But then again, you've never lasted as long as you did before. I think my research into the foreplay and fornication habits of the adult human may have been what worked. Shall I try some of my other newfound knowledge on you to see if you can rise to round two?" She'd never been this bold in her sex life with William and the power it made her feel surged through her. She straddled his hips and lowered herself over his cock.

A smile lifted the sides of his lips. "I'm up to the lesson, if you're up to teaching me."

"Hold on to your starched shirt, I'm about to ride you until you cry uncle."

"Giddyup, cowgirl." He bucked beneath her, sheathing himself in her warmth. She rose on her knees and lowered herself, her breasts bobbing in the steady rhythm of his thrusts.

William grabbed her hips and lifted her up and down, slamming her down on him, until she felt his balls slapping against her anus.

He'd never filled her so fully. "Are you…sure…you're my—" She gasped and arched her back, her breathing coming in rapid jerky intakes.

William pulled her hard against him, his face strained in part agony, part ecstasy as his cock throbbed his release inside her.

Completely drained of any strength, Briana lay against his chest, sucking in air and willing her heart rate to calm into a normal beat.

With him still inside her, she felt her eyelids drooping low and knew she would fall asleep within seconds. "William?"

"Yes, Briana?"

"Will you be the same when I wake up?"

"I don't know, Briana. You do have a remarkable affect on my libido."

"I mean will you still act like you care—not just the sex—but like you still love me?"

He smoothed a lock of hair from her face and kissed the tip of her nose. "Yes, Briana." He hesitated a moment before pulling her closer. "I'll love you as long as I live."

That's all she ever wanted. To be loved. Briana smiled and drifted to sleep, content in William's words and satiated in his lovemaking. Tomorrow she could make her decision whether or not to leave. At this point, she didn't know if she could trust him with her heart. Would he let her down again?

Andre dressed quietly in the next room the following morning. He hadn't wanted to wake Briana after their late-night foray into the lusty delights of each other's bodies. The harsh light of day presented sharp reminder of his mission and why he had to focus on the business at hand. He tucked the radio headset in his ear and switched the button on.

"Sean, you awake?"

"That you, Andre?" A sleepy female voice came across the line. "About time you tuned back in. You're about to have company. Right about—"

A soft knock at the door interrupted Melody's warning. Andre swore softly. He wasn't ready to deal with anyone yet. But then, he was supposed to be ready all the time. One beautiful blonde in the next room had him completely off-kilter today.

Tugging at his tie with one hand, Andre strode for the door and yanked it open.

Framed in the entrance was an overly endowed, big-haired young woman with bright red lipstick and long, clawlike fingernails. William Payton's assistant and lover, Tanya Bates. "Mr. Payton, are you ready to go?" She rose on her tiptoes and stared around Andre to the room beyond, before she leaned forward and whispered, "Is she still asleep?"

"Yes." He backed a step, Tanya's perfume assaulting his senses with its cheap bitter aroma.

"Good." Tanya shoved him backward into the interior of the room and launched herself into his arms, wrapping her long legs around his waist. Her short skirt rode up revealing her lack of undergarments and a dark thatch of pubic hair. "If we hurry, we can do it before we go to the meetings."

Andre reached behind him and unlocked, with difficulty, her legs from around him and pushed her feet to the floor.

"Not now, Tanya. I'm feeling a little ill." At least in his response he was telling the truth. That William had been fucking his assistant with his wife in the next room, made the bile rise in his belly.

"I missed you last night." Tanya pouted. "You said you were coming to see me in my room."

"Something held me up." An understatement to say the least. How he'd love to see the expression on her face if he were free to say, *I dropped dead at your door.*

A glance at the fake color of her strawberry blonde hair and the surgically enhanced breasts was enough to make him want to punch a dead man. How could Payton prefer a bimbo to his own beautiful wife?

But he wasn't there to question why Payton was an ass to Briana. He had a treaty to sign and three countries to save. Then he could leave and get back to his vacation.

Only the vacation wasn't looking as relaxing and revitalizing as he'd once envisioned. Andre couldn't imagine himself lying on the beach worrying about how Briana took the "death" of her husband.

Would she fall apart and commit suicide like Patina Gorchev?

Andre shook his head. Briana was a strong woman, despite her lousy choice of a husband. She'd probably follow through on her plan to go to the Virgin Islands.

Tanya wound her arms around his neck and licked his chin from tip to earlobe. "Want to scoot back to my room before you go down to the negotiations?"

A shiver of revulsion slithered along Andre's spine. With deliberate movements, he clasped Tanya's arms and set her away from him. "Not no, but hell no."

"You don't have to be so mean, you know." Tanya's full lower lip pushed out in a melodramatic pout. "It's not as if we hadn't done it with your wife in the other room before."

Andre turned his back to Tanya and counted to ten. Payton was lower than an ass, he was contemptible as a human male. Screwing his assistant with his wife in the other room. "Leave."

"But I just got here and we have to appear downstairs in twenty minutes." She rubbed her breasts against his shoulder. "Just enough time to sneak in a quickie."

"Leave, now." He turned and leveled a killer look on her — one that left no room for misinterpretation.

The "lady" emitted a distinctly unladylike snort and stomped her foot. "I don't know what's wrong with you. You're not acting normal, if you ask me."

"I agree. Normally, you'd take your flirtations out of our room instead of flaunting them in front of your wife." Briana stood framed in the doorway to her bedroom, a red oriental-patterned robe tied around her middle.

Andre inhaled slowly and let out the air in his lungs in a long, steady stream. His gaze never left Briana, but his words were directed toward his proxy's assistant. "Leave, Tanya."

Tanya's eyes narrowed at Briana and, pursing her lips, she turned toward the door. "Game time in twenty, *Mr.* Payton." The door swung closed a little harder than necessary and Andre cringed.

With a step toward the beautiful woman in her red robe, he held out his hand. "Briana—"

Her shoulders shifted back and her chin tilted upward. "Don't."

"But you need to know."

"All I know is what my eyes and heart tell me. Last night was nothing but a lie. If you can have an affair with that...that...tart, you can't possibly still love me. I'm leaving."

"Briana—"

"Goodbye, William."

Why he couldn't walk away and let her continue to think her husband was a philandering bastard, Andre didn't know. But he couldn't stand the hurt in her eyes, the fleeting flash of longing he witnessed before her lips tightened and her entire face closed up like a door being slammed shut.

If he behaved like the professional Chameleon, he'd let her go. Her husband's death would be less traumatic if she assumed he was a complete jerk—which he was. When Andre should have left the room immediately, he didn't. His feet propelled him toward Briana and he caught up with her as she reached for the handle to her door.

With a deep breath, he closed his hand over hers and wrapped an arm around her waist. "I don't love her."

Her body stiffened. "Can you tell me you haven't been screwing her? Can you?" She turned to face him, her lips close enough for him to taste if he leaned down to claim them. But with her eyes flashing fire, he didn't dare.

What could Andre say to make it right between them? He couldn't shake off the magic of what they shared last night and he didn't want to. At the same time, he couldn't deny William Payton slept with his assistant. Part of him wanted to let Briana think the worst of Payton, the easier for her to get over him when he "died". Yet, as he stared down into her blue eyes, he couldn't hurt her even more.

"Yes, I slept with her."

Her bottom lip trembled. "And you'll do it again, won't you?" She wasn't asking him a question, her words were more a statement. How long had William Payton been cheating on his wife? Obviously long enough she knew he would never change. "I guess last night was a romp in the sack to keep me happy, right?"

"Briana, what we shared last night couldn't be classified as a romp. It was beautiful, sexy and incomparable."

"But not enough to make you stop sleeping with Tanya." The skin between her brows wrinkled and her eyes pooled with unshed tears. "Where did we go wrong, William? Were we ever in love?"

What could Andre say to her? He didn't know William's motivations for marrying Briana. Perhaps there had been love in the beginning. "I don't know," he answered honestly. "All I do know is that I would rather spend the rest of my life with you than any other woman." He lowered his voice and tugged her close. "You ignite my soul."

Her gaze scanned his face, a glimmer of hope softening the frown etched in her forehead. "I wish I could believe you."

The aroma of her shampoo tantalized his senses, a reminder of the time spent making love throughout the night. With her already so close, a slight jerk pulled her into his embrace and his lips descended on hers.

Fiery currents sped along his neuropathways, shooting blood and sexual tension south to his groin, engorging his cock to uncomfortable proportions in his suit pants. If he didn't have her now, he would explode in a messy display of adolescent vigor. "Briana, I swear on my mother's grave, I will never cheat on you again. You are the only woman I could love in a million years, I only wish I'd found out sooner. Believe me when I say, I'll love you forever."

"If only I could trust your words." She sighed against his lips. "But they are only words."

"Then let me show you how I feel."

Her eyes widened. "Now? Don't you have a treaty to sign?"

"Damn the treaty! I want you." He pushed the robe from her shoulders and it drifted to the floor in a silken pool. She stood before him naked and glorious.

"Just because we make love, won't change my mind." Her tone was less committed than it had been when she told him she was going to leave.

"I'll take that chance." After a kiss pressed to the tip of her nose, he skimmed his lips across her cheekbone and nipped at her earlobe.

Briana moaned and leaned into him. "You don't love me."

"Wanna bet?" While his lips continued his assault down the graceful curve of her neck, his hands warmed the skin lower still, cupping her breasts.

"I should kick you out." Her eyes squeezed shut and she pushed her breasts more fully into his fingers.

"But you can't." He bent down and lifted her into his arms, striding toward the bedroom where he laid her across the bed. "You're beautiful, Briana."

"And you're fully clothed." Her eyebrows rose, the corner of her mouth curling.

"As you so rightly put it, I have other obligations. But first—" He dropped to his knees and pulled her legs over his shoulders until her ass scooted to the edge of the bed. "First, I will pleasure you."

"Not fair. I don't plan on changing my mind," she said leaning up on her elbows.

After the first swipe of his tongue across her clit, she fell back and succumbed to his magic.

Five minutes later, she screamed out his name. William's name. The reminder returned Andre to earth with a physical thud. He wasn't there to make the ambassador's widow come. A room full of delegates awaited his presence. Thousands of people needed that treaty to preserve their homes, lives and families.

Gently, he slid her legs from his shoulders, stood and straightened his suit. "I have to go."

"I know."

"I wish I didn't."

"But you do." Briana grabbed the edge of the cream satin comforter and pulled it around her naked body. "Just go."

The time had come in his job to cut loose. He'd never see Briana after the treaty was signed. The team would make sure William Payton's body showed up in some convenient place, there'd be an autopsy performed by special agents disguised as local medical examiners and Payton would be buried. His widow would get on with her life. Without Payton, without Andre.

Damn. More than anything, Andre wanted to close and lock the door—shut out the rest of the world and live in the moment with Briana. To hell with everyone else.

But he couldn't. He'd come to do a job and it was, as Tanya put it, game time.

"Goodbye, Briana." He turned and left the room, Briana's last hurt gaze haunting him all the way down to the conference room.

"Hey, Andre," Sean said into his ear.

Shit, he'd completely forgotten his team was tuned in. How much had they heard?

"You know you violated protocol, don't you?"

"You heard?"

"Every last moan." Andre could hear the amusement in his friend's voice. "Thanks, man. You made my day."

"Great." He straightened his tie and stepped into the negotiations room. "Let's get this over with."

Chapter Four

ॐ

Briana settled into her seat in first class on the airplane bound from Miami to the Virgin Islands. The funeral had taken a lot more out of her than she thought it would. For a woman on the verge of leaving her husband, she couldn't believe he was dead. Worse still, she missed him. After a ten-year disaster of a marriage, she shouldn't have missed him so much. But that last night together had been different.

Had William known he was going to die? She'd pondered this question at least a hundred times in the past month. Maybe the laidback pace and warm sun would ease her mind and make her more relaxed. A smile tipped the corners of her lips.

"Is this your first time to the Virgin Islands?" a warm, sexy voice said from the seat next to her.

With her head still leaning back against the seat, she eased her eyes open and stared at a dark-haired man with incredibly blue eyes. Wow, how had she missed him when she'd come on board? He was positively beautiful. "Yes. This is my first time."

"Mine too." He smiled across at her, his face open and friendly. "I hear the beaches are second to none. I can't wait to curl my toes in the sand."

"Me too." Her smile opened wide and the sun shining through the airplane window seemed brighter. "Are you meeting someone there?"

"I'm on my own." He held out his hand. "I'm Andre Batello, and you are?"

"Briana Payton. Happy to meet you." And she really was happy to meet him, yet something about this man seemed oddly familiar. "Do I know you?"

"Maybe." He smiled a secret, Mona Lisa-like smile before he settled back against the seat next to her. "Maybe in another life."

About the Author

෪

Email: mylajackson@earthlink.net

Website: www.mylajackson.com

Myla welcomes mail from readers. You can write to her c/o Ellora's Cave Publishing at 1056 Home Avenue, Akron, OH 44310-3502.

Also by Myla Jackson

෪

Trouble With Harry

CALL ME BARBARIAN

Liddy Midnight

Chapter One
Apollonia, on the rim of the Old Empire
Year 52 of the Solitary Age

სა

I entered the imperial box and paused to greet my father and Dasch, his prime adviser. The two men were deep in conversation and barely registered my presence, although a warmth entered my father's eyes when he glanced up. I overheard a reference to ships and knew they were discussing the current plans for what to do when space travel resumed. I doubted it would happen, and certainly not as soon as they expected.

The last spaceship came and went long before I was born. In over fifty years there had been no news and no explanation. After a period of hope that proved fruitless, we descended into civil war before plague plunged us into a downward technological spiral. We lost more than a third of our population. Battles raged through agricultural areas that still had not recovered. Many of our resources, from certain crops to every refinery, had been wiped out in a few short years. Our societies could no longer support the conveniences my grandparents had taken for granted. Instant communication across long distances, machines that performed household tasks, and unfamiliar substances like orange juice were mere myths. I was happy that I'd never miss what I had never known.

Heat from the sunny arena poured over me. The box was crowded. In the nearly two years I spent in the north, first as the prince's bride and then as a widow securing the interests of my eldest stepson, my brothers had churned out more spare heirs than the Empire could ever expect to need. The palace, damaged in an earthquake shortly before I returned from Serac and still under reconstruction, was bursting at the seams with them all. Their presence here, away from the attraction of the working carpenters and stone masons, was expected.

I stumbled over children on the way to my seat. My best friend arrived soon after and swept me into a hug.

"Thank the gods you're already here, Cedilla! I'd hate to have to wait for you in the corridor. I've been looking forward to this more than you'd believe." Tilda gazed out over the amphitheater before she settled back against the embroidered silk cushions to grin at me. She had changed little in the time I'd been away. "This is so much more comfortable than the commoners' benches."

Never having sat anywhere other than in the imperial box, I couldn't say whether my friend was right but I nodded as I relaxed beside her. The large pillows were as soft as those throughout the palace and servants awaited our orders; my father would accept nothing less. In that, as in so many things, we were in perfect agreement.

Tilda and I had talked ourselves out the afternoon before and now sat together in silent harmony. A mild breeze kissed my face, ruffling my curls in its passage. The feather-soft fabric of my gown caressed my skin, such a contrast to the heavy clothes I'd worn in northern climes. I tilted my head and breathed in the scents of home. Hot sand, floral perfumes, and the salt tang of the sea.

Life was good.

The gossiping voices of my brothers washed over me and their children tumbled around us. Bright banners bearing the imperial arms snapped aloft in the wind. Sunlight reflecting off the pale sand of the arena made me squint even under the canopy. A trickle of sweat ran down between my breasts and I plucked at my bodice. The fine silk stuck to my heated skin. A servant moved in to fan me. The drying perspiration cooled my skin and I reveled in the contrast between heat and cold.

Tilda and I were the only women in the imperial box. My father sat above us on his throne. He smiled and nodded when our eyes met. Although the epitome of a hardened warrior, he had a smile that took years off his face and turned him into the most handsome man I'd ever seen. He gestured to a servant, who brought us goblets of iced *paretti* juice. The cool, tart liquid slid smoothly down my throat and quenched my thirst.

"What is entertainment like in Hostilia? Would I enjoy it?" Tilda never traveled. Such behavior was unseemly for young women.

Unless you were a princess and your father's favorite child.

My birth gave me access to experiences most other women would never know, like the ice in my juice. A gift for diplomacy had led to both my short-lived marriage and the necessity of leaving my husband's heir firmly in control when I returned home. Diplomacy would likely determine my second husband as well. Both my brothers had failed to inherit that attribute from our father. Although they were spitting images of him, he had passed his level head and skill at business and intrigue on to me.

"They don't call their land Hostilia, they call it Serac. And yes, you would enjoy it." I'd missed my friend's chatter. I'd missed the tumult of the busy capital. And the entertainment of the arena. "Seracans are fond of lively music and raucous plays, but consider displays of physical prowess, such as this, to be barbaric."

Call me a barbarian, then. I adore watching acrobats strut their stuff, showing off flexibility and balance as they perform for the crowd. I thrill to the beat of the drums as warriors try their best to win without maiming their opponents.

A dance troupe from Sudania, once our southern territory and now an independent neighbor, entered the arena. Tilda and I spent their time on stage leaning forward and clapping with delight. The dancers incorporated elephants and buffalo into their routines, leaping from their backs and somersaulting between them. Quite the best performance I'd seen in several years. A wonderful spectacle. I added a handful of gold to the coins thrown onto the sand at the end. A group of children scampered to scoop up the money, turning somersaults as they ran back and forth.

"I shall miss this."

"Oh, Tilda, are you finally going to visit your sister in Bitterland?" Perhaps my influence had helped her father loosen the leash he kept her on.

She frowned. "No, I meant when I'm married."

An icy hand gripped my heart. "Don't tell me you're to wed? You said nothing yesterday!" Surely the Pirellis had not snared a husband for Tilda last evening.

Once she wed, her friendship with me would change. We could only meet in private, and tradition would require her to be veiled at all times. Marriage and widowhood had not done the same to me, for I was the favored—and only— daughter of the Emperor.

"Of course I am!" Overdone indignation in her voice alerted me to her teasing. "You know I want children and a house of my own, but relax. It will be later rather than sooner. We'll enjoy many more shows together, my friend." Her eyes sparkled as she sipped her iced juice. "Last night, the ward president came to dinner with his son to look me over but apparently they were not impressed. A lavish gift accompanied the no-thank-you note this morning, so Father's not too upset."

"Good. I would double it to keep you with me a while longer, you know."

Tilda's father was a chef, which was how we met as toddlers. As our friendship grew her family had prospered, until now her father ruled over his own empire of pots and pans in the royal kitchens, turning out sumptuous feasts and delicacies fit for kings, princes and of course my father. She was my one true friend, someone I knew would always tell me the truth and not what I wanted to hear.

"I know. You're my best friend. I'll miss you."

"Oh, look! The gladiators are up next! You should hear the buzz among the women, about the two brothers from Sudania. They are quite the swordsmen, if you know what I mean." Her arch expression made me look at her a little more closely.

"Really?"

Before I could pursue this line of inquiry, fighters entered the arena and I became distracted, too busy admiring their oiled muscles and strutting bodies to start up a gossip session. As a rule, I understand, gladiators are a vain and rutting lot, but oh, are they gorgeous!

The southern brothers led the second round. From the moment they stepped forward, they dominated the arena. They moved with confidence and a charismatic quality that kept all eyes on them. Their peers and opponents paled in comparison. My pulse quickened and I could not tear my attention away, even when Tilda touched my elbow.

I could understand the excitement generated by their bouts in the ring, for they were in truly excellent shape. Not overdeveloped, as some bodies in the arena appear, but balanced and fluid in their movements. I admired their tanned skin and what looked to be strong profiles, although their faces were mostly hidden by their half-helmets.

Dark hair flowed down their backs, worn longer than is customary in the ring—especially as they favored trident and net as weapons. Those permit the wielder to capture his opponent's weapon and render it useless, then move in to grapple hand to hand. Close fighting can be dangerous with long hair, as it gives an opponent something to grip. Flexible as eels, the brothers eluded every attempt to hold them and won the ensuing wrestling matches in short order.

Flowers and coins showered into the arena as the crowd awarded them the victories. They had mastered what I call the "winning strut", the victory lap that every winner takes around the arena, to cheers and catcalls.

When they turned to acknowledge the Emperor and removed their helmets, my breath caught in my chest.

They were the most beautiful men I'd ever seen. Their strong profiles proved to be a compelling combination of planes and angles that added up to what should have been harsh features but instead had a unique and stark beauty.

The nearest one swept his gaze across my family and came to rest on me. I nearly fell into his dark eyes. Something hitched within me, something I had never felt before. A recognition, a sense of kinship.

Lust followed quickly. Intense heat blossomed between my legs and rose to pool in my womb. My nipples pebbled beneath my silken bodice and an ache began to weigh down my breasts. My husband had evoked such a response with kisses and caresses. How could this happen with but a look?

The gladiator's expression changed, from victory to astonishment and wonder. I read on his face the emotions that poured through me.

Sweet oracle! I had never experienced anything like this. The delicious heat grew and expanded, rising to engulf my torso. I wanted more. I wanted him in a way that both elated and disturbed me.

He lifted a hand to me. Without volition, despite the fact that he stood yards below me in the arena, I rose to my feet and took a step forward.

Stinging pain forced me to my knees on the bench in front of me. The skin between my breasts burned as though a lit torch had been thrust against me. Agony lanced through me, agony like that of a thousand wasps caught within my garments and stinging their way to freedom.

Chapter Two

ℬ

Fluttering my hands across my left breast, I tried to skim off whatever was hurting me. I failed. As a last resort, I wrenched off my bodice, the fragile silk parting beneath my frenzied fingers.

Tilda set up a screeching that drew everyone's attention to her — and to me. I tried to shush her but could force no sound from my throat.

When I looked down, it was to find a rash forming, a vivid red mark, rapidly darkening to royal purple. Welts rose under my fingers, forming an ornate pattern that sent a chill down my spine even as my chest flamed in pain strong enough to pitch me forward, retching in agony.

This was no insect bite.

This had to be a spell of some sort.

My mind raced, trying to understand what was happening. Who might I have offended — or did this have to do with my work on my father's behalf? We had no mages in our land, although stories of them elsewhere abounded. An enemy might have purchased revenge upon my father for something. The gods knew he had stepped on many toes over the years.

My father rose and stepped from the dais down into the family seats. He gripped my upper arm and wrenched me to my feet. "Come," he ordered, including Dasch in his command. Two guards supported me and we followed as he ducked beneath the curtains that masked the door.

I could barely walk on my trembling legs. The soldiers dragged me along as we left the arena. Silent and stalking like an angry cat, my father led us to a small chamber. He barked at the guards. "Leave us!"

Unable to support myself, I sagged against the wall and hugged my burning chest. I struggled to overcome the pain and discovered that, somewhere on the journey from the imperial box, desire had returned and now mingled with my agony. When I managed to raise my head and face him, I met his cold eyes. His stony expression helped me focus my attention on him.

"It seems your mother was a whore. You are no child of mine."

I reeled from the lash of his words. He might as well have slapped me in the face. I waited for an explanation, huddled in misery and confusion. What did he mean, my meek, mild mother was unfaithful to him? What in all the hells did that have to do with whatever was happening to me?

What *was* happening to me? I caught a glimpse of Dasch by the door. He appeared just as baffled as I was.

My father stared at me in silence. Was that a flash of hurt and anguish in his eyes?

"Father, please, explain—"

"Oh, I'll explain, all right." His voice was icy. I searched his face but found none of the warmth I was used to. I'd imagined the emotions I thought I'd just seen.

My beloved father had become a terrifying stranger.

Mere hours ago, we were closeted in his study, laughing together as we reviewed my reports from the neighboring realm to the north. Last night he had sent me to bed with his customary kiss on the brow and the wish that I had been a son so I could inherit his throne. I gulped back tears and tried to concentrate on his words. This had to make sense, somehow.

"This—" he spat the word and jerked a hand at my chest, "is the mark of the southern kings. When one of these barbarians first meets their destined mate, the foul magic of their soul springs forth in such a mark." He paused and his scornful gaze swept over me. "Somewhere out there, in the assemblage or among the performers, a Sudanian man bears the same mark. You should find him.

"Dasch, you are here in your capacity as Senate leader." His voice grew formal. "As of today, I withdraw my blood-claim of Cedilla as daughter and revoke her imperial status."

He flung open the door and summoned the guards. "Escort this woman from the amphitheater." He spoke in a tight voice, with an emotional detachment I had heard countless times when he dismissed a subject from court.

The soldiers betrayed their training and openly gaped. I did the same. This was my father, the man I loved more than anyone in the world. I had devoted my life to supporting and serving him. What was he doing? How could he be so heartless?

Pride kept me on my feet when the pain of the brand on my skin was eclipsed by a deeper hurt right beneath it, in my heart.

Pride kept my mouth shut, when I wanted to plead with him, to beg to know how he could do this.

The last I saw and heard of my father was the swing of his robe and the slap of his sandals on the stone floor as he returned to the imperial box. Before following, Dasch touched me on the arm and murmured, "I am so sorry." He didn't look at me.

The guards discharged their duty, escorting me in silence to a lower door that led to a filthy alley. I was glad when they locked the door behind me. I couldn't bear their pitying glances.

By now, the pain had subsided. I had heard that only a thin line lies between pain and pleasure. For a moment, I teetered there, balanced between the ache of the mark and a different ache, a sharp and urgent need, that grew deep within me.

Need won out. Desire surged up, freed of the bonds of pain.

I had to leave the alley. The stench of the refuse turned my stomach and I was already suffering. Where could I go? I had no home, no family. Tilda would help me but she was beyond my reach, still in the imperial box. No doubt wondering what had become of me.

Every step moved my thighs against each other, increasing the pulsing need that skittered through me. Heightened desire tightened my nipples almost painfully and drenched my pussy. I reached the mouth of the alley and faltered. Simply the presence of the soft silk on my skin fueled my need for greater pleasure. By all the gods, this was nigh unbearable.

Tilda's mother would take me in. She'd be at home, as proper wives always were. Head down, working to master the passions that roared through me, I turned left into the street.

And bumped into someone. A moment later, I was caught and held between two men. I didn't need to look to know who had found me. I did anyway, hesitant to trust my instincts. Yes, I recognized that sculpted chin. One of the twins from the south turned his head and grinned down at me.

Immediately, the burning need eased. I relaxed against their broad chests, knowing somehow that I was safe. That left only the confusion to deal with.

What had just happened? I'd known blinding pain and then my father repudiated me. No, not my father, according to him. But he was my father, in every sense of the word that mattered. A sob stuck in my throat.

Dimly I heard the men speak. Their voices rumbled into me, soothing and familiar in the most unsettling way. "We have found her, brother."

Chapter Three

ஓ

The bustling street gave way to a quiet alley, and they stopped to unlatch a door. After a quick survey of the street, they carried me inside and shut it behind them. I was gently set on my feet and steadied with two arms about my waist, one from each side.

"Cedilla, love, this is where we live."

We crossed a modest courtyard, entering a room on the far side.

"You will be safe here. I promise."

"And I."

I looked around at the modest furnishings. Several straight chairs, a table, a bench, and a large bed flanked by matching chests. So different from my rooms at the palace. Which I would never see again. Nor would I ever be a part of the large family I'd loved since birth.

Grief filled me and confusion welled up anew. I thrust the grief aside. Time enough for that when I was settled and safe. I had nowhere to go, nothing to do. How would I live? This morning, I had dressed in my favorite gown and the jewelry my father had gifted me with upon my last natal day. The jewelry was unfortunately my most modest and the gown now hung from my shoulders in ruins.

They stared, openly admiring me. The lust shining in their eyes should have bothered me more than it did. Instead of embarrassment, desire filled me. May the gods help me, I wanted them to take me, to sink their hard cocks into my pussy and slake my rampaging lust. I tamped it down by force of my will, crossed my arms over my naked breasts and studied my saviors.

Alike as only twins could be, the two of them stood a handspan taller than my father. Each now wore his long hair clubbed at the nape, wrapped in a leather thong that hung down his back. As were all gladiators, they were bare-chested. And more gorgeous than I had thought, now that I was close enough to touch them.

My gaze fastened on the identical marks their chests bore. I looked down, peeling my hand far enough away to examine the mark that had formed on my skin.

All three matched perfectly.

I am a princess. I am intelligent. I will solve this mystery, I vowed. I will find a way to return to my life at the palace.

They were men. They wanted me as much as I wanted them, by the impressive erections visible through their shorts. We were destined mates, according to my father. *They represent a new life for you*, a small voice inside me said. Ignoring it was not as easy as I expected.

Summoning my best autocrat's voice, I ordered, "Find me something to wear and tell me what this means."

I had learned well the ways of the palace. A minute later, I wore a loose, soft linen shirt and we were seated around the small table.

"I am Asterix."

"And I am Apostroph."

"And you are twins."

"Aye. We come from the south, where such things," Asterix indicated their chests, "are common."

I stared at his mark. Intricate and pulsing with life, it was more attractive than I would have expected the tangible evidence of a spell to be. "I am unfamiliar with this. Is it magic?"

"Some say yes, some say no. All agree that its appearance confirms the bearers have found their perfect mates. A family passes it through the male line. If a man does not meet his destined mate, the mark will not appear but the gene is still passed on. Genealogical records indicate that it is the father who provides the gene to his descendants." He shrugged and the mark on his skin rippled. "If that makes sense."

"I think I understand. I can only bear the mark if my father — or his father or someone back in his father's line — has also borne the mark at some time." I gazed off into the distance, trying to avoid the distraction their gleaming bodies presented. Not breathing the pheromone-laden air proved more of a challenge. "Because my father, or rather the Emperor, does not have this in his father's line, he knows some other man must have sired me. Ergo, he names my mother a whore. As she is not here to defend herself or explain how it happened, we will never know the circumstances, of whether she was willing or not. I'll have to find a way to check the palace records and see who was at court in the Sudania delegation at the time I was conceived."

"Correct. Brother, she is not only beautiful, she is smart! We have been blessed."

"Whoa! What does that mean, 'We'? That you are both my destined mates? How can that be?"

"Sometimes it happens." He shrugged. "There is more to the mark, though."

"And that is?"

"Once the marks rise, we are bound. Now that we have found you, we will never find release with another woman." He pursed his lips in thought. "I'm not sure about you, if you can climax with another man."

"We were told this by our father, and he glossed over some of the story that didn't pertain to us."

"I see," I said, although I didn't. Typical male, to be unconcerned with the ramifications for the woman. I had to say, though, that the two of them were looking better all the time. Could it be that the mark was affecting my judgment? I ran my hand over the ridges and whorls beneath the linen shirt while I examined the matching mark on Apostroph, who sat to my right.

The design was gorgeous, a complicated knot pattern that formed an overall seashell shape within a circle larger than my fist. His skin was bronzed by exposure to the sun, while mine was still white between the ruddy threads of the knotwork. I'd seen that much before I donned their shirt.

I frowned and stroked my mark. A shaft of desire speared through me. I traced the knot and heat flared beneath my touch. Sensation grew, to warm my breasts and pebble my nipples.

Apostroph watched the movement of my hand, shifting on his stool. Could it be that his mark responded as well, even though I was not touching him?

"I have heard nothing of this before today, though I shared my brothers' lessons in history and biology. Where did this gene originate?"

Asterix answered. "We come from the very southern part of Sudania. Long ago, when our ancestors first settled the hills, they found old settlements, established long ago and nearly abandoned."

I frowned. "Nearly?"

"There were a few remaining people. They knew the land and the best ways to cultivate, where to hunt. We adopted them into our families. With them came the mark."

I reviewed the planetary history I'd been taught, made some quick calculations and shook my head. "That's impossible. That area was settled within twenty years of the first colony. To have been there that long before you, they would have to be indigenous people. Nonhuman. That means genetically incompatible." Just because we lost interstellar contact before I was born did not mean I was lacking in education — or curiosity. Some books survived and the palace had quite a library. My brothers had been more interested in racing and whoring than in reading.

They exchanged looks. "That is for a xenobiologist to decide. We only know that the families who took them in gave rise to the marks within two generations."

"And they explained to us what the marks mean. That can't be coincidence. It has to have come from them."

"Why can I not sit still?" I demanded.

"You are feeling the urge of the mark, to be joined with your mates. We feel the same."

"Well, it's damned uncomfortable!"

"We know."

I chewed my lower lip and considered the situation. "If we join, will that invoke the binding of the marks, that we must stay together?"

Asterix shook his head. "The binding has already occurred. All we can do now is give in to it."

"That's unacceptable! What if I don't want to be tied to you both for life?"

"None of us has a choice. We are bound, just as you are, and we also had no say." He frowned. "But how will you live, and what will you do for money, if you leave us?"

"There must be something I can do. I could work for a foreign delegation."

"I thought that women in your society are invisible."

"They are." Gloom fell over me. I had forgotten about the special privileges I held as a favored princess. No one in the Midland government would speak to me now. I had formerly moved in a man's world but was now banned from that status.

"She is intelligent," Asterix stated. "She could find some sort of work, behind closed doors where she can use her brain without offending anyone."

"We would care for her well. She would be foolish to leave us."

"Hello?" I snapped my fingers in front of Apostroph's face. "Don't speak of me as if I'm not here. And don't I have a say in this?"

"None of us may choose." His smile was grim. "You may become a beloved mate, cherished and wanting for nothing. Or you may try to find work and live on your own. You know more of your society than we do. What do women do to provide for themselves, women who are without a family?"

I knew the answer to that. Our society was one of double standards, requiring complete obedience and chastity from women of good repute while men of all ranks took pleasure where they would with women of ill repute. Without status or means, I would join the ranks of the latter, and said as much.

"So you would become a sexual plaything, in the market or a brothel. Many men would pay dearly to sink their cocks into your soft princess's body."

That prospect made me physically ill. The idea might have repelled me in the past but not to the degree it now did. Much as I didn't want to believe it, there might be something to this bonding claim.

"I don't want to hide in the house. I am accustomed to being outside, doing what needs to be done. If I marry you, and join with you, will you force me to abide by society's strictures?"

Asterix smiled and took my hand. "That is not our way. In Sudania, women are our equals. It is only here in the Midlands that your gender is sequestered. We make an excellent living here as gladiators, but if it is your wish, we will return home where you will be more comfortable."

I looked around at the simple room they rented. Although a resident of the palace, I kept up my knowledge of prices in the market and real estate values. How else was one to judge the affairs of commoners? My father had taught me that the level of an effective fine often has more to do with the transgressor's means than the severity of the transgression.

"How much is an excellent living?"

"We clear about six thousand tessars a month."

I whistled. That was more than the Pellinis spent to support their entire household. "And how much did you earn at your previous work in Sudania?"

"Less than a tenth of that."

"You volunteer to give that up, to make me happy?"

"And more."

"You are our hearts now. If you are not happy, we are not happy."

There were worse men to be bound to, of that I was certain. If I couldn't live in the palace as a princess, it appeared I had landed on my feet. Mentally, I ticked off the advantages of life with the twins.

They were willing to sacrifice a lot for my happiness.

They were wealthy—for now. If we went south, that could change. I wondered how much they had saved, since their lodgings clearly weren't straining their budget.

They had shown me nothing but kindness and concern that I understand what was happening to us. I was sure many other men in this situation wouldn't have wasted time in explanations, they'd have taken me straight to bed.

Last but by no means least, they were drop-dead gorgeous.

I became distracted by reminding myself just how gorgeous they were, ogling them shamelessly while they ogled me in return.

Eventually Apostroph cleared his throat. "We can choose to make your life smooth, and you can choose to help us. We have no choice about the marks themselves and their effect on us. We will not be happy unless we make you ours and provide for you."

The prospect of sex with both of them made me weak, but weak with desire and not fear. I reached out and took each one by the hand. They instantly linked fingers with me. Their firm and sure grips radiated comfort and security. I had just lost everything I had known and been carried off by two men I'd never seen before. How could I feel so calm in their presence?

"And why waste time? Come, let us explore the benefits of our bond." Asterix rose and pulled me to my feet, exchanging a look with his twin that told me they were in total agreement.

"I still cannot believe that the Emperor cast me off so easily. I was his favorite child, or so he claimed."

"Men in power are accustomed to making swift decisions that often save their lives." It was then that I realized the most amazing thing. Asterix felt compassion for me, an emotion that quickly turned to need. And I felt it, too, in both of them. Desire rose in them, and in me as well, fueled by the collective marks we bore.

Chapter Four

ֆ≎

They had to protect me. And seduce me. The former I accepted. The latter I was beginning to warm to. Well, more than warm to. I was getting quite hot about it. So were they, from the condition of their erect cocks.

The first time we kissed, it was a mingling of the three of us, our mouths melding and parting as we shared our passion. They tasted of sun and dust. They might have showered quickly before they found me, but some of the atmosphere of the arena lingered.

Sweet oracle, the headiness of their tongues invading my mouth exceeded all pleasures I had known before. We took our time, exploring the myriad textures and flavors of each other's flesh. My body expanded beneath their touches, opening like a flower seeking the heat of the sun. They warmed me with their hands and mouths. I gushed fluid like a heavy dew.

I ended up sprawled across the bed with one of them on each side of me. We were all panting, our hearts beating hard. I thought I heard them, thumping in unison, but how could that be?

Asterix moved to kneel above my head, capturing my hands in his. His twin—how could any woman deserve two such fine specimens?—rolled atop me. He parted my legs with his knees and bent to kiss the tips of my breasts, leaving wet spots that chilled and further puckered the taut peaks. Asterix rubbed the dampness away before he pulled and rolled my nipples, one after the other.

I wanted to capture the moment and hold it forever. One poised above me, his hard cock pointing at my frothing curls. The other holding my hands in one of his and torturing my breasts with his clever fingers.

Apostroph entered me with care, first gently nudging the entrance to my pussy with the head of his cock. His eyes glazed and he moaned as he sank a teasing inch into me. "The friction of your hair is exquisite." I wriggled my hips and his moan became a groan. "Oh, sweet Cedilla, you're going to kill me."

"If you don't hurry up, I just might." I raised my legs and wrapped them around his hips, pulling him closer.

He jerked forward in response, stretching and filling me as most of his cock drove home. I tightened my inner muscles and grinned when he shuddered and thrust harder. His cock reached my womb. It was my turn to moan as I reveled in the feel of his thick, hard shaft buried inside me.

Asterix leaned forward and whispered, "Remember me?" I met his wicked eyes as he seized one nipple in a firm grip and held it. At the same time, Apostroph withdrew halfway and flicked my clit with his finger.

Heat sizzled through me, from Asterix's pinch to Apostroph's cock as he plunged back into me. The breath rushed out of me in a hoarse cry.

Asterix laughed softly, a carefree sound that spurred his brother on to piston his cock in and out of me in long, smooth, fast strokes. The unrelenting pressure at my breast became building heat, in contrast to the give and take of Apostroph's fucking. I lost control of my breath, sobbing as the mark on my breast pulsed in time with strokes of the hard, thick cock that filled me.

Higher and higher I reached, feeling the impending climax as it neared. Sparkling lights danced in front of my eyes. My sobs became cries.

Asterix began rolling my poor, sweetly tortured nipple between his thumb and finger. In a flash of lightning, pleasure exploded from my pussy, skittering up my spine and flooding across my skin. My thighs hugged Apostroph, pulling him close. He burrowed deeper than I thought possible and arched his back, bellowing as our orgasms swept over us together.

Apostroph fell on me, capturing my lips in a hard kiss. I didn't even have the energy to wrap my arms around him. I lay beneath him, eyes closed, enjoying his warm weight on me.

After a moment, he roused and levered himself off me. "By the entire pantheon, I have never had a fuck like that."

"Nor I."

We both looked up at Asterix.

"What?" He was wiping cum from the sheet. "I shared it all, even though I wasn't the one buried to the hilt in her. I felt the grip of her hot cunt just as you did, brother. We're linked in ways I never expected." He tossed the cloth to the floor and grinned. "Our father didn't begin to cover the extent of the ties that bind us."

We rested a bit and recovered, wrapped around each other.

During my brief marriage, my experienced husband had taught me the pleasures of sex. I was a willing pupil and thrived under his tender tutelage. My time as a widow, busy with my stepson's affairs and mindful of the need to remain above reproach, had frozen my sexuality. Now, encouraged by the two men fate had bound to me, I had regained the physical joy I had once known.

I sat up and blinked. The room had grown dark while we engaged in bedplay. I could barely see the other side of the room and no light came through the cracks around the shutters.

"Let's have some light," he suggested. "I want to be able to see you."

"See what you're doing?"

"No, see your beautiful face. I love to look at you, Cedilla."

"As do I." Apostroph struck a match and lit a lantern as well as several candles. One gave off a wonderful fragrance. He smiled sheepishly. "Our one extravagance. It reminds me of our mother."

"It's lovely."

"Not as lovely as you." Asterix came and cupped my face in his hands. "I fear we have neglected the romance part of this very odd courtship."

How sweet of him to notice. This whole situation was odd indeed. Events had unfolded with the cart careening along well before the horse, as one might say. I somehow knew that the more I learned about these two, the more I would come to love them. Perhaps the mark was influencing my thinking, but I wasn't sure it could have happened any other way.

Apostroph handed me a goblet of wine. I breathed in the bouquet and raised my eyebrows. I recognized the vintage and knew the cost. "Another extravagance?"

Asterix laughed and took another goblet from his brother. "No, fine wine is a necessity, not a luxury. Only a fool drinks swill when he can afford ambrosia."

Apostroph held up his goblet in a toast. "And only a fool spends his last penny on anything other than ambrosia."

I had to laugh with them. "I'll drink to that."

Asterix grew serious again. "I'd rather drink to you, and to us as a whole. May our family be prosperous."

"And may we live long in bliss."

A lump blocked my throat for a moment. No one had ever voiced a nicer sentiment. "Hear, hear," I managed to croak. A sip of wine washed down the emotion clogging my throat. Another made sure it stayed down. Before I realized it, I had drunk it all.

Apostroph got up and refilled our goblets. "I heard you were married." Before he joined us on the bed again, he dipped his finger into the wine and dribbled a few ruby drops across my breast.

Asterix bent his head to lap them up. Three leisurely passes of his tongue were followed by a long draw on my nipple. Heat licked through me. He latched on to my nipple again, teasing the peak with flicks of his tongue.

I shuddered before I could answer him. "To a northern prince. He was much older, with a passel of children from his first two wives."

Apostroph took my goblet before I spilled it. "Busy man."

"Wonderful man," I corrected him. "He was kind and gentle with me, and I grew to love him in the short time we had together."

Mentioning him now did not hurt the way it had the day before, when I discussed my brief stint as a wife with Tilda.

Apostroph held the wine up, making me stretch to reach it. The grip Asterix kept on my breast pulled against my efforts and a quite pleasurable sensation streaked from his mouth to my womb. By the gods, what else could they show me? I had a sneaking suspicion we might not leave the bed for days.

"How did you deal with a ready-made family?"

"Fairly easily. It's not as though I had to act as a wet-nurse." Asterix tugged on my nipple and snickered. "Or change nappies myself. I've been around children all of my life. I even was one once myself!" They didn't laugh at my joke. I frowned at them until they each managed a weak chuckle. "The palace is full of children, more now than when I left, but there have always been cousins or relatives who bring their offspring along."

"Didn't it concern you, that any children you had would not inherit?" Apostroph put the cup down and licked his fingers. When he was free of wine, he nudged my legs apart and began tracing my labia with his thumb.

I smiled and shifted my weight to permit him better access. "I knew my husband's heart was faltering when I agreed to the marriage, although his horse threw him before it gave out. Odds were I would outlive him by a good span. Any children we had would have returned here with me after his death. And his children are nice." I moaned as Apostroph parted my short curls and cool air washed over my pussy lips. "Oh, that's nice—don't stop." Asterix moved his attentions to my other breast and I gasped as he nipped at the tip. "Helping his son learn the ropes of court survival was no chore. He's quick and good with people. He'll do well."

"And you now have a firm ally to the north."

"Indeed." I could only manage one word. Asterix was laving one breast with his tongue and massaging the other. Apostroph thrust two fingers inside me and began to caress the walls of my pussy with light strokes.

Asterix lifted his head. "Would you have done so if you didn't like his son?"

I gathered my wits and gifted him with my sunniest smile. "Of course. Everyone wins. That's the whole point of diplomacy. It just helped that I like him."

I fell back across the pillow I'd been leaning against. My back arched, thrusting my breasts upward. I watched as they each closed a mouth around one nipple. Identical heads at my breasts. The idea that I had two husbands, two lovers, when most women were in the opposite situation, being but one wife of several, brought a gush of cream to my pussy.

"Mmm..." Apostroph hummed and scissored his fingers, sending incredible vibrations streaming along my nerves. Lightning sizzled across me, just under my skin. He thrust deep inside me and pressed on a place that made the lightning dance faster. The two of them began to tug on my nipples in coordination, one right after the other.

Sweet oracle, could I have an orgasm from their mouths alone?

It seemed I could.

Chapter Five

ဆ

I stretched, enjoying the slide of skin across skin and the heat of the men on either side of me. No one waited for me to give them orders. No one watched me to see what I would do. No one knew where I was.

Not only that, for the first time in my life, I was completely relaxed.

Not for long. Asterix began to move, tracing patterns on my arm. "When you've recovered, I need to stake my claim. Feeling it through the bond isn't quite the same as loving you in reality."

I rolled over and smiled into his serious eyes. "And just what does your mark need?" I grasped his penis, which stirred and began to harden in my hand. "Shall I suck your cock? Would you like that?"

"I'd love that, but I'd rather be inside your pussy." His breathing hitched. "I want to see how you really feel."

"I think I can manage that."

Asterix tossed the rest of his wine back in a gulp. Setting the goblet on the table, he came to stand before me wearing a gentle smile. "Now, let the wooing begin."

His lips carried the lingering taste of the wine. I opened my mouth and our tongues thrust and parried until we were both giggling like children.

"Potent wine," Apostroph murmured as he pressed up against my back. His cock, already stiff, nestled in the cleft of my ass.

Asterix lifted his head and corrected him, "Potent woman."

Apostroph nibbled on my shoulder. His hands slipped under my arms and he reached forward to cup my breasts. Asterix kissed me again, while his hand trailed across my hip to linger at the patch of curls between my thighs.

With two fingers, he traced my pussy lips until he found my clit. The fingers parted, one rubbing each side of the sensitive nub. A light squeeze made my hips jerk forward, seeking more. "Sweet heaven," I hissed as he moved lower and delved into the juices I released at his touch.

Apostroph's cock rode up and down as he leaned forward and breathed softly into my ear. "Feel how exciting you are, how beautiful and how sexy." He squeezed my breasts and I shivered in delight.

The room around us faded into a haze. My reality contracted to the three of us.

Asterix knelt between my spread legs. I was more than ready for him to drill me with his cock. A little thicker than his twin's, his erection was just as long and just as pulsing with need. I sat up and ran a finger over the veins and he pulled my hand away with a gasp.

"No! I don't want to come too soon!" He pushed me backward until I lay down again.

This time it was Apostroph who waited to hold me still, although he did it by pressing on my shoulders and not by restraining my hands. Asterix smiled his wicked smile, and I knew he was going to take his revenge for tempting him. I couldn't wait to see what he had in store for me. Although he was punishing me, I knew it would be something I would enjoy.

I didn't have to wait long. He loomed over me, still smiling. With one hand, he grabbed his cock and slid just the tip up and down the outside of my pussy lips. When he reached the top, he circled my clit several times before starting over.

The sensations were incredible. It wasn't long before I was more inflamed than I'd ever been, and he was as well. He shuddered with each movement, and I recalled what Apostroph had said about the friction. I tried to make him take me by raising my hips but he only pulled away.

I was almost sobbing with need before he took pity on me and gave me a taste of his thick shaft. He leaned forward until just the very tip slid inside me. I had thought Apostroph filled me completely, but Asterix promised to stretch me to my limits. I was more than ready, my pussy lips sucking at him as he gave me a bit more.

"Oh gods!" I cried out as he withdrew slightly before pushing back into me. He did that several times more, teasing me until I was ready to burst. Every time he pulled out and slid back in, delight beckoned and danced before me, just out of reach. Gasping, I began rising to meet him, trying to slide up and down the length of his driving shaft.

Through the bond, I shared his struggle to hold on to a measure of control. We rolled over until I was on top. Taking one side of my ass in each hand, he thrust every thick, hard inch he had up into my pussy. We both groaned our satisfaction.

His grip pulled my ass cheeks wide apart. Apostroph slid a hand down my back and I jerked in shock when his oiled finger probed my anus. Shock changed to desire as he slowly entered me there, where I had never imagined penetration would feel so good.

The sensations emanating from his finger were delicious. I reared back against him, only to be pulled back down onto Asterix's cock. Oh, sweet oracle, Apostroph added another finger, then two. This was more than I'd be able to tolerate.

"Relax," he urged and I did my best. To my surprise, the pleasure-pain eased, becoming pure pleasure.

Asterix lifted me up and fastened his mouth around one of my nipples. One strong suck accompanied by the scrape of his teeth took my attention off what was happening behind me.

Until the head of Apostroph's cock eased into my anal passage. More slowly than Asterix had, he pushed in a little at a time, while Asterix kept pounding his hard shaft into my cunt. At last, I accommodated them both.

They moved in counterpoint, one thrusting in while the other withdrew. Violinists, I thought, playing a lively tune, with me as their instrument. We moved in harmony and the music intensified with each stroke.

I could not only imagine what they felt, I shared in the sensation of two cocks rasping across one another, separated by the wall of my pussy.

The pleasure was too intense to be borne. They were going to fuck me into an early death. One of the Earth cultures, according to a book I found tucked behind the stacks in the palace library, called the moment of orgasm *the little death*. I feared this would prove to be much more than that, and they might have to bury us still locked together, in a very large casket.

There was no way this could last forever. I came first, plunging headlong into a shuddering orgasm that clenched my teeth and curled my toes. I screamed their names, over and over, as I gripped them both in uncontrollable spasms.

"Come for me, sweet Cedilla." As Apostroph growled against my neck, he gripped my hips and began thrusting into my ass with rapid, powerful strokes that triggered another incredible climax. "Yes, that's it, come for me again!" He drove deep one last time and filled me with hot cum.

Beneath me, Asterix roared his release and the bed thudded against the wall hard enough to jostle the table and the lamp. As shadowed light flickered across us, I cried out at the intensity of the pleasure we shared. Asterix flooded my pussy with his jetting cum and I returned the favor, my juices flowing out, mixed with his. I swore the whole structure shook around us, echoing our throes of passion.

We collapsed into a moaning tangle. I buried my face against Asterix, shaking with the aftermath of the most incredible fuck of my life. Although both cocks were still deep inside me, none of us could move. We fell asleep that way.

Chapter Six

ඪ

When we awakened sometime later I could barely walk. Muscles I didn't know I had ached whenever I moved. While Apostroph prepared our breakfast, Asterix treated me to a full body massage, using oils he swore kept the gladiators in fighting trim. I supposed they should know more about healing and recovery than anyone else, so I put myself in his capable hands. Plus, I had little choice. I could trust him or suffer. I've never been a fan of suffering.

The man had magic hands. In less than half an hour, I was moving freely, with no trace of pain. Except between my legs, and that was something that would take time to heal. Asterix readily admitted he knew little about feminine discomfort.

My life as the wife of gladiators began with a sumptuous feast of fruit and bread, with half a haunch of leftover roasted meat. Apparently all gladiators ate well.

We ate still tangled on the bed. Asterix and I had never bothered with dressing. Apostroph stripped off his shorts and joined us.

Pounding on the door interrupted us. Nearby shouting accompanied the pounding, echoed by fainter voices some distance away.

"What in all the hells is going on?" Apostroph stumbled to his feet, pulling on a pair of shorts he had just removed. I pulled the sheet up over the two of us left in bed.

Asterix held his head in both hands. He looked the worse for wear, but then, he'd been the one we'd plied with wine. When he looked up and met my eyes, I gave him my best sympathetic smile. I could tell he wasn't fooled.

Apostroph yanked the door open and Dasch all but fell across the threshold. At least, the man looked a lot like the Senator, but under the soot and ash it was hard to tell.

"Cedilla," he croaked, "I thank the gods you are safe. You must return." He was Dasch, but Dasch as I'd never seen him. His hands trembled and his skin was pale beneath the grime.

"Asterix, get him some water." I shoved the sheet aside and reached for the nearest shirt. Heedless of its wrinkles and possible stains, I wrapped it around me and began doing up the buttons. "Sit down, Senator, and tell me why you bothered to track me here. You heard the Emperor. I am outcast, no longer part of the imperial family."

Asterix brought a mug of water and guided the Senator to a chair. Behind me, I heard Apostroph rummage for clothes. Their aplomb pleased me. I would hate to be bound to men without any sense.

"By the gods, you sound just like him." Dasch dropped into the chair with a splat. A puff of ash rose from his garments. "The quake — the aftershocks — the palace collapsed." His voice broke and tears rose in his eyes. One fell, leaving a clean trail down his cheek.

I frowned in confusion. "The quake?" I had enough sense left in my pleasure-sotted brain to not blurt out my surprise at not having noticed an earthquake.

So the earth had moved in truth as we fucked ourselves senseless. Earthquakes were not unknown in the capital. Small tremors were commonplace. This shouldn't have been serious, given the magnitude of the one that had brought down a portion of the palace several months before. Dasch's state of distress, to say nothing of his disarray, said otherwise.

"Your father is dead."

My heart stuttered in my chest and my eyes filled with tears. My grief was overwhelming—and unexpected. How could I feel such deep loss at his death? The man had disowned me. It seemed one day without him as a father mattered little when I had loved him for years.

Asterix and Apostroph came to stand on either side of me, slipping their arms around my waist. I clung to them. Somehow I knew they understood. My sorrow eased with just their presence.

My spine stiffened and my father's training kicked in. Although none of his blood ran in my veins, he had been my father in every way that counted. "Why come to me?"

"The new mortar being used in the palace repairs failed, and its collapse brought down more of the older structure. The roof over the private quarters shattered and fell. All but your brother Macron died, and he sustained a serious head injury. Babbles complete nonsense. Every last one of the imperial family who was worth anything is dead. Except for you." He paused to run his hand over his face, obliterating the evidence of tears. "You are the only one left. You must take the throne and hold it."

"Nonsense. There have to be others."

"No. They were all there. Your brothers, your nephews, even your nieces. You saw how they slept, crammed into close quarters until the renovations were completed. We have searched since the quake stopped and found only Macron and bodies."

"I am not the Emperor's daughter. I have no right."

A crafty gleam, one I had seen often, came into his eyes. "But you are your mother's daughter. Through the maternal line, you have a claim on the throne not only of the Midlands, but that of Bitterland as well. No one will contest your bloodright."

Dasch was correct. My mother's family was royalty. How could I have forgotten that? My maternal grandmother had come from one of the Empire's first families, one with ties to the throne. One of my uncles controlled Bitterland. He had five wives but no children. I was his titular heir although I never expected to rule. We were about the same age and it was more likely that a son of mine would inherit that throne.

My thoughts raced. "How much damage is there elsewhere?"

"Little enough, from what I hear. On the way here, I saw a few houses that caved in. The masons working on the palace tell me the new mortar in the interior walls had yet to set fully and so a small quake was enough to bring it down." Dasch stared up at me. "We need your leadership. We need it now. Finding you wasted valuable time. There is panic in some parts of the city, and it will only grow as rumors spread."

"You were born for this," Apostroph whispered.

"There has been no time to inform the Senate of your father's decision yesterday to denounce you." Dasch rose to his feet and assumed the confident stance he used when orating on the Senate floor. "You and I and those two guards are the only ones who know."

"And their captain," I reminded him.

He made a dismissive gesture. "If they did as they were ordered. That can be contained."

Asterix tightened his grip on my waist. "We will be with you every step of the way."

"You don't understand, loves, consorts here are hidden, invisible. Outside of the family, they do not exist."

The twins exchanged a worried look. "We thought that was wives."

I looked at Dasch, whose expression had changed to one of distaste.

"You have two consorts?"

Wordlessly, the three of us pulled aside our garments to show him the marks.

He sat down again. Hard. "This changes things."

"How much? You heard the Emperor say these are the marks of the southern kings." I gave the twins a minute shake of my head and they shut their mouths. No need to disillusion Dasch, not when it would work to our advantage. "Does it not reinforce the claim of royalty?"

"But two husbands—it isn't done!"

"An Empress hasn't been done, either. How badly do you need my help?"

He ran a trembling hand over his sober face. Despite the dirt and dishevelment, he was still a formidable figure. I hid a smile. Whatever he decided, the rest of the Senate would follow. I had no need to woo the masses; convincing this one man would suffice.

"The palace might not be the only structure that collapsed. Have you sent messengers to check on your peers? How many advisers are missing and presumed dead?"

Dasch paled again. "I had no time to think of that, once I realized the palace was gone. We were all tearing at the rubble and searching for survivors. My concern was to secure the Empire, and the Emperor is the Empire."

"Two husbands, and they will remain at my side, on daily display." I pressed the issue. There would be time enough later to change the rules completely and bring the wives out of their homes. "If not, we go south to my husbands' home. I cannot expect them to live a life I would find intolerable."

The Senate leader stared at us. I met his gaze steadily. If I did not win this battle of wills, I would forever be a pawn.

Finally he turned to examine the men who flanked me, taking their measure. I watched different emotions flicker through his eyes.

A man may school his features but his eyes will betray his thoughts. How often had I heard my father say that? I squelched the grief that rose within me. The best way I could honor the memory of my father was to take his place, as he had often wished I could do. He had taught me to negotiate well, and I could do no less than take it on my terms. It helped that I held all the cards.

Dasch realized that as the thought ran through my mind. I watched as resignation came into his eyes, followed by resolve. I relaxed imperceptibly and managed to conceal my triumph.

He rose and straightened, shaking out his clothes. We stepped back to avoid the resulting dust cloud.

"I apologize, Your Highness." He bowed. "With your permission, I will return in a bit with an armed escort to return you to your rightful place."

I held out my hand and, after a hesitation, he took it. "I appreciate the formality, dear Dasch, but we are alone now. I hope that you will continue to be as good a friend and adviser to me as you were to my father. May the gods smile on his soul."

"I am so glad we didn't lose you, too. The Emperor always said you were worth far more than both your brothers rolled into one." When I grinned at him, he grinned back. "Let me see if we can salvage anything from your quarters. You appear to be in need of suitable garments."

"And jewelry. Don't forget the emeralds. They go with the cream silk, if that survived."

"Your maid was dismissed last evening. I'll have her summoned and she will take care of you. It will mean a promotion for her, now that you are Empress."

"I'm not crowned yet."

"We'll take care of that this afternoon or tomorrow morning."

"I'd rather you accounted for the full Senate first."

"This cannot wait. You have been back too short a time to know everything. Your grandmother's family has been plotting to overthrow your father." He grinned and suddenly looked years younger. "What a coup this will be! A member of their family on the throne, but one who owes them nothing." He rubbed his hands together in anticipation. "I look forward to giving them the news personally."

"After the coronation."

"Yes. Afterwards. We only need a quorum, and I can raise that immediately." He rubbed his chin and eyed Apostroph and Asterix. "Two consorts' crowns may present a problem."

"Not at all. Doesn't my father have several matching pendants with the imperial seal on them?"

"Three, I believe." He sounded more like his old self. The prospect of confounding my mother's family's ambitions was going a long way to ease the pain over the death of his friend and Emperor.

"Then use them for all of us, and add the crown for me. Find two matching chairs somewhere."

"The throne did not survive."

"There you go! Find three chairs from somewhere, and just mount one higher than the others. We'll manage."

Apostroph spoke up. "It will be a quick ceremony anyway, won't it?"

"The city needs search and rescue teams organized and dispatched as soon as possible," his brother added. "We can draft the gladiators to help."

Dasch nodded. "I believe we will manage. It may take me an hour or more to gather the guards and your possessions."

"We'll make ourselves ready," I assured him and ushered him out the door.

After he closed the street door behind him, I locked our door and broke into a happy dance. My lovers joined me, the three of us holding hands and whirling around the room.

We fell in a breathless heap on the bed. Eyes closed, head spinning with both triumph and the vertigo of the dance, I lay cradled in their arms. My hand fell on the raised ridges of one of their marks and I stroked it. Heat blossomed in response, warming my mark and sending a glow of desire through me.

Lips met mine and I opened in invitation. Asterix, from the taste. Apostroph shifted me so I straddled his brother's hips and began licking the back of my neck. When he moved to nuzzle my ear, I angled my head to give him better access.

He took the advantage and suckled my earlobe. A thrill ran down to my breast, peaking my nipple. Asterix reached up and tweaked the hardened tip. I descended with them into a world of pure sensation.

Eyes still closed, I was hard-pressed to know who was doing what. Hands caressed my skin. Fingers massaged erogenous zones and dipped into my pussy. Tongues stroked and teased my nipples and clit.

I ended up on my knees, ass in the air while one of them licked and sucked on my pussy.

"Dasch will be back soon."

"Mmmm," was the only response I was capable of making.

"Nice tactic, threatening to go home with us. It provided leverage at just the right time and worked out well."

"Who says I was threatening?"

They both stilled.

"I would go with you wherever you go." A horrible thought struck me. "Oh, gods, I never thought to ask. You do want to rule with me, don't you?"

"Turn down a throne? Regardless of what your people think, the marks we bear are not the sign of Sudania's royal family. At home, we are simple farmers."

"And your talents would be wasted at that. You are far too intelligent to spend your days ankle-deep in fertilizer."

"How would you have us spend our days?"

"By my side, hearing petitions and planning for the good of the Midlands. And your nights? No question there. Balls-deep in me."

"I think we can manage that."

"Can you handle being called names for marrying two men, and foreigners at that?"

"Oh, I decided long ago that I was not the average Midlander. Call me barbarian or whatever, it matters not to me. Besides, with you two hulking gladiators at my side, who's going to say anything to my face?"

They laughed and drew me into an embrace.

Life was good.

It still is.

The End

About the Author

෬

Liddy Midnight lives, loves, works and writes in the woods of eastern Pennsylvania, surrounded by lush greenery and wildlife. Although raccoons, possums, skunks and the occasional fox eat the cat food on her back porch, she's no more than half an hour from some of the finest shopping in the country. Situated in this best of all possible worlds, how could she write anything other than romance?

Liddy welcomes mail from readers. You can write to her c/o Ellora's Cave Publishing at 1056 Home Avenue, Akron OH 44310-3502.

Also by Liddy Midnight

ℰꙘ

Fire and Ice
In Moonlight (*anthology*)
Small Magick
Transformations (*anthology*)

By Liddy Midnight writing as Annalise

ℰꙘ

Equinox II (*anthology*)
Venus Rising

SPONTANEOUS COMBUSTION

Nicole Austin

Dedication

∽

To Teri who so graciously has offered her friendship. Thank you for making the time in your busy life to read for me and offer your valuable opinion.

Trademarks Acknowledgement

~

The author acknowledges the trademarked status and trademark owners of the following wordmarks mentioned in this work of fiction:

Slip N' Slide: Wham-O, Inc.

Barbie: Mattel, INC.

Corvette: General Motors Corporation

Heimlich Maneuver: EDUMED, Inc.

Mensa: American Mensa Limited

Chapter One

ഔ

"Tell me your deepest, darkest fantasies."

The words were breathed in a husky, sultry tone against Maddy's ear. Warm breath caressed her neck, raising the fine hairs at her nape and sending chills coursing down her spine.

She didn't have to turn around, knowing instantly to whom that deep sexy baritone voice belonged. How she would love to provide explicit graphic details of her most intimate fantasies for him. Or better yet, maybe they could act them out.

"Come on. Tell me, babe. What is it? Being bound to the bed, or maybe oiled up on a Slip N' Slide? Do you dream of sweet lovemaking, or hard fucking? One lover or several?"

Icy shivers prickled along her skin. Just the sound of his voice, his erotic words, had her nipples puckered and pressing against the bodice of her little black dress. She had worn it in hopes of catching his eye. Not that he would ever notice Maddy as a woman. His buddy, sure. A woman, never. His words were all in jest as usual, right?

"How much have you had to drink tonight, Jake?" she questioned, then gasped as he licked a hot wet path along the ultrasensitive skin behind her ear.

"Stop it, Jake!" Maddy squealed in protest. Of course, stopping him was the last thing she wanted to do. But giving in meant risking both heart and soul. She couldn't stand the thought of being rejected by this man, the only one who really mattered.

Jake Cruise had been her best friend and neighbor since college. They had shared everything. Well, almost everything. She couldn't share her true desires with him, could she? As if he'd ever want to have sex with her. He was such a tease.

Maddy gave herself a mental shake. What was she thinking? Of course she couldn't. It would ruin their friendship. Probably freak him out to hear her dark, forbidden passions.

"Come on, Maddy. Tell me," he pleaded.

"I don't have dark fantasies, Jake. You know I'm a good girl."

Yeah, right! Liar, liar, pants on fire!

If Jake didn't stop whispering in her ear, Maddy's panties just might catch on fire. Heat surged through her blood, pooling in her swollen labia. Her panties were soaked in her creamy juices. At least she was in the right place to have the fire put out if she went up in flames. Half the guys from the firehouse were scattered throughout the rowdy pub.

Man, the train of her naughty thoughts was out of control. If she were the devout good girl her parents wanted her to be, Maddy would be spending a lot of time in the confessional, saying a lot of Hail Marys. It certainly was a good thing her dark thoughts were private. If anyone in her family knew the things that ran through her mind she'd be labeled a wicked bad girl. She was not a bad girl. She just had some bad thoughts once in a while, right?

I am a good girl!

Well, she'd been raised to be a good little Catholic girl. It was just her baser carnal desires that made her feel like a bad girl. Maddy had done everything she could to keep them suppressed. Good, intelligent girls just didn't think about the things that haunted her mind late at night, many of them involving Jake and a few of their closest friends dominating her sexually.

Truth be told, Maddy had been in lust with Jake since the first time she had laid eyes on him across their quiet street. Standing in his driveway, he'd been wearing only a pair of red swim trunks while washing his pride and joy, a shiny blue convertible Corvette. Jesus, the man made her sweat. He'd looked like a shiny-bronzed god standing there, caressed by golden rays of sunlight. He was perfect.

If only I was his idea of a goddess!

But she was so not his type. Jake went for the typical blonde Barbie doll types with large breasts, impossibly thin waists, long legs, and low IQs. Maddy was far, far removed from that image. Her hair was shoulder-length, fiery red and extremely curly. Her breasts, while pert and firm, barely filled out a C cup. She wore a curvy size fourteen, considered her legs to be only average, and held a PhD. Although she knew men thought her to be pretty, she could never measure up to one of the beauties that usually captured Jake's attention.

"Come on, Red. You can tell your ol' friend Jake."

I want you, Jake. I fantasize about you all night, every damn night. Hard, fast, and dangerously wild fucking. I want you to take control, and lavish me with more pleasure than I can handle.

Sure, that would go over well. Not! She could never tell him her true desires and fantasies. Not when Jake continually tried to set her up with boring, nerdy, three-piece suit desk jockeys. How could she ever make him understand that was not what she wanted or needed?

No, she didn't want some boring average guy, with a boring average job, and absolutely no sex appeal. There had to be chemistry. Heck, she wanted to see sparks fly. To feel the electric jolts of lightning that surged through her body every time Jake casually laid a hand on her arm. Like they did every time she was near the totally hot, adventurous bad boy currently whispering in her ear. God, if only he were truly attempting to seduce her.

Now that really was a fantasy. Jake liked to joke and pal around with Maddy. He treated her like a little sister. Actually, more like one of the guys. They went to action movies together, hung out having wings and beer with the other guys from the firehouse, and participated in extreme sports. She had even gone to a strip club with the guys once. Now that had been embarrassing.

"Do you dream of a big, hard cock sliding in and out of your slick heat?" he asked in a husky tone. "Or maybe it is dual penetration that gets you wet. Maybe you want to be forced onto your knees and made to take my cock past those pouty lips, right here in the pub with everyone watching." His voice became raspy, filled with need, driving her to the edge of reason.

Oh God, yes! Please!

She wanted to scream out that answer, drop to her knees and part her lips. To just once take a chance, be a little bit wicked. Or maybe even a lot wicked. Experience the fervor of unleashed animalistic lusts.

Maddy bit back a moan as one of her favorite fantasies came to mind. She was trapped in her bedroom, calling out for help. Panic set in when she'd awoken to a fire. Then she heard his sultry voice from the other side of the door. Jake chopped through the wood with rhythmic swings of a sharp axe, talking soothingly the whole time.

When she could finally see him, sweat glistened on his bronze, muscular flesh. Each movement set rippling muscles moving sinuously beneath his slick skin. Mmm…his yellow turnout pants were slung low over narrow hips, red suspenders over broad, bare shoulders. Smears of dirt here and there on that muscular chest, dark hair spread like a lush pelt over the wide expanse of gloriously male hard body.

A five o'clock shadow darkened his square jaw and firm upper lip. God, those were the most kissable lips, pleasantly plump but not overly so. The pale white flesh of the scar slashing across his right cheek only enhanced his rakish bad boy looks, giving his face character. While no one would ever call Jake a pretty boy, he definitely was rugged and sexy as all get out.

"It's okay, babe. I'm here now," he would reassure.

His jet-black hair always appeared slightly mussed up, the silky strands hanging over one sapphire blue eye, cascading down onto his shoulders. The smoldering look of desire in those gorgeous eyes as she slowly moved to his side put a seductive sway into her curvy hips and made her burn. If the room weren't already on fire, that look in his eyes alone would certainly spark some flames. She would look past his shoulder and see the other guys, similarly half turned out, standing in the doorway.

Okay, so no firefighter would respond to an emergency bare-chested, wearing only half his gear, but hey, this was a fantasy after all. And in Maddy's wet dreams they always showed up just in time—hot, horny, and half dressed.

Of course, she was no wilting daisy that needed rescuing. Maddy considered herself to be a tough broad, totally capable of taking care of herself in almost any situation. Not in her fantasy though.

Placing both hands on his magnificently sculpted pecs, Maddy would slowly slide the suspenders down sinewy arms, letting her fingertips graze over every curve and sinew. Then she would drop to her knees, sliding her hands over rippling abs to pull his pants down. Jake would stand before her in the body-hugging boxer briefs he favored, pants pooled around his boots. The formfitting underwear did nothing to hide the impressive package so wonderfully displayed along his hip.

She was always wearing a silky hunter green chemise in these heated visions. With an impressive display of strength, Jake would tear the thin garment in his haste to uncover the feminine wonders that lay beneath. Then several pairs of large, thick-fingered hands would touch and tease every fevered inch of flesh as they all pleasured her.

"Tell me what you're thinking that's getting you so hot and bothered. What's bringing that sexy little smile to your gorgeous lips, raising your heart rate?"

Damn her pale, freckled, redhead's complexion. Maddy could feel a bright red flush burning on her cheeks and neck. The heated embarrassment of being caught fantasizing spread all the way down to her breasts. She felt flushed all over. A deer caught in the hot, bright glare of oncoming headlights.

They really needed to turn down the air conditioner in this place. With a great effort of will she was barely able to restrain the need to fan herself with her hand.

This time his lips moved enticingly against the shell of her ear as he leaned in close. The musky scent of her arousal rose heavily in the heated air surrounding them. She prayed that he would not notice, but knew she was not going to be that lucky. Jake was currently nuzzling her hair and down her neck, only stopping when he reached the thin strap of her dress. For a brief moment Maddy thought she felt the wet heat of his tongue on her shoulder, but she must be mistaken.

He leaned back, intense blue eyes meeting hers in the mirror behind the bar, piercing the outer calm she struggled to project. She looked over her shoulder, mesmerized as the pink tip of his tongue peeked out between those sensual lips, then traced a wet path over the comely curves. Maddy spotted several of their friends closely watching every move they made.

"Jake!"

Twisting around on the barstool, planting both hands against the solid wall of his chest, she shoved at him. He stood statue still. "You are such a pest. Why don't you go bother someone else?" She made a show of looking around the crowded bar. "Where's this week's Barbie doll gone off to anyway?"

His penetrating gaze never left her face. "Candy prefers the ritzy clubs downtown. Said she wouldn't be caught dead hanging out in a dive like this." A little shrug of indifference briefly drew up his broad shoulders.

That figured. A local joint like O'Rourke's Pub certainly was not Candy's style. It was the favorite hangout of the local cops and firefighters. Amazing how it suited Maddy so well. Sweet, bleached blonde airheads just didn't fit in at the rowdy pub.

She wanted to laugh out loud over that thought. Why were women who were not very intelligent always referred to as sweet? And why were all Jake's women named after foods and drinks anyway? The most recent names flashed through her mind. Brandy, Brie, Cherry, Ginger, Sherry. And Maddy's personal all-time favorite, Honey. Why any parent would name their daughter Honey was beyond her. That is, unless they wanted her to grow up to become a stripper.

"Come on, Red. Tell me what turns you on."

Y O U! You turn me on, Jake.

Her annoying friend was just not letting up tonight. Okay, time for a subject change. "I wonder if Candy's gone off to join the other female foods," Maddy giggled. "Ambrosia, Cookie, Peaches, Melba ..." She broke into a fit of hysterical laughter which made her eyes water as she doubled over. "You…you must be…so hungry…all the time," she gasped out between fits of laughter.

Two of the guys standing closest to them heard her joke. Luke guffawed and Tom slapped his thigh before howling with laughter. The look on Jake's face just made her laugh harder. He seemed genuinely offended, even hurt. Well, it served him right.

"Making fun of the girls I date is not going to make me forget the topic, Maddy," he chastised.

Damn, busted. Leave it to Jake not to be distracted by her antics. "Jake Cruise, I would not tell you my fantasies, even if I did have any."

A serious, worried look crossed his face. God, how she loved that face. She was tempted to reach out and smooth the dark locks of hair away from his forehead, then gently soothe the deep lines furrowed there with her fingertips. Something always stopped her though. Regardless of all they had shared, there had never been anything sexual between them. No matter how much she'd always wanted him, Jake never had been and never would be hers.

"Come on. Good little Catholic girls usually have the wildest fantasies. If you won't tell then I'll guess. And if I get it right…if I turn you on…well, then we go home and act it out."

Maddy nearly choked on her mouthful of beer. That would have been great. It would have aspirated down into her lungs and brought on a major coughing fit. Knowing Jake, he'd try to do the Heimlich maneuver on her or something.

Of course, Jake knew exactly how to get under Maddy's skin. Growing up the youngest of six children, the only girl, she'd been teased and tormented beyond belief. Her brothers were all so rough and tumble, into one-upping each other. Being the baby of the group, the only girl, she'd always had to prove herself. Go one step further than her brothers, show she was tougher.

It had been obvious in the wild stunts she was willing to participate in with the guys. All they had to do was make an offhand comment that a woman wouldn't be able to do something, and she had to prove them wrong. The guys all knew what a dare did to her. Regardless that she understood the psychology involved, dares were something Maddy could not walk away from. It went right back to trying to fit in with her brothers, prove that she was good enough to hang around with them. If he dared her now she was doomed.

"Come on, babe. What's the chance I'll get it right?"

"Yeah, like you could possibly understand what an intelligent, sophisticated woman desires. You've been hanging out with the food bimbos a little too long, Jake. There is no way you'd figure out what I fantasize about."

Okay, that was probably pushing too far. Now he was bound to say the one thing that would put steel into her spine and force her hand. And she really had it coming after her taunting words. Why did she push him on this?

"I dare you. What's the chance of me getting it right, slim to none?"

He gently pushed her knees apart and moved to stand between her legs, nice and close. Too damn close. The scent of sandalwood and testosterone-ridden male heat made her nostrils flare.

Oooooh, what a brat. He knew exactly what those words did to her. It didn't matter that she was a well-educated intellectual woman with her doctorate in psychology. Challenge her, make it a dare, and there was no way she could resist. Especially when she figured the odds were in her favor. Heck, just thinking about the guys he'd set her up with over the years boosted her confidence. Jake didn't truly know what she wanted. No way!

Chapter Two

ﾞﾚ

The luck of the Irish had failed Maddy. That was how she now found herself being driven home to act out the most outrageous fantasy with her best friend. She sat on the passenger side of Jake's Vette, clutching her purse over her now panty-free mound.

Crap, crap, crap, and double crap! She was supposed to be smarter than this. Yeah, like her high IQ, PhD, and Mensa membership did her any good in this situation. How the hell was she supposed to have fantasy sex for one night with Jake, and then ever be able to look him in the eye again?

Come on, Miss Smarty Pants. Figure a way out of this hole you dug for yourself, and fast. Okay, time to put on the thinking cap. In about two minutes they would be home, and Jake was expecting to fulfill one very erotic fantasy.

Instead of working on a solution, Maddy kept replaying their conversation over and over again in her mind. Jake's deep raspy voice softly speaking close to her ear, his hot breath kicking up her internal temperature. The way he looked deep into her eyes, but it seemed more as if he was looking straight into her very soul.

"*I know what you want, Maddy. What you need,*" he'd cockily stated. "*And I am the one man who can give it to you, because it's what I want, what I need, too.*" The look in his eyes had turned hungry, feral. "*Don't you worry about a thing, babe. I'm going to make it so good for you.*"

Then he proceeded to reach into the deepest, darkest recesses of her soul and draw out every secret longing, every hidden desire. She felt as if he'd waltzed straight into her dreams, capturing her most intimate longings.

"You dream about dark, wild fucking. You want to be tied up, outside. Somewhere off the beaten path, yet public. You want to be stripped naked, body and soul, out where anyone could walk by and maybe even join in the fun. To submit yourself completely, turning over all responsibility for your pleasure to another.

"I will drive you so wild with my fingers, lips, and tongue that you'll be screaming my name. You will beg me to stop, and plead for me to finish you off with the very next breath. I'll keep you hanging on edge until you entrust me with everything."

"You're wrong, Jake," she had lied. *"I don't want any of that."*

If he didn't know her so well, Maddy could have pulled off the lie that she had not been turned on by his fantasy scenario. But the jerk had held her wrist the whole time, felt the changes in her pulse. He'd even measured the increase in her respiratory rate as her breathing became fast and shallow. And there was no hiding the heat rising from between her legs. Not when he stood wedged so closely between her thighs.

She had nearly melted into a puddle at his feet. Leaning close, his fingers had casually brushed over one painfully swollen nipple. Maddy had not been able to suppress her needy moan. The fingers of his other hand settled down on her knee, and then trailed a scorching path up her thigh. And if that wasn't enough, Jake had really shocked her with his next words.

"Are you wet for me, Maddy?" The heat pouring off his big body had nearly branded her skin. *"I can smell your sweet scent, babe."*

She had sputtered and gasped like one of his brainless food bimbos. *"Jake Cruise, you are a rude, arrogant prick,"* she'd declared, voice full of righteous indignation.

He'd just laughed. *"I'm sorry, Red. I must have misunderstood. Did you just say you want to see my enormous, amazing dick? If you said anything else you've just earned a spanking."*

A spanking? That idea certainly had potential. She had always wondered how it would feel. Would the initial sting transition into a slow burn? Would it make Jake as hot as the idea made her?

When he had finally stopped laughing, Jake continued to drive her absolutely out of her mind. The hand that had rested at the hem of her short dress, dangerously close to the apex of her legs, began to move upwards once again. The material slid salaciously over her thighs, leaving way too much leg bare.

"There's only one way to prove whether you were turned on or not. I'll have to check if your panties are dry."

Maddy had nearly fainted right then and there. Although she'd never been one prone to syncopal episodes before, Jake was really getting to her. *"No way, no how,"* she'd said, slapping his wandering hand away.

He just laughed at her again. *"Okay. Then go to the bathroom, slip off your panties, and bring them back to me."*

"When hell freezes over, Jake."

Her spine had stiffened, there was no way she'd give him her panties. Not just because she'd creamed them either. Then he'd hit her in her stubborn pride, striking a fatal blow.

"Okay, babe. I'm sorry. Should have known you couldn't take the heat, follow through on the dare you accepted. It was a little too much for you. Never mind."

And then he'd struck the final nail into her coffin.

"I've got this friend that's more your speed. Greg's a junior accountant with an up-and-coming career. I'll set you guys up for a

date sometime next week. He is real stand-up good guy. Someone just perfect for you."

Maddy knew he was playing her, but now her back was against the wall and she came out swinging.

"Fine, I'll prove to you it didn't turn me on."

"Good. Run on over to the ladies' room like a good little girl and bring me back my prize."

It had been a command, not a request. And what other choice had she had? It was either let him slide his hand all the way up under her dress in front of everyone, or go to the bathroom and take off her panties in private. Just the thought of putting her wet panties into his hand sent a fresh gush of juices over her pussy lips.

As they'd left the pub, Maddy had felt like all eyes were on them and everyone knew exactly what they were about to do. They'd made the rounds, saying goodnight to their friends. Luke had hugged her tightly and whispered in her ear. "If you need rescuing from that rogue, just call me, honey. I'll come and save you. Whisk you away somewhere safe and warm."

Now where the hell had that come from? Did he know something she didn't?

* * * * *

Jake couldn't hold back the wide grin that spread across his face every time he surreptitiously looked at Maddy from the corner of his eye. For once he'd finally gotten to the confident, intelligent, tough as nails woman who'd been making him crazy for longer than he could remember. Broken past her proper little façade.

He'd figured out some time ago that if he was ever going to get to Maddy, he'd have to use what he knew about her, push her past her barriers.

She was so nervous that she couldn't sit still. Each time she wiggled her butt against the leather seat a little more of her thigh was revealed, driving him to distraction. She held a white-knuckle grip on her purse while he casually rubbed her silky, wet ivory panties against his cheek, and under his nose. Hell, he primarily did it because he could tell it was making her nuts, taking her out of her comfort zone.

He couldn't wait to get her naked, spread open the soft folds of her pussy and taste her sweet cream. His cock was harder than the steel pole in the firehouse just from the scent of her arousal permeating the air, saturating the scrap of material. He never would have imagined her wearing such sexy, lace-trimmed panties.

Thankfully it had taken her awhile in the bathroom to work up enough courage to bring them to him. During that time Jake had make arrangements with two of their friends. Together they would make this a night that Dr. Madailein Flannagan would never forget. But first he needed to gather some supplies.

Pulling up into his driveway, Jake shut off the engine and turned toward Maddy. She just continued to stare out the windshield, refusing to look at him. Her nervousness almost made him want to let her off the hook. Almost, but no dice. Not when he finally had her just where he wanted her.

Damn, how he loved everything about Maddy. He would have had her long before now if she weren't so far out of his league. Smart good girls like her deserved a hell of a lot more than someone like him. Facts are facts. Jake only had a high school diploma and firefighter certification.

So he'd held himself back all this time, marking time dating the silly flavors of the week. He just couldn't wait any more. He had to have Maddy, put his mark on her. And there was no turning back now. He had every intention of making her his. If she would have him, he would treat her like a princess, give her anything she desired. There was nothing he wouldn't do to ensure her happiness.

"Look at me, babe," he ordered.

She complied with a reluctant, deliberate turn of her head, staring somewhere in the vicinity of his chin.

"Up here, babe." He waited for her to finally look him in the eye before continuing. If she was going to submit to him, she had to learn to do as told.

"I'm going inside to pick up a few things." He gave her a stern look. "Don't even think about moving out of that seat. If you're not sitting right there when I come back out I'll have no choice but to spank that luscious ass of yours."

"You wouldn't dare," Maddy gasped, and dropped her gaze once again.

Jake took her chin in his hand, bringing her eyes back to his own. "Don't doubt me, Madailein. Have you ever known me to not follow through on something I've said? Think about it. And as a little precaution I'll be setting the car alarm. It will go off if you open the door."

Her gorgeous hazel eyes widened in surprise. The pupils were so dilated Jake could barely make out much of their normally warm green color. "Stay put, babe," he warned, never breaking eye contact.

Jake hit the garage door remote then climbed out of the low-slung sports car. Once inside the house, he grabbed a small nylon duffel bag from the bedroom and tossed in various items. Back in the garage he rummaged around for some rope. He glanced surreptitiously over at the car. Maddy still sat exactly where he'd left her, fidgeting uncomfortably. Good, let her sweat.

Just thinking about what he had planned made his cock press painfully against his jeans. He'd waited so long to finally pin her down. There was no way he would let her wiggle out of making good on the dare. Sure he felt a little bit guilty seeing how nervous she had become, but that was not going to change his plans.

Maddy was the kind of woman whom he could picture being his perfect life partner. Her easygoing, adventurous personality complemented him so well. They loved to do all the same things, rock climbing, rappelling, skydiving, both water and snow skiing. Heck, there wasn't anything she was afraid to try. And she usually excelled at all physical challenges.

Fiercely independent and dominating in her work as a therapist, she projected strength and power. Yet deep inside he saw her need to turn over control during sex, the need to submit her body and needs to the right partner.

And what a body. The exact things she hated about herself were the features that Jake loved. Nothing felt better than one of those springy red curls wrapped around his finger. Mmm…and all those glorious curves. Nothing would please him more than to lose several hours just tracing each and every contour.

The diets she was always on made him want to scream. For a woman so confident in every other area of her life, Jake didn't understand why she was so insecure about that gorgeous body. Hell, last year Maddy had nearly starved herself on some crazy cabbage soup diet to lose only ten pounds.

The alarm chirped as he deactivated it, suppressing a smile at her having submitted in this small way. "Good girl," he praised when he climbed back into the car. "Now we're going to have some fun."

Panic shone in Maddy's wide-eyed, somewhat glassy gaze. Jake silently cussed himself. He was being a bastard, but there was no turning back. He needed her too much. Hell, he'd needed her for way too long. Now that he had her in his grasp there was no way he was letting her slip free.

He had to give her credit. She remained quiet during the short trip to nearby Kinsey Park, finally speaking when the car was parked in the deepest shadows of the empty lot, the engine turned off.

"Jake, I can't do this."

With a deep sigh he took her hand, giving it a gentle squeeze. "Yes you can, babe. I'll be with you the whole time. All you have to do is relax and enjoy. Give yourself over to my care."

"But, Jake…"

"Shh, Maddy. No more talking unless I ask you a question, or give you permission first. I'm in charge now. You just follow my instructions. Trying something new can't hurt you. If you don't like something that I do, you have permission to tell me and I'll stop. I won't do it again unless you ask me to.

"Your job tonight is to just let go. Turn over care for your body and pleasure to me. I know you trust me, otherwise you would never have jumped out of a plane with nothing but me and a piece of nylon to get you safely back on the ground."

Jake held his breath. He half expected her to fight him on this, show her steely backbone and stubborn pride. Damn, if she turned him down now he'd fucking die. He'd never wanted a woman so much before. His desire for Maddy was like a burning ache deep within his soul that only she could relieve. But he'd walk away if she didn't trust him, since trust was so essential in any relationship.

For several moments she just sat there, deep in thought. He began to worry that she would back out of their deal until she nodded her head.

"I trust you, Jake."

With just those four simple words he felt like the luckiest man alive. He wanted to shout and throw his fist up in the air in triumph. Instead, he just nodded back. She was his now. His to love and care for. His to pleasure and dominate.

"Good. Come on, let's go."

Jake slung the bag over his shoulder. He carried a flashlight in one hand, the other he kept around Maddy's waist for support. Walking over the rough terrain of the dark runners' path in four-inch fuck-me heels made her somewhat unsteady. Before long they reached a small clearing, never seeing another soul along the way. No one used the park at night, which was exactly what made it perfect.

Four areas in the park were set up to perform different exercise activities. The idea was to run along the four-mile trail and stop to perform the exercises in each clearing along the way. The one where they stood now suited Jake's purposes just fine.

Guiding Maddy to the middle of the clearing, he dropped the bag at the base of the chin-up bar. It had a wooden frame with a metal pole across the top and was just what he needed. He'd fantasized about tying Maddy up here every morning during his workout. The frame featured several sets of holes bored into the wood along its length allowing users to adjust for height differences.

It was a warm night, so he knew that Maddy's shivering was not due to the temperature. Pulling her up against his chest, Jake tried to soothe her nerves. "It's okay, babe. We'll take things slow. Just relax."

She came to him willingly, leaning into the shelter and warmth of his body. With slow motions, Jake stroked his hands over her back and the silky skin of her bare arms. Just like a little kitten she snuggled up against him, rubbing her cheek against his chest.

Damn! It was sheer heaven to finally hold her close as something other than just a friend.

After several minutes, Jake cupped her beautiful face in his big hands. Lowering his head slowly, he held her eyes with his own until they were too close to focus. At first he just brushed his lips over the warm fullness of her mouth. Then he used his tongue to trace the generous curves before sliding along the seam, seeking entrance.

Maddy's lips parted on a sigh. What started out as an easy, tender discovery quickly built into burning passion. Jake wanted to holler with joy as he felt Maddy give herself over to his kiss. Their tongues twirled and tasted while their lips sucked each other deeper. It felt so good to finally taste what he had endlessly longed for.

Damn! It was even better than anything he'd imagined.

While she let him take the lead, Maddy was in no way passive. She sucked on his tongue, inviting him for a deeper tasting. God, did she taste good. Her mouth was hot, warm, wet, and very receptive to his advances. He could taste the dark amber beer they had drunk earlier. Underneath that were the deep, sensual flavors of warm summer sunshine and willing woman.

"God, babe. We've wasted so much time waiting." The heat steadily built between them. Soon they were sealed together from shoulder to knee, but it still wasn't close enough. Her firm breasts were pressed into his chest, the soft flesh of her belly cradling his throbbing cock. Intense warmth radiated from every curve of her soft body. If he didn't get inside her heat soon he just might die.

Their hands were everywhere, exploring, inciting need. They still had way too many clothes on, but not for long. Pulling himself back was the most difficult thing he'd ever done, but hell if he'd do this half-assed. He wanted the joy of seeing Maddy subjugate herself before him. Her acquiescence to both their needs was a beautiful gift that he wanted to fully enjoy.

"Strip for me," he demanded.

He saw the defiance in the tight set of her shoulders, the deep furrowed lines across her forehead. This would be a turning point for them. Either she would submit to his demands, or they would not be able to continue.

"Do it. Now," he ordered in a tone that left no room for discussion.

A multitude of emotions played across her sweet face in a matter of seconds. He waited without breathing as she came to a decision at this important stage in the game.

Maddy's hand shook as she reached around for the zipper at her nape. She lowered it with slow, deliberate movements, her eyes downcast. Hesitating for only a moment, she shrugged her creamy shoulders, letting the straps slide down her arms.

"Look at me, babe." The words came out slightly harsh. Maddy's slightly timid green eyes jerked upward to meet his own intense gaze.

"Continue," he said, giving her a slight nod.

While Jake was not truly into the Dom/sub lifestyle, he would expect her to comply with his wishes concerning their newly developing sexual relationship without hesitation. Soon enough she'd learn that compliance would lead to the fulfillment of pleasure beyond her wildest dreams when they played this way.

Maddy could be as fiercely independent as she wanted outside of the bedroom, or park as it were. Hell, he applauded her self-reliance out in the world, but he would be top dog in everything sexual.

Chapter Three

ဢ

With a provocative wiggle of her curvy hips, Maddy pushed the dark material over her pearly, freckled flesh, allowing it to pool around her ankles. Good Lord, the woman had no idea how her inherent sensuality literally radiated from every beautiful inch of supple flesh. It was her utter unawareness of both her intoxicating sensuality and feminine allure that attracted Jake. She was nothing like the vain, self-absorbed women he tended to date.

With her dress lying pooled at her feet, Jake stood back to drink in the glorious sight of her voluptuous curves. Pearly white skin was dotted with scattered freckles. He wanted to taste each and every delectable spot. Her breasts stood firm and proud, nipples pebbled beneath the lacy white strapless bra that matched the panties in his pocket. Nothing fake there.

There was just enough moonlight for him to see each peak and valley of Maddy's gorgeous body. His eyes were unerringly drawn to the dark red triangle of curly hair at the apex of her thighs.

"You are so beautiful, Maddy. Absolutely perfect," he said with a growl. "I'm going to tease and taste every inch of opalescent skin as you melt in my mouth."

"Jake!"

"It's okay, babe. I'm right here. Take off the bra, now." He could not suppress a moan when her full, gorgeous breasts were revealed through slow, sensual movements. Jake felt like he'd die of thirst if he didn't drink from her sweet flesh soon.

Moving forward he captured a distended, pretty coral-colored nipple between his lips, licking and sucking. At the same time he pinched and twirled the other firm bud between his fingers. The soft sounds of unbridled pleasure bubbling up from the back of Maddy's throat were nearly his undoing.

Damn! His erection was becoming almost painful. Jake wanted to thrust into her intense heat, make himself a permanent part of Maddy.

No. He would not rush this. Tonight would be a night neither of them would ever forget. He would raise her desire for him to an all-consuming level, binding them together.

He lavished each breast with equal attention, kneaded the firm globes while sucking the elongated coral peaks into his mouth. Pressing both breasts together, Jake sucked and licked both nipples simultaneously.

Maddy's head dropped back between her shoulders as she cried out her pleasure to the moon. The sight of her graceful neck extended and allowing unfettered access was too big a lure. Jake worked his way up, stopping to tease the hollow at the base of her throat. As his tongue tasted the salty-sweet skin he could feel the frantic pace of her wildly accelerated pulse.

Her devilish little hands began to roam his body, pushing his shirt off his shoulders after working the buttons free. When her wandering fingers found the bulge in his jeans she teased his throbbing erection mercilessly. His cock jerked against the barrier of his jeans, desiring a more intimate caress.

The scent of her arousal was killing him. No more waiting. He had to taste the sweet juices coating the swollen lips of her pussy, *now!* As he dropped to his knees, Jake pressed her legs wider apart with his shoulders. Using his thumbs, he gently spread apart her luscious pink lips before deeply breathing in her scent. The soft, swollen folds glistened with her juices.

"Damn, babe. You are so wet."

She cried out and grabbed onto his shoulders for support as his tongue slid over her tender lips. He licked, teased and tasted everywhere but the one place she wanted him most. His mumbled moans of male appreciation sent tremors through her body making her shake with the combined pleasure and need for more.

"Jake, please," she gasped.

"Mmm. I could drink in your hot juices all night, babe," he praised just before slipping a finger into her drenched pussy. The walls tightened on the digit while her strong pelvic muscles contracted, drawing him deeper. He added a second finger at the same time his lips closed around her pulsing clit. Jake continued to suck and lap at the little bundle of nerves while finger-fucking Maddy as she convulsed in an explosive orgasm.

"Oh my god!" The sensations exploding through her body were beyond description. Jake had ignited a blazing fire that expanded out through every fiber of her being. Maddy let the intense feelings overtake her body and mind. She remained encapsulated in her own little world of heavenly pleasure for what could have been hours or just a few minutes.

When her awareness finally settled back to the clearing she was shocked to find herself totally immobilized, tied to the chin-up bar by several lengths of soft cotton rope. The rope was looped through the holes in the wood frame, securing her ankles and spreading her legs wide. Her arms were stretched high above her head, leaving her exposed, helpless.

Sweet Jesus! She hadn't even realized that they had moved and now she found herself captured. The good girl was screaming inside her head. *This is bad. Naked, tied up in a public place, Jake in control of the situation.*

Maddy whipped her head around wildly, hair flying over her face. Where the hell was Jake, anyway? *Dear Lord, please tell me he didn't leave me here, trussed up and completely defenseless, raw and laid bare.*

She felt like a newborn babe, stripped bare down to her very soul, jumbled emotions spiraling out of control. It felt like everything that happened in her life prior to this moment was meaningless, null and void. Reality and what was important to her had changed between one heartbeat and the next.

Maddy struggled not to panic. She had to use her brain if she were to survive this crazy situation. Relaxing her shoulders she craned her neck as far backward as possible, searching for any signs of her captor. If she ever managed to get free that man would face her wrath. How dare he rearrange her very existence then disappear.

Finally catching sight of him several feet away over her left shoulder, Maddy let out a sigh of relief, but the feeling was quickly overridden by anger. The arrogant prick was talking on his cell phone. How could any call be so important as to interrupt what was happening between them?

"Jake Cruise," she sternly growled. "If you don't untie me right now…"

"Just settle down, babe," he casually called back.

After mumbling a few more words into the cell phone he slowly walked over to inspect his handiwork. Maddy struggled for a few moments against her bonds until he whispered in her ear from somewhere behind her back. Her whole body tensed as his velvety voice caressed her shoulder.

"You look breathtaking with the moonlight casting a silvery glow over your bare skin." His fingers trailed from her shoulder and down her spine, creating wild shivers through her heated flesh. "Just relax, feel, enjoy."

When his fingers reached the bottom of her spine, Jake traced along her waistline. The muscles in her abdomen contracted as his butterfly soft touch stroked over the soft little swell.

"I want to see you truly let go, Maddy. Just let instinct take over," he breathed against her neck. His devilish fingers traced the outer curve of her breasts before teasing her now supersensitive nipples. The way her breasts fit so perfectly within his large warm hands registered in some distant part of her mind. She felt complete, a sense of everything coming together flawlessly.

The good girl continued to scream at her, trying to make her feel shame and guilt. Yet every touch, every seductive word only increased her feelings of rightness. Submitting to Jake's touch was the most wonderful, beautiful thing she'd ever done.

His warm, firm lips and hot, wet tongue slid down her neck leaving behind a fiery path. "You need to let go of your pious beliefs and open up to your darker side. Allow yourself to experience what you truly desire."

Maddy wasn't sure if she could do that. Yet here she was — restrained, naked and open, right out where anyone could stumble upon them. It was sinful, wanton. Shockingly, just thinking about what she'd already allowed Jake to do brought a fresh flood of hot juices sliding down her vaginal walls, spreading over swollen folds. There was no way something that felt so right could be wrong.

The devilish man kissed, licked, and nipped a path down her back. After a particularly hard bite on her left ass cheek, he soothed the pain away with a gentle lick.

She cried out sharply as his tongue delved into the crevice between her cheeks. Jake's hands massaged and spread her ass wide for his loving. Slowly, heatedly the downward path continued. Then he did the most unexpectedly taboo thing. The wicked man ran his hot tongue in a circle around her puckered anus.

"Oh my god!" she screamed. "Jake, what the hell are you doing?"

She'd lost control of her breathing, gasping and panting in an effort to draw in much-needed oxygen. Her breasts jiggled wildly as Maddy struggled against the sensations rioting through her body, and continued to fight the battle being waged in her mind.

Before she could protest further, his sinful tongue plunged into the small, tight hole. Maddy did not have enough breath left to scream this time. Every muscle and tendon tightened, then relaxed under his expert ministrations. One hand remained massaging her ass as two fingers from the other one slipped into the slick heat of her pussy.

All her vast capabilities for thought left as Maddy became a mindless mass of nerve endings. The battle of good versus bad died in that instant. Her entire world narrowed down to the sensations that started in her pelvis and shot quickly through the rest of her ravished body. Totally unaware, she pleaded mindlessly for more of everything — harder, faster, and deeper.

* * * * *

Jake lost count of how many times Maddy reached orgasm. His ears had begun to ring from her unbridled pleasure-filled cries. All his adult life he'd dreamed of finding such a passionate woman who would respond so openly to his lovemaking. Although he had suspected Maddy held dark, lustful desires similar to his own, he had never imagined they would connect on such a soul-deep level.

Grabbing a tube of lubricant from his duffel bag, Jake began working a finger into her tight back channel. The near volcanic heat he discovered there drove him to the brink of his control. Tight muscles along the narrow channel spasmed against the digit.

He circled her clit with the fingers of the other hand while adding a second finger to her tight ass. Her needy little moans and whimpers nearly had his cock bursting out of the confining jeans he wore. There was no way he could take them off before he had Maddy ready without losing any remaining thin semblance of control.

Scissoring his fingers, Jake stretched her tight channel, preparing her to take his cock. God, she had the most perfect ass. The firm globes were perfectly rounded, soft skin and firm muscle.

Suddenly, Maddy stiffened, every muscle in her body tensing.

"Oh god, Jake. I hear someone…"

Her words died in her throat when Luke and Tom made their way into the clearing, stopping short at their first glimpse of her stretched out in the moonlight.

"Holy fucking shit," one of them gasped.

"Gawd damn," the other huskily groaned.

Maddy struggled against her bonds futilely. The two men slowly moved forward taking in the glorious sight. Jake barely paused in his preparations. If he didn't get his cock in her soon he just might blow his wad in his pants, or explode from the painful erection.

"You are so beautiful, honey," Luke praised. "We're gonna make you feel so good."

Tom tripped over an exposed tree root and nearly face planted. He couldn't take his eyes off her long enough to watch where he was walking. All four of them burst out in riotous laughter, breaking the tension that hung heavily in the crisp night air.

Strangled cries bubbled up from Maddy's throat as Jake added a third finger to those invading her ass. "About time you boys showed up," he growled from between clenched teeth. His jaw was fast becoming sore due to his efforts to hold back.

"Holy shit! The three of you planned this," Maddy cried.

The uncharacteristic cursing, rather than the accusation, had the three men pausing. Luke was the first one composed enough to respond.

"You say no, and we walk away, Maddy." Sincerity was clear in his chocolate brown eyes, along with his deep desire that she not ask that of him.

For several breathless moments the men waited for her response. Looking into Tom's and Luke's hopeful eyes, she realized that they would turn away if she did not agree. Her gaze swept over the two rugged firefighters waiting before her. Luke with his short, sandy blond hair and dark puppy-dog eyes. Tom with his perpetually tousled brown hair and smoky gray eyes. Both were incredibly muscular and fit. Handsome, trusted friends whom she had often fantasized about.

That's what it all came down to in the end. They were trusted friends whom she had desired as long as she'd known them. None of them would intentionally hurt her. They were offering intense pleasure beyond anything she could imagine.

Maddy let her eyes wander appreciatively over the two hunks waiting patiently for her response. Luke was a few inches taller than Tom, who had the stockier build of the pair.

Both men had incredible bodies, and were unselfconsciously sporting large bulges between their legs.

Mentally, Maddy slapped a hand over the good girl's mouth, shutting up her constant ranting. There was no way she could pass up such a generous, once-in-a-lifetime offer to achieve untold satisfaction. They would indulge her in every pleasure of the flesh, and there would be no recriminations.

Meeting each man's intense gaze first, Maddy responded to her friends the only way she could. "Please, don't go. I want this, all three of you."

Luke boldly walked right up to her, cupping her face in his hands and seized her mouth in a deep kiss. Jake slowly resumed his preparations. Tom stood mesmerized for several moments before beginning to strip out of his clothes.

Jake couldn't take any more. The sound of his zipper seemed impossibly loud in the quiet night. He barely allowed his fingers to make contact while generously coating his dick with lubricant. He was so close to the edge that it was not going to take much to throw him over.

Luke worked on removing his clothes, never taking his mouth from Maddy's for long. Tom moved in close and began tending to her swollen, achy breasts. When he sucked a diamond-hard nipple deeply into his mouth, Maddy moaned into Luke's kiss.

Being as gentle as he could tolerate, Jake pressed the head of his cock against her tight little rosebud. Tom moved back and forth between her nipples as Luke dropped to his knees and began tongue-fucking her.

The multiple stimulations had Maddy jerking and writhing against her bonds. One forceful movement impaled two inches of his straining cock into the intense heat of her tight channel.

"Ah, fuck," he cursed. "Maddy, babe, you've got to hold still."

She was unable to articulate actual words, mumbling pure nonsense. When Luke's teeth closed gently against her clit she exploded, hips bucking wildly, impaling another three inches of Jake's throbbing cock.

Jake gasped for every breath, his chest laboring hard as he struggled to hold back his climax. Maddy slammed back against him wildly, sheathing him balls-deep and snapping his control. With a wild roar he began fucking her spasming channel hard and deep, fast and mindless.

Luke stood, quickly donning a condom and burying his cock in her slick heat with one hard thrust. Incredible sensations from the added tightness and friction against his shaft sent him soaring, triggering Jake's climax. He couldn't move as her pelvic muscles clamped down tight, holding him captive. The soft, full cheeks of her ass flexed and rippled with the powerful spasms surging through her gorgeous body.

After filling her tight channel with his hot cum he could only wait for her body to release him. When finally free, Jake fell to his knees. He'd never experienced anything so earth-shattering before. Maddy had sucked him dry.

Lying back in the grass, Jake watched as Tom stepped into place behind Maddy, put on a condom, and lubed up his straining cock. Her ass was well lubed and open from Jake, so Tom was able to slide into her ass nice and easy.

Maddy's cries and whimpers filled the night. Watching their two friends fuck Maddy senseless was having a distinct effect on Jake. Never would he have imagined becoming hard again so soon after such a powerful climax. Yet that is exactly what was happening.

He rose on shaky legs, moving to her side. Gently capturing her chin, he turned her face toward him. "Damn, babe. You look so sexy. Your beautiful face is shining with passion while they fuck you. Every luscious inch of your skin is slick with desire. Feel them, Maddy! Their big cocks slamming in and out of your heat, filling you up to bursting."

Jake could not imagine a more beautiful sight. He had never seen anything so compelling in his life. The image of Maddy consumed with passion, body and soul bare for all to see. He kissed her deeply, drinking in her lusty response until she once again shattered, pulling the two men along with her for the tumultuous ride.

She came hard, her glorious body trembling with overwhelming pleasure as her screams echoed around the clearing. Pumping his cock in his hand, Jake came again watching the woman he loved succumb to such blissful ecstasy.

Once they all recovered, he had every intention of staking his claim, binding Maddy to him. While it had been an amazing experience to watch her complete and total surrender to the blazing desires of her body, it would never happen again. She belonged to him now, and no other man would ever touch her again.

As the other men fell away from her, Maddy collapsed bonelessly, held up only by the rope securing her to the wooden frame. The three men worked her free of her bonds and gently lay her down on a blanket where they tended to her needs. They put her dress on, sans undergarments, and Jake pocketed her bra. Then he carried her satiated body the entire one-mile walk back to his car.

Chapter Four

80

The heavenly aromas of coffee and bacon penetrated through deep layers of sleep, gently waking Maddy. For a few minutes she tried to drift back down, but the various persistent aches in her muscles demanded attention. It felt like she'd spent an entire day rock climbing.

As her mind began to focus she felt a warm, solid heat pressed against her back, and she snuggled in deeper. She'd just started to drift contentedly back down to sleep when thick fingers plucked at her nipple, bringing the flattened nub to life. Maddy's eyes popped open wide as the realization that she was in bed with someone filtered through her sleep-fogged brain. From the feel of the body she was held firmly against it was a big somebody with a rather large erection.

Blinking rapidly against the sudden influx of bright light, she struggled to figure out where the hell she was. The unfamiliar masculine surroundings eventually took shape and substance. Heavy, dark wood furniture and hunter green bedding. Posters depicting extreme sports hanging on tan walls.

OHMYGOD, OHMYGOD, OHMYGOD!

She was in Jake Cruise's bedroom, lying in his bed. That must mean the man playing with her nipple, sending lightning-hot sensations straight down to her already dampening pussy must be…

"Wake up, sleepyhead, while your breakfast is still hot," he mumbled against her ear, then his devilish tongue began tracing an intricate pattern along her neck. Tremors of anticipation and remembered bliss coursed through her tired body. His fingers absently toyed with a fat spiral of her sleep-mussed hair.

Events from the night before came back in little bits and pieces. A hot blush spread over Maddy's cheeks as she remembered hanging completely naked from the chin-up bar in Kinsey Park while Luke, Tom, and Jake tortured her in such delightful and decadent ways.

However, the most amazing thing Maddy remembered was the tender, loving way Jake had treated her. That and the way those gorgeous sapphire eyes had gazed at her with such love and possession.

The thought of him regretting what had passed between them was more than she could bear. Add in a strong dose of guilt over what she'd allowed them to do, and her whole body stiffened. This could only turn out badly.

Okay, mind, start functioning.

She'd never been good at the awkward morning-after episodes. Heck, she'd never faced a morning after with a friend before. How did one handle something like this without ruining a friendship? Probably best to just face the music.

Maddy rolled over to face Jake, praying that it was only the two of them. Facing Luke and Tom at the same time would be difficult. Doing so naked with morning breath was not something she wanted to contemplate. The breath froze in her throat as she caught sight of her bronzed god. Her lover. There was no doubt that she loved him to the point of distraction. Always had.

His glorious jet-black hair was still rumpled from sleep, sticking up in clumps. Golden rays of late morning sun made the silky strands shine. She knew that they would feel cool sliding through her fingers. Maddy drank in the sight of his rugged, hard features as her fingers traced the path of the white scar over his right cheek. God, how she loved his handsome face.

"'Bout time you came back to the land of the living. I was beginning to worry," he said, favoring her with a devastating smile.

His intense, penetrating blue gaze reached straight into her heart. How was she supposed to go back to just being friends? Of course, the answer was obvious. She couldn't. Her heart belonged to Jake. There was no turning back. She had given him everything last night.

"Damn, babe. You look like a deer caught in headlights. Relax, Maddy. Everything's all right." One big hand traced soothing shapes over her back. If only she could just be casual about the situation, act like one of the cool, calm food bimbos. But that was not her. She was cursed by being practical, serious, an overachieving intellectual.

"No. No, it's not! Everything has changed, Jake..." she blurted out.

He placed a finger against her lips, stopping her words. "Shhh. There is no reason to feel awkward around me, babe. Sure, things changed last night, but it was a change for the better."

Looking into his eyes she detected love, possessiveness, and desire. "You're mine now, Maddy. What happened last night will never happen again. No other man will ever touch you, make love to you. End of story," he growled.

Thank you, God.

While being pleasured by the three handsome men had been incredible, Maddy was not sure she could handle such an intense experience again. Relief washed through her tensed muscles with the knowledge that she'd never be faced with such a situation again. Jake appeared to be staking a claim on her.

Cradling her head in his big hands, Jake tenderly kissed away her anxiety. God help her, but the man sure knew how to kiss. Her entire body heated in seconds, melting all resistance, along with her bones.

They really were perfect together. Did she dare hope this would turn into something more, something permanent? Sex had never been casual for Maddy. Deep emotions were involved. She was so much better with books and knowledge than fickle emotions.

Their kisses turned fevered as passion once again took hold. This time Jake built their need slowly, carrying Maddy away on wave after wave of pure desire. She longed to feel his cock cradled deep within her pussy. To feel complete, one with this sexy man. No past experiences could have prepared her for how right it felt to be in his arms, to share his kiss.

When Jake finally ended the kiss he could hardly breathe. Maddy affected him in a way no other woman could. Setting his soul on fire, she made him dream of things he'd never wanted, marriage and children. Never before had he fucked a woman without a condom. With Maddy everything was different. He could not stand the thought of even such a thin barrier coming between them.

The love shining in the depths of her sparkling eyes filled him with emotions that were fresh and new. Things he'd never experienced before. How he loved this woman. Her easy intelligence, sharp wit, adventurous spirit, and beautiful soul. There was no way he would allow her to close him out now.

Without a word, Jake rose from the bed. He extended a hand, drawing Maddy to his side. He wanted to take care of her, and that would start right now with feeding her breakfast.

Initially she protested leaving the bedroom naked, but Jake quickly quashed her reluctance by letting her know there was no way he would allow that luscious body to be hidden from him. They walked silently, fingers intertwined, into the small kitchen.

After seating her at the table, Jake piled the food onto plates. He'd made crisp bacon, three-cheese and portobello mushroom omelets, fresh fruit, and wheat toast. After setting the food on the table he poured two large mugs of the strong coffee he preferred.

Their conversation was light and casual, just as it had always been between them. Neither felt obligated to fill in the gaps with senseless chatter. They were comfortable enough together that silence was not bothersome.

Watching Maddy enjoy the meal he'd prepared brought him great joy. She was not one of those women who picked at only low-fat foods without really eating. Maddy enjoyed good food, and ate with an obvious pleasure, which was refreshing.

Just watching her pouty lips move as she chewed, and the fork slid in and out of her mouth had his cock hardening. When her pink tongue peeked out to gather up an errant drop of food from the corner of her mouth he couldn't help groaning. He could imagine nothing better than seeing those ripe lips close over the head of his straining cock. That pink tongue swirling around the length of his shaft.

Those sweet green eyes peeking at him over the top of her coffee mug held a question. Well, he certainly had an answer for the little siren.

The chair scraped against the tile floor as Jake rose. He moved slowly around the table, keeping her gaze pinned to his own, silently communicating his desires. As he moved, he took his hard and ready cock into his hand, pumping the shaft in a slow, steady motion.

Maddy swallowed hard when he stopped before her. To her credit, her gaze never faltered. She continued to watch the intense need playing across his expressive eyes.

"Down on your knees, babe," he commanded.

After only a brief hesitation, Maddy gracefully slid from the chair, kneeling before him. There was no doubt she knew what he wanted. That sweet little tongue peeked out, then slid over her sumptuous rosy lips, leaving them glistening. Her breath came out with a slow hiss as her gaze swept down his body, fixing on the erection only inches from her lovely mouth.

Slender fingers wrapped around his shaft as she took over, pumping in the same rhythm he had established. Jake felt like he'd died and gone to heaven when the warmth of her tongue flicked over the pearly drop of come which had leaked from the slit. She took his length between those pouty lips, the warm perfection of her mouth enveloping him, and his knees nearly gave out.

Jake stared down at her sweet, round face to find a look of unadulterated delight. Her small moans vibrated against his sensitive flesh as she devoured him like a special treat. Those beautiful eyes were so dilated with passion that he could barely discern the normal warm green color. It was all too much, felt too good.

His need for Maddy increased tenfold as she drove him to the brink of insanity. With a rough growl, Jake pulled back from the sweet depths of her talented mouth. A whimper of displeasure left her lips as she tried to recapture his cock. Taking hold of her arms, he pulled her to her feet.

One sweep of his arm cleared the table. His swift motions startled a squeal out of Maddy as he grasped her hips and lifted her, and plopped her unceremoniously down where their breakfast had been only moments before.

Balancing her on the edge of the table, knees draped over his forearms, Jake buried his cock balls-deep in one long, gentle motion. They both held their breath for several heartbeats, reveling in the completeness of their joining. The fit was perfect in every way.

Maddy became lost as Jake set a slow pace, nearly pulling free with each withdrawal, filling her completely with each advance. The slow glide of friction over her sensitive inner walls felt magical. She knew in that moment there would never be another man for her. Jake was the missing half of her soul. The connection between them deepened as they slowly made love.

The pace built gradually as they moved together toward the pinnacle of pleasure. Her muscles protested each withdrawal by tightening around his cock, pulling him deeper. She needed more. She needed his heart, his love, binding them together as surely as their bodies were bound.

"Jake," she gasped.

Her breathing was ragged, and she found herself barely able to form words. "Stop," Maddy cried.

Jake stilled, a look of concern crossing his hard features.

"Shit, babe," he panted. "Don't make me stop now. I don't know if I can."

"Please. Just hold still for a minute." Using her muscular legs, Maddy held him locked deeply within her body. "I have to ask, have to know." The words were difficult to speak when he'd made her so breathless.

"What? What is it, Maddy?"

The loving tenderness in his eyes as Jake stroked a hand over her cheek made her falter yet again. She knew she'd just have to say this quick, get it over with. "Jake. I need you."

The strained emotions in her voice brought a look of concern to his face. "I'm right here, babe."

She placed a finger over his lips to quiet him, and Jake sucked the tip into the warmth of his mouth. His tongue swirled over her finger as he sucked it in and out, imitating the act he wanted to complete.

"I can't just fuck you, Jake. I need more. I need your love, always," she quickly blurted out.

Great, now he looked confused. This was not going well. Maddy figured she might as well just say what she meant and get it over with.

"Jake, will you marry me?"

Shock turned his eyes a cold, lifeless shade for a moment. Then it was Maddy's turn to be shocked as he burst out in joyous laughter.

"Damn it, babe. I'm supposed to ask that question on bended knee, ring in hand. Now what the hell are we supposed to tell our grandkids when they ask about how I proposed? I sure can't tell them I was buried balls-deep inside you on the kitchen table, and that you asked me." His eyes darkened, desire quickly returning. "Have no doubt, Madailein Flannagan. We are most certainly making love. And just as soon as we are finished here, I'll be making you Mrs. Jake Cruise."

Each word was punctuated by a hard, deep thrust, filling her completely. Her heart swelled with happiness. The only response Maddy could manage was to tighten her muscles around him, pulling him even deeper, and a breathless, "Yes."

About the Author

≈

Nicole Austin lives on the sheltered Gulf Coast of Florida, where inspiration can be readily found sitting under a big shade umbrella on the beach while sipping cold margaritas. A voracious reader, she never goes anywhere without a book. All those delicious romances combined with a vivid imagination naturally created steamy fantasies and characters in her mind.

Discovering Ellora's Cave paved the path to freeing them as well as manifesting an intoxicating passion for romantica. The positive response of family and friends to her stories propelled Nicole into an incredible world where fantasy comes boldly to life. Now she stays busy working as a certified CT scan technologist, finishing her third college degree, reading, writing, and keeping up with family. Oh yeah, and did we mention all the hard work involved with research? Well, that's the fun job—certainly a labor of love.

Nicole welcomes mail from readers. You can write to her c/o Ellora's Cave Publishing at 1056 Home Avenue, Akron OH 44310-3502.

Also by Nicole Austin

ဆာ

Passionate Realities
Savannah's Vision

DRAGONMAGIC

Allyson James

Chapter One

🔊

Arys felt his dragon body turn inside out, then there was a bright light and he was standing, naked, on two human legs inside a cozy, one-room cottage.

"Damn witch," he growled at the voluptuous woman bent over the fire. "What do you want now?"

The witch Clymenestra stood up calmly, eyeing him with her usual smugness. Arys was tall, with bronze-colored skin over hard muscle, waist-length white-blond hair, and dragon silver eyes. Clymenestra looked him over like she owned him.

The bitch knew his true name and could call him from Dragonspace anytime she liked. *Not forever, darling,* he thought. *Not forever.*

"I need dragon's blood," she said, letting her gaze rove his body.

"Always blood. What is your spell this time?"

"Never you mind." She looked at him with dark, possessive eyes. "I hold you, dragon, and you'll give me your blood." She smiled. "I'm always willing to pay for it."

He knew her thighs were wet with her cream, her opening hot, anticipating. Arys' cock was already swollen and hard, standing straight out from his body. His long hair warmed his back, but his arms prickled with cold in the night air. Human skin was too damn thin.

Clymenestra had bound him to her with the magic of his name — but one day, one day, he'd be free. He knew the secret of his freedom, she didn't.

"So you called me all the way from Dragonspace for a drop of blood?" he growled. "I was deep in important business."

"Two drops. And you were lying on your back in the snow, sunning yourself. Silver dragons are the laziest things in creation."

Arys didn't deny this. In his dragon form, he lived to eat and hoard and mate as often as possible. He also worked his own kind of magic, which was lightning fast, like a fiery needle in his brain.

He loved dragon magic. Human magic was too much like work.

He watched the witch gather up the ingredients for her spell, checking and double-checking the cracked parchment book spread out on her wooden table. She ground herbs with a mortar and pestle, her muscles working as she smashed the herbs into a paste.

So much effort simply to work one little spell. Of course, her tedious magic worked on Arys—she could yank him from the dragon world whenever she wished.

But all human magic required a price. Arys picked up a knife, eager to get on with her payment. "Ready?"

She ground a few moments longer, then set aside her pestle. "Ready."

He quickly sliced his palm and let two drops of blood fall into the bowl she held out. Magic gathered and danced above it, faint magic, not very strong.

He peered into the bowl, seeing nothing more than green bits of leaf stained dark with blood. "Is that it?"

"No. I need more."

He frowned and held out his hand again. "More blood?"

"Not from you. I need a maiden."

"A maiden? What for?"

Clymenestra looked up at him, impatient. "Never mind, I said. I need maiden's blood. So I want you to bring me a maiden."

His blood was pumping hard with lust, his mind barely registering the odd request. "Right *now*?"

She looked him over, from the top of his head to the soles of his bare feet. "Maybe later."

"Good." He closed his hand, annoyed at the tiny pain of the cut. Dragon hide was so much tougher than human skin.

Clymenestra put down the bowl as Arys approached her. Her dark eyes went completely black as her excitement mounted.

Arys grabbed the top of her loose dress and ripped it open. She was naked underneath—of course, she'd be ready. Her breasts were firm and upright, the nipples round and dark. Her taut belly held a jewel in its navel. Beneath that, her quim curved between her legs, a shimmer of pale hair twisting through it.

Arys tossed the dress aside, snaked his hand through her hair, and forced her to her knees.

Clymenestra's eyes widened with joy as she closed her mouth around his enormous cock and began to suck.

* * * * *

A witch's lot is to be exiled—to live far from others. The words echoed in Naida's mind as she stopped on the path through the woods to catch her breath again.

What kept her going, and kept her from despair, was the excitement of finally confronting her rising latent powers. At least, she thought they were rising latent powers. Hence, her journey to Clymenestra to seek the witch's opinion.

Or, Naida thought, *I might just be insane.*

In that case, I can sit comfortably by the fire and talk to myself while others bring me cups of tea. She grimaced, her sense of humor no longer comforting her.

But she knew the words that called power to her. She'd known the right moment to grab Farmer Beluh and yank him from his barn. The roof had groaned and fallen in a second later.

When her father's lamb had been born dead, suffocated in its struggle to enter the world, she'd called the words to push air back into its lungs. The lamb had shaken its head, climbed to its newborn feet and bleated for its mother.

These occurrences could be dismissed as coincidence or luck—she might have heard the timbers of the barn creaking just in time, and when she pushed on the lamb's chest, she might have encouraged its lungs to not give up.

She could have dismissed the events except she *hadn't* heard the timbers, she had only touched the lamb, and she had the dreams.

The dreams were so vivid that afterward, the waking world seemed sluggish and not real. In her sleep, white-hot power called to her and frightened her. She could not recall details of the dreams when she awoke, but she remembered pain and elation, and she always woke very aroused.

Her quim would be creamy wet, her opening burning. She'd have to press her hands hard against herself until she found release. She muffled her sounds in the pillows, lest she wake her sisters and brothers, who slept with her in the loft of her father's farmhouse.

After her release came and dark joy receded to sweet lethargy, she couldn't resist putting her fingers to her mouth, tasting the wild flavor of her own come.

She loved the dreams, yet feared them. She wanted the power that called to her, though she knew she'd lose everything to get it.

Naida held her side as she climbed the hill to the house in the clearing. *Or maybe,* she reminded herself, *I'm just insane.*

She reached Clymenestra's cottage, a cozy white-washed affair with a well-kept thatched roof. The men of the village would do anything for Clymenestra, freely. Clymenestra never paid in coin or eggs or hens, though she would occasionally do a spell to heal. Naida never knew why, and the men would not speak of it.

Naida's palms went slick with sweat as she neared the door. What would Clymenestra say? Would she smile and be glad that Naida was now a witch? Or would she laugh and tell Naida that she simply liked to touch herself under the quilts after her dreams?

But she had to know.

Naida lifted her hand to knock, then dropped it. She had never been to Clymenestra's cottage and did not know what to expect.

A well-stocked window box hung from the tiny window next to the door, holding scented five-pointed summer flowers. Naida gripped the box and rose on her toes to look through the window's thick pane.

What she saw inside made her gulp with shock and lose her balance. She grabbed at the window box to stay upright, feeling splinters drive into her fingers.

Clymenestra, her thick blonde hair caught in a knot at the nape of her neck, knelt before a huge man who stood in front of her, naked.

The man had silver-blond hair that hung down to just above his backside. His hair shimmered like true silver, glittering and beautiful. His hips were narrow, taut with muscle, what she could see of his backside a pleasing curve. His chest was sculpted muscle, as though he'd been chiseled by the goddess in bone and sinew. He clenched his fists, knotting biceps that gleamed with his sweat in the firelight.

Naida could see his cock, which was enormous, thick and long. The end of it rested in Clymenestra's mouth, and she was happily suckling it.

Something dark fluttered in Naida's belly. The man's face was square, sharp, and a little odd-looking, but most attractive. Not handsome, but fierce and hard, and his eyes…

His eyes were breathtaking. They were silver and large, luminous with their own light. While she stood, gaping, he turned his head and his silver gaze rested right on her.

Her heart banged in her chest. He saw her, and he smiled. His grin was infectious, tugging at her, telling her that he liked her watching and invited her to continue.

She couldn't have looked away if she tried.

Clymenestra's tongue laved his cock all over. Seeing the huge thing stuck in Clymenestra's mouth, and the man's balls drawn hard and tight, made Naida's knees shake.

She wanted to slide her hand under her dress and touch herself like she did in bed. Never mind she was outside and very rudely watching what was meant to be private between Clymenestra and her—

Her what? Lover? Husband? Was he another witch? He certainly looked like no man she'd ever seen before.

He placed a hand on Clymenestra's forehead and abruptly withdrew himself from her mouth.

"No," Naida heard Clymenestra plead through the glass. "I want to swallow you."

"Later," he said. He had a rumbling bass voice, a powerful man's voice. It also held a hint of something else — something wild and hot, and why did she think of *flying*?

He snatched a piece of cloth from the bed, wrenched Clymenestra to her feet, and tied the cloth around her eyes, blindfolding her.

The witch gasped with excitement. Her hands went to her bare nipples, fingers squeezing them. Naida knew exactly what Clymenestra felt, the same sense of aliveness Naida experienced every night in her dreams.

But Naida thought she knew why the man had blindfolded Clymenestra. He didn't want Clymenestra to see Naida at the window.

He wanted Naida to stay and watch, and didn't want Clymenestra to grow angry and send Naida away.

That he wanted Naida to watch him made her more excited still. *Why should he want me to?* she wondered.

He did, though. He guided Clymenestra to the edge of the low trestle bed and pushed her down on her back. As Clymenestra fell willingly, he grabbed a piece of twine from her worktable and used it to bind her hands in front of her.

Clymenestra offered no peep of protest. She squirmed on the bed, smiling, aroused and needy.

The silver-haired man climbed onto the bed, hovering over her on hands and knees. He yanked Clymenestra's thighs apart and bent down, opening his mouth over her cunt.

Naida squeezed the flowerbox, her own quim pulsing. She imagined his tongue on *her*, imagined feeling the hot slice going inside her where only her fingers had ever been. It would be the sweetest heaven.

Clymenestra writhed beneath his mouth. The witch's naked body was shapely and beautiful; Naida thought of her own softer limbs with some regret. Clymenestra reached for the man, but was hampered by her bonds. She moaned.

The man licked and licked, his hands spreading Clymenestra's legs as wide as they could go.

Naida wanted desperately to touch herself, to make her fingers do what the man's tongue did to Clymenestra. But if she lost her grip on the flowerbox, she'd fall and miss everything. She bit her lip and squeezed her legs together tighter, tighter.

Clymenestra screamed. She bumped on the bed, wriggling and moaning, her face twisted in ecstasy.

The man backed away. He grasped Clymenestra's hips and flipped her over, facedown. He lifted her hips, pulled her back toward him, then rammed his very long cock straight into her waiting quim.

It was raw, brutal sex. The man pumped into her, his hips working, broad hands brown on Clymenestra's white hips. Clymenestra went on screaming.

The man continued a long time, stroking her, fucking her, while Naida held on to the flowerbox, her eyes wide, watching hungrily.

The man threw his head back and groaned as he came. Clymenestra's screams had wound into breathy moans by this time.

He pumped a few more times, then withdrew.

Clymenestra collapsed on the bed. The man stood above her, breathing hard, his cock still rampant, wet and glistening.

"Oh," Clymenestra moaned. "Arys."

He glanced over at the window, brawny shoulders moving, and he winked.

With a sudden wrench, the flowerbox came away from the wall. Naida stifled a shriek as she went down, flowerbox and all, to the mud below.

Shaking, she scrambled to her feet, her hands stinging with splinters. Without waiting to see whether the couple inside had heard her, she sprinted away into the darkness of the woods.

Chapter Two

"What was that?" Clymenestra asked from the bed, her voice hoarse.

Arys untied her bonds and pulled off the blindfold. "Nothing." He shrugged. "Probably an owl. Do you want me to hunt?"

"No." She groaned as she slid off the bed and got to her feet. She walked away from him, snatching another dress from a hook as she went back to the table. "Go find me a maiden. I need to finish the spell."

Clymenestra was always like this. Fuck, then get back to work, almost like she forgot about the fucking the moment she got off the bed.

The girl peeking in the window, now, she'd looked most appreciative. She'd also looked curious, astonished and interested, more emotions than he ever saw in Clymenestra.

Clymenestra liked sex, but she didn't like men. Or dragons. She had no use for women at all. She might have tried to hurt the sweetheart at the window, and that would have been a shame.

Clymenestra shrugged on the dress and started grinding herbs again, clearly finished with him. Arys opened the chest that stood in the far corner and took out the old breeches and threadbare shirt Clymenestra kept for him in case he had to wander around outside.

I am enslaved to a witch who can't even bother to get me new clothes, he thought in disgust.

Keeping a neutral expression, he pulled on the breeches and buttoned the fly. "Hunting a maiden," he said. "This will be fun."

"Arys." Clymenestra looked up. "I need her to still *be* a maiden when she gets here, understand?"

He slid on the shirt and settled it over his body. "I do know what *maiden* means, witch."

"And I do know how randy you are."

"Hey, I'm young. I'm sowing my wild oats." That's how the bitch had caught him in the first place. He hadn't been paying attention, until there she was, speaking his true name...

She glanced up, a curious light in her eyes. "Just how old are you?"

"Nine hundred and seventy-two."

She laughed. "A mere stripling, are you? I'd love to see you full grown."

"I *am* full grown." He decided not to explain. Clymenestra was a fool and there was no use explaining things to fools.

He straightened the shirt, not bothering to tie it closed, and went to the door. On the threshold he paused. "Dragons mate for life, you know."

"Yes, you mate all the time. You've told me."

"No," he said slowly. "I mean when a dragon finds his life-mate, it's forever. No one else matters from that time forward."

Her brows arched. "Are you proposing to me, Arys?"

"Never," he growled, his afterglow evaporating. Clymenestra understood nothing beyond her own pleasure, the shallowest kind of person.

He closed the door on her cool laughter and started down the path, barefoot. Clymenestra hadn't provided boots.

He stepped on a sharp twig almost immediately.

"*Ow*," he snarled. "I hate these *feet*."

* * * * *

Naida had stopped running. She sat on a boulder, which was sharp on her backside, trying to catch her breath.

She would be a fool to run at breakneck speed through the night woods, and she knew it. Not to mention the wolves she might attract. But she ran instinctively. What she'd seen in Clymenestra's cottage had unnerved her and aroused her and confused her.

The beautiful man had winked at her, as though he knew how wet and excited she was, as though he knew the wild thoughts that raced through her mind, as though they were friends sharing a secret.

She thought of his huge cock, and Clymenestra licking it all over, a wide smile on her face. What would it be like to have that cock in her own mouth, to feel the warm tip bump her lips?

She drew in a long, ragged breath. She'd likely never get the chance to know. He was Clymenestra's lover, and the witch had him, and that was that. Naida's father would likely marry her to one of the local farmers' sons, probably Angus, who liked to drink beer and belch a lot.

No tall, beautiful man with silver eyes for her.

Naida felt foolish now for hurrying toward Clymenestra's house, excited and eager to learn whether she was a witch. She wondered if the man would after all reveal that Naida had spied on them, and whether Clymenestra would be angry.

She decided she'd better make her way home. The moon was huge and luminous tonight, lighting the woods a little, but it was still nearly black under the densest trees. She was not afraid of the dark, she never had been, but she was cautious. A wolf, bear or wild boar would not care how brave she was, only how fast she could run.

As if it had heard her, a wolf appeared from between the trees and hesitated at the edge of the small clearing in which she sat. He sniffed, nose working, eyes gleaming yellow in the moonlight.

Naida stilled. "Oh, goddess," she murmured. "Please let him have just eaten a big meal."

The wolf took one step into the clearing, his eyes on Naida.

If I have magic, this would be good time to learn how to use it.

But she hadn't the faintest idea what to do. *Cast a spell? Will it to be gone?* She didn't know.

The wolf took another step toward her, oblivious of her frantic thoughts. A twig snapped in the woods behind the wolf, followed by a muffled *Ow*.

The wolf did a curious thing. Instead of fleeing the intrusion—a wolf was not fool enough to take on two people at once—it sat down and looked behind it as though waiting.

The silver-haired man from Clymenestra's cottage appeared on the path. He walked toward the wolf, unafraid and unconcerned.

Naida sat, mesmerized, as the man called Arys stopped two feet from the wolf and met its gaze. The wolf studied him intently, as though trying to understand something, then it rose from its haunches, turned, and slipped away into the woods.

Naida let out her breath. "Thank the goddess it wasn't hungry."

"He is hungry," the man said. His words were slightly accented, as though he came from a foreign land. "I asked him to look for you and protect you from harm."

Her eyes widened. "You asked him?"

"To look for you, yes. But I did not really need to. I felt you. You reek of power."

He strolled to her, his silver eyes swimming with sparks like fireflies on a summer night. The plain homespun breeches and linen shirt he wore could not disguise the raw sexuality of him, which struck her like an avalanche.

He sat down next to her on the boulder. His skin smelled damp and fresh and his hair was slicked back from his forehead, dark with water.

"I reek?" she asked faintly.

"Of power. Strong power. I felt it when you were at the window." He smiled, one corner of his mouth lifting. "You smell nice, though. Like a maiden."

She did not know what to say to this. "Why are you all wet?" she asked.

"I had a swim in a moonlit pool. Would you like to join me?" He watched her eagerly, hand extended, as though he'd like nothing better than to strip with her and dive into a warm pool in the middle of the woods.

She saw the red streak across his palm. "You're hurt." She caught his hand, turning it toward the light.

"'Tis nothing."

"But if you don't wrap it, it could take sick." She dipped her hand into her pocket and brought out the clean kerchief she always kept with her. She wrapped it deftly around his hand, tucking in the ends.

When she looked up, she found his gaze on her, unnervingly close. His body was warm and hard, his strange eyes studying her intently.

"A beautiful maiden with a kind heart," he said softly. "The very thing to ensnare a dragon."

She looked away, curling her fingers in her skirt. "Do not talk about dragons. Everything has been so very strange tonight. I do not want to hear Clymenestra's lover tell me he has seen dragons."

"Of course I have seen dragons. I *am* a dragon."

She shook her head, red braids dancing. "No, please don't tell me."

"Why not? I am a silver dragon. I am Arys."

"Who?"

"Arys." He waited for her to be impressed, then deflated. "Oh, never mind. Why did Clymenestra have to enslave me in *this* world?"

Naida looked up, indignant. "Clymenestra enslaved you?"

"Yes." Arys lifted Naida's hand and kissed it. "But don't worry, I'll be free of her soon."

The warmth of his mouth shot heat through her body. She still ached from unreleased tension, her quim throbbing and damp. Even her run through the woods and the encounter with the wolf had not eased her completely.

"She should not have," Naida said.

His smile returned. "You are sweet. It was my own fault. A moment of foolishness, a hundred years of slavery."

"A hundred years?" Her mouth went dry.

"In my dragon lands, I am still free. But whenever she calls me, I must come. I have no choice. I'll be free, though, very soon."

"You sound certain."

"'Tis certain," he said, looking wise. "For everything that is taken, something must be released. I try to tell her. She does not listen."

It was easy to believe him. Sitting in the moonlit clearing, his feral eyes on her, after her own dreams of bright power, all this did not seem so strange.

She understood nothing, but at the moment it was not necessary to understand. Only to be here with him was important.

"You said I reeked of power."

He licked her palm, his tongue a hot streak. "I taste it on you, as well. Are you not a witch?"

"I do not know. That is why I was coming to see Clymenestra. To ask her what to do."

He smiled, hot and wicked. "And you saw us fucking instead. Do you enjoy watching?"

Her face heated. "No. That is, I never...I couldn't look away for some reason. I do not know why."

"You needed to see. Your body is ripe for it, and you crave it."

"How do you know that?"

"How could I not know?" He still held her hand, the night air biting where he'd licked her palm. "I smell your need, I sense it. That is why I blindfolded Clymenestra and let you watch."

He was right, she wanted him. She'd envisioned herself in Clymenestra's place, first having his tongue deep inside her, then spreading her legs to receive him.

Swallowing, she withdrew her hand from his, clasped the skirt of her dress, and inched it upward. "Will you touch me, Arys?" she whispered.

He pressed a kiss to the side of her mouth. She turned her head and let her lips meet his. His mouth was hot and felt good, his tongue, caressing.

"What is your name?" he murmured.

"Naida."

He placed his hand, large, calloused and warm, on her thigh. As he kissed her, he brushed the skirt out of the way and pressed his first two fingers to her quim.

She gasped aloud at the new sensation. He moved his fingers, stroking, circling her opening and stirring the cream there.

"Naida," he said. "Like the Naiad. A lady of the water."

He opened his mouth, drawing her tongue into him. She'd never tasted the inside of a man's mouth before. He was spicy, a little like nutmeg. When she stuck her tongue in farther, chasing the taste, he began to suckle it.

Dark feeling swirled at the base of her spine. She opened her legs, welcoming his fingers inside her. She thought of his cock, long and hard and ready. She wanted that inside her, too.

"Please," she whispered.

"Please what?"

"Please, I want..." She grew confused. What did she want? Love. Lust. Him. Magic.

He watched her with strange silver eyes, beautiful and intense.

"You said you sensed my magic," she said. "What did you mean?"

He traced her opening, rubbing fingertips along the petals of her quim. She squirmed with need.

"Strong magic," he said. "Sharp and hot. Raw power. Very dangerous."

"I don't want to be dangerous."

He smiled. "I like you dangerous. When I fuck you, it will be wild and intense—and dangerous." He licked her cheek. "And then you'll fuck me."

If any of the farm boys had said that to her, she'd have screamed or fainted or run away. Maybe all three.

But she sat still, feeling the burn of his tongue on her skin, his fingers plying sensations all along her pussy, and wanted him.

"Will you?" she asked. "Arys? Will you fuck me?"

The word felt strange on her lips, but she liked it. *Fuck.* It was rather freeing to say it. "Fuck," she whispered again.

"No."

She jumped. "What?"

He stroked two fingers in and out of her, blunt, raw sensation that promised so much. "I must take you to Clymenestra. She wants a maiden, and you must be a maiden when you arrive."

Her heart began to pound in sharp, panicked beats. "Why must you take me to Clymenestra? I do not want to go to her. I changed my mind."

"She tells me I must take you to her, and I cannot disobey. She holds me, but not for much longer."

"Can we wait then, until you are free of her?"

He shook his head. "No."

He went on stroking her, thumb teasing her clit while his fingers pressed inside her.

"I don't want to go to her, Arys," she tried. "I am afraid of her. I would rather face the wolves and try to get home than go back to her."

"The wolves will not harm you. I told them to leave you alone. But I will take you with me to Clymenestra."

She clenched her teeth. She wanted nothing more than to sit here and let him play, while her cream flowed all over his fingers, but she made herself return to sanity.

She pushed his hand from her, and stood up, breaking all contact with him. He watched her, not very alarmed. "What if I refuse to go?"

"Then I will take you by force." He said it matter-of-factly.

"You have just told me I had powerful magic, that I was dangerous. I might hurt you."

"I know." He grinned. His eyes sparkled with anticipation. "This is going to be fun."

Chapter Three

ು

Arys watched Naida stare at him, her beautiful brown-green eyes wide with alarm.

Then she whirled around and ran from him, heading into the woods. Her skirt hitched up, revealing her plump, shapely legs, and her thick braid of red hair bumped against her back.

Arys stood up, blood pumping. Her hot come still clung to his fingers, and he licked them clean, taking a moment to savor the taste of her.

What a lady. He would take Naida to Clymenestra as he was compelled, but then he'd show little Naida the wildest lovemaking the universe had ever known. He'd tell her who she was and what she had to do to free him from Clymenestra the big, bad witch.

He started to run after her. Oh, this hunting would be good. He could easily outrun her, and the sweet morsel would be his in the end.

He stepped on a sharp rock. "Damn!" He danced in a little circle, cursing in pain. *Wolf. Stop her!*

I'm eating dinner, came the thought back.

Is food all you think about? Stop her, now.

He heard a snarl in his mind then silence as the wolf loped off after Naida.

Arys caught up to her not far from the clearing. She stood on the path, panting, staring anxiously at the silver-furred wolf barring her way.

Arys came up behind her and slid his arms around her waist. His heavy cock, thick with wanting, nudged her through their clothes.

"Is he your friend?" she asked shakily.

"Maybe."

The wolf was a fearsome sight, tall and yellow-eyed, its jaws stained red from whatever animal it had caught.

"Go away now," Arys told him.

Sure. No problem. Call anytime. I'll drop everything and come running. Just for you. The wolf stalked away, its thoughts dying into low-pitched mutters.

"Will all the wolves in the forest help you?" Naida asked.

"Probably."

"Then I have no chance."

"No," he said.

She suddenly elbowed him in the ribs, twisted from him, and ran. He caught up to her in three strides, laughing as he scooped her into his arms and spun around with her.

"I think I love you, Naida of the water. Now let's find some."

He could slide sideways through space if he needed to, and he did so now. In a few moments, he was back at the pool he'd swum in earlier, the moonlight bright on its surface.

He thumped Naida back to her feet. She clung to him, alarmed and breathless. "What did you do?"

"Dragon magic. Want to see some more?"

"I'm not sure I do."

"This will be easy. Watch."

He thought of what he wanted, and suddenly, Naida's dress and underdress vanished from her body and landed harmlessly in a pile a few feet from them.

She shrieked and clutched her arms over her chest. "That wasn't fair."

He grinned, tilting his head, looking his fill. "Goddess of the moon, but you're beautiful."

She had a lovely body, plump and curved, her breasts round with dark, lush tips. Her pussy, too, was cute, brushed with fiery red hair to match the curls on her head. His cock jumped. He had never been partial to human women, but she was the finest thing he'd ever seen.

"Swim with me," he said. He stripped off his clothes in the usual way and dove into the silvered pool.

When he surfaced, he saw her watching him, her look appreciative. She might be frightened and shy and uncertain, but she liked looking at his body. He'd seen that when she'd peered avidly through Clymenestra's window.

He thought she'd try to run away again, but she stepped to the edge of the pool, raised her arms above her head, and dove in, her body a graceful curve.

She surfaced, water cascading from her. Water beaded on her lips and her lashes and on the skin of her neck.

He stepped to her and slid his hands around her hips. "Naida," he said against her mouth. "Do your magic now."

Her breath tasted like honey. "I don't know how."

"You want Clymenestra to show you?"

"Yes."

"She can't." He swiped his tongue across her lips. "Clymenestra's magic is of the earth. Yours is of the air, like lightning, or white fire in your mind. You have the dreams, don't you? Of being elsewhere, of knowing something different than this?"

Her eyes rounded. "How did you know?"

"My magic is the same. Concentrate. Try to make something happen."

She closed her eyes. Her face grew calm, and he felt the power inside her begin to crackle and glow.

Suddenly he found himself flying backward through the air. He landed in the water again, *smack*, his backside stinging.

He struggled to his feet, shoving his wet hair from his face, laughing.

Naida gasped. "Did I do that?"

"Yes, sweetling."

"Oh." She looked startled, then slightly pleased. "I have no idea how."

"I do. I will teach you."

"Will you?" Her eyes were wide, luminous.

"Of course. I can teach how to control your magic and use it when you need it." He grinned. "And then you'll learn how beautiful your body is, and how much I can pleasure it."

She gave him a skeptical look. "What has that got to do with magic?"

"Much, sweet Naida. Very much."

He placed his hands on her shoulders, finding them soft, his fingers indenting her flesh. She was lush and beautiful, and his cock, which had already been hard, swelled to its tightest point.

He bent and swirled his tongue over her left shoulder, trailing it to her neck, then to her ear. He dipped inside, knowing the hot sensation that would flow through her. "Put your hands around my cock," he said.

She swallowed, eyes darting sideways at him as he continued to lick the shell of her ear. Then, lovely sensation, she put tentative fingers on his very needy cock.

"Take it." He nibbled her earlobe. "Put your hands all the way around it."

She nodded once, her pretty red hair tickling his nose. And then, *goddess, I love you*, she closed both hands around him.

His hips involuntarily jerked, his cock wanting the sensation of her squeezing him. He stilled, forcing himself to go slowly. No sense scaring her away. "Part your legs," he said.

Another sideways glance. "I thought I had to remain a maiden."

"You will. I am going to show you what it is to be pleasured, and teach you to pleasure me."

"Oh." Her eyes darkened in anticipation, the pulse at her throat jumping. Slowly, as though still uncertain, she moved her feet apart.

He slid one hand to the curls of her pussy, swirling his fingertips through delightfully wiry hair as he'd done earlier in the clearing. He spread his fingers, nudging her to part her legs farther.

She drew in a breath, eyes widening.

"Do you like it?" he whispered.

"Yes."

He opened her a little more, feathering his touch along the folds, then he slid one finger inside her, finding her juices already flowing for him.

He swirled his finger, pressing it deeper inside than he had been able to before, feeling the exquisite tightness of her cunt. It excited him. Even as a dragon, he'd never known a virgin.

Naida turned her head, her lips hot against his. "It feels like when I touch myself, but better."

He happily imagined her with her hand pressed to her pussy. Her eyes would be heavy with desire, her head lolling back, her red hair spilling over her. She'd stroke and stroke, moans escaping her parted red lips.

"You feel nice," he murmured, and slid a second finger into her.

She groaned and tightened her hand around his cock.

"Like this," he said. He guided her fingers to his tip then closed his hand around hers and stroked down to the base. The sensation burned and tingled, and he felt the building pressure of his seed.

He released her hand, letting her have a go on her own. She let her fingers drift to the tip, then, sweet girl, squeezed him down his full length, just like he'd taught her.

"Oh, love," he breathed. "You learn fast."

He scooped her to him, letting the buoyancy of the water lighten her. He let his third finger join the others, pressing deep inside her. She was wet in there, and hot and tight. He wanted to be inside her, and not just with his fingers.

"Why does Clymenestra want me?" Naida murmured.

"She needs your blood. But do not worry, I'll not let her hurt you."

She lifted her head. "How will you stop her, if you must obey her?"

"I have ways. Now, stop talking."

Obediently, she closed her mouth. He laced his tongue over her lips, prodding the closed line like his fingers prodded her opening.

"I want to show you so many things," he whispered. He angled his fingers to press forward on the inside of her walls. "Things like that."

She gasped. "Arys, what are you doing to me?"

"Showing you pleasure."

"Too much. I can't..."

"Yes, you can." He slid his tongue over her lips again, dipping inside. He kissed her chin, her cheek, and the hollow beneath her eye. "You taste good, Naida."

She'd gotten the idea of how to rub his cock, though he could tell she really did not know what she was doing. Her grip moved up and down like he'd taught her, but she also explored him in quick little strokes. She found the sensitive place beneath his tip, the warm tightness of his balls, the place behind his scrotum that excited him.

As she played with him, he played with her, fucking her with his fingers. The walls of her cunt squeezed him, harder and harder as she grew more excited.

"*Arys.*"

"Have you ever come before?" he whispered against her skin.

She nodded, eyes closed. "In bed. Alone."

"It's much better when someone else takes you there. Do you want me to take you there?"

"Yes." The word came out a groan. "*Please.*"

"All right. Hold on."

She tightened her grip on his cock at the same time she slid her arm around his shoulder. He wriggled his fingers inside her, pressing forward against the walls of her cunt to find her place of greatest pleasure.

At the same time, he moved his thumb over her clit, teasing and circling. She was so wet with cream that his fingers were soaked with it.

He moved his other hand to the warm space between her buttocks and dipped his forefinger between her cheeks, finding her anal star.

Her head fell back. "Goddess, what do I feel?"

"You feel me." Arys pressed a kiss to her forehead, a strange tenderness washing over him. "You feel me feeling you."

Slowly, so as not to hurt her, he dipped the tip of his forefinger into her ass.

She squeezed his cock, hard. In response, he slipped his finger farther into her ass, until she let out a strangled moan.

Goddess, he wanted her so bad. He felt the constraint of the order Clymenestra had given him. He could sense the witch's magic around him, like a net of fiery threads, compelling him to obey.

He strained against it, wanting Naida, knowing she could free him if he could just — get — through.

"Too late," he groaned. "Oh, too late."

Naida screamed. Her juices flowed hot around his fingers, sweet come, *oh, yes, love*. She bucked and rocked against his hand, her hold on his cock an iron-firm grip.

"Naida. *Fuck*." His climax took him hard. His seed shot into the water as he pumped and pumped through Naida's grip.

Her spicy scent surrounded him, her skin sweet under his tongue. He kept pumping, wishing her hand was her pussy, all warm and wet around him.

Clymenestra was going to pay for every thrust that he could not have inside Naida. He treasured this woman, and every sound of excitement she made, and Clymenestra would not let him have her.

Not for long.

Naida cried his name. She rubbed herself against him like she wanted to climb inside him, nails biting his back. He guided her hand to his scrotum, cupping her fingers around it while he moved his hips to release the last of his come.

Breathing hard, he gathered her against him. "Naida. Love."

Her own climax broke, dying off into breathy little sighs. They held each other for a long time, her hand still on his cock, his fingers still buried inside her pussy.

"I've never felt like this before," she murmured.

"Neither have I, sweet love."

Arys kissed her lips. She returned the kiss with faint, shaking pressure, her mouth weak.

It was new to him, this tenderness, coming hard on the heels of the best climax he'd ever had in his dragon life. "Neither have I."

Chapter Four

&

Naida swallowed as Clymenestra's house came into view. Arys' hand in hers was strong, and when he looked back and gave her a smile she felt slightly comforted. But only slightly.

She understood now that Arys would not let Clymenestra hurt her. And yet he still brought Naida here, unable to disobey Clymenestra's commands.

Naida felt flushed and open and warm from his hands and mouth on her. She should be ashamed, she thought, but she wasn't. The warm glow that pulsed through her body was more than pleasure. She did not understand why or how, but she'd fallen in love with Arys.

And why not? He turned his head and gazed at her, his smile warm and wicked. He was beautiful, and he made her laugh, and the way he looked at her...

She knew better than to think he could possibly return the feeling. He was Clymenestra's lover, Clymenestra's slave. Clymenestra had a lush and enticing body, and Arys had to obey her.

After Clymenestra had taken from Naida what she wanted, everything would be done. Naida would return home, trying to come up with a clever explanation for why she'd been gone all night, and this would be over. She'd likely never see Arys again.

That thought brought an ache to her heart.

They approached the house. The window box still lay broken near the threshold.

At the door, Arys stopped. He slid his arm around Naida's waist and kissed her gently. "I am pleased I found you this night, Naida of the water. All will be well, I promise."

Without waiting for her reply, he opened the door. Keeping his strong hand on the small of her back, he guided Naida inside.

Clymenestra's cottage smelled of lavender and patchouli, sandalwood and poppy. The witch herself stood at the sturdy table in the middle of the room, chopping herbs with a wicked-looking knife.

She did not bother to look up as they came in. "You brought her? Good. Tell her to stand over there." She pointed with the knife to the space beside the bed.

"It's all right," Arys said in Naida's ear as he led her across the room. "I'll not let her hurt you. And then, when she's done, I will be free."

Naida did not really understand why he was so confident, but the strength of his voice, coupled with the heat from his hand, calmed her a little. As long as Arys was with her, she could face anything.

Clymenestra straightened up, knife in hand. She stared at Naida, then her face changed, irritation giving way to surprised delight.

"Oh," she said. "Clever Arys to bring me *this* one."

"I am very clever," Arys said, his voice rumbling. "You should remember that."

Clymenestra ignored him. "Do not worry, my dear. I need your blood, but only a drop or two. Of course..." she neared Naida and touched her cheek with a cool hand. "Your blood will be special."

She licked her finger and drew it across Naida's lips. Naida recoiled, cringing against Arys behind her.

"She's mine," Arys growled. "I saw her first."

Clymenestra laughed. "I care not what you do with her, Arys, *after* I am finished. Have her, do what you like."

"Oh, I'll do whatever I like when you're finished," Arys said.

Clymenestra shot him a puzzled look. Arys simply smiled a wonderful, dazzling smile that said he knew much better than Clymenestra what the world was really all about.

Clymenestra didn't bother trying to understand. "Lie down," she said to Naida. "You might want to take off your dress, first."

Naida started. "You said a drop or two. Why should I have to lie down?"

"A drop or two," Clymenestra replied impatiently, "from a maiden's hand in the moment she ceases to be a maiden. That means you need to deflower her, Arys."

She turned away, unconcerned. Arys scowled at her back. "You didn't bother mentioning this before."

"I did not think I had to. Don't tell me you don't want to deflower her, because I won't believe you."

"She is not for your use. She isn't your slave."

Clymenestra smiled a nasty smile. "No, but you are. I command you to fuck her, slave. There is a convenient bed next to you. I'll take the blood as soon as you break her hymen, then you can have her to your heart's content."

Arys folded his arms across his broad chest. "This I will not do."

Clymenestra gave him a disbelieving look. "But she's a lovely thing. I am surprised that you don't want to ravish her."

"What is between Naida and me is between Naida and me," Arys said. "It's nothing to do with you. She's a maiden, and a sweet lady, and I'll not let you foul her with your magic."

Clymenestra stared at him a moment, as though amazed a docile pet cat had grown claws, then her eyes narrowed. "Oh, yes you will. You will do anything I like, anytime I like."

"Not this time," Arys said.

Clymenestra closed her eyes. Naida slid her hand into Arys' large one, suddenly worried.

Clymenestra balled her fists, drew a long breath, then opened her mouth. From her parted lips came a musical, rather beautiful chant, full of long and nonsense syllables.

The sounds filled the air like smoke, hanging in the scented cottage. They wound among the beams, flowing into Naida's ears, filling her body with music. She felt the syllables try to grasp her, but they could not, and slid away.

Arys suddenly released Naida and clamped his hands over his ears. "*Damn witch.*"

His face white, he sank to his knees, his eyes wide with shock. The silver color of his irises drained nearly to white. His whole body shook, his strong, muscular frame racked with tremors.

Naida realized that the words that had tried to grasp her had found purchase inside Arys. They held him like fiery bands, wrapping him in pain. She did not know how she understood this, but she did.

"Stop!" she cried.

Clymenestra did not move. Naida strode forward and seized the witch by the shoulders. "Stop. Leave him alone. I'll do your stupid spell."

Clymenestra closed her mouth. The musical words slowly faded, floating away like dying snowfall. She raised her head, opened her eyes, and smiled. "Excellent," she said. "I knew I could count on you."

* * * * *

Beautiful Naida stripped her dress from her body and stood naked in the cottage's heated air.

Arys forgot a moment about Clymenestra and her spells, and the needle-hot agony that had laced every bone and sinew while Clymenestra chanted his true name.

Naida was all that was beauty. He'd seen her in the moonlit pool, when his hands floated all over her lovely body, but this room was bright, firelight touching her and flushing her skin.

She had plump limbs, tapering to delicate wrists and ankles, hands a little rough from her farm work, feet dainty in shabby leather shoes. Her waist nipped in over round hips, buttocks full and lovely.

He admired her sweet, pretty ass that he'd touched and filled with his finger. Some day he'd fill it with his cock. He'd teach her to take it little by little, until he could slide in full length.

Her breasts were round and plump, dark areolas tightening to points in anticipation of what they would do. Her neck was long and lovely, bared by the braid that kept her red hair confined.

Clymenestra smiled, sweeping her own appreciative gaze over Naida. Annoying woman.

Arys stripped off his shirt and breeches, tossing the threadbare clothes aside. If all went as planned, that was the last time he'd have to wear them. He saw Naida's gaze flick to his muscled chest and then down, and her eyes widen. He grinned to himself. His cock had inflated in a big way.

"Lie on the bed," he told her. "Spread your legs for me."

She glanced at him in trepidation, but obeyed. Her buttocks swayed enticingly and her breasts swung as she crawled onto the bed. She lay down, arranging herself comfortably, and moved her legs a few inches apart.

Beautiful sight. He wouldn't hurt her though, never that. He'd go slow, get her used to him, make her so wet and slippery and use his dragon magic so that she'd not feel a maiden's pain.

He climbed upon the bed with her. She watched him, concern in her green-brown eyes.

"Did she hurt you?" she whispered as he knelt over her.

"Not too much. Don't worry, sweetheart."

She ran her hands over his broad shoulders and he realized she was trying to soothe him. "She should not have hurt you," she said.

He leaned down and kissed her lips. "You are sweet, Naida. But never mind about me. I need you to open your legs a little more."

She complied. She did not look at Clymenestra, who'd moved back to her worktable, but at Arys. Her eyes fixed on him, watching him, trusting him.

Trust. He'd never had the pleasure of someone's trust before.

"It won't hurt, love, I promise," he said.

Clymenestra approached them, silver bowl in hand. "I do hope it hurts. I need her to scream."

"Too bad." Arys lowered himself onto her. Naida's scent surrounded him, sweet, heady, and spicy. He was losing focus, forgetting about the hot room and Clymenestra and the too-rough blanket under his knees. "Do not listen, Naida. Look only at me."

Naida did. He could get lost in her eyes, green-brown and framed with dark lashes, and her skin that warmed him.

He ran his hands down her sides, swirling fingers over the bones of her hips, dipping to her thighs and spreading them wide. He brought his legs together and lowered himself to her.

"Lift your hips a little." He splayed his hand across her opening, sliding fingers through her cream. He dipped a finger inside, then brought it to his mouth and sucked it clean. "I love tasting you."

She pressed her fingers to his biceps, rubbing them a little. He fused his dragon magic to her mind, gently shutting it to pain. Clymenestra would not get Naida's pain.

"Ready?" he whispered.

Naida swallowed, her throat working. She nodded.

He sensed Clymenestra hovering next to the bed, a bowl and small silver knife held ready. Naida stretched out her hand.

"Take me, love," Arys said, then very slowly, he slid himself inside her.

He felt the change in her instantly. Her eyes widened and she gasped, the walls of her cunt closing in on him tight, *so tight*.

Her whole body jerked, and not in hurt. Infused with her mind, he felt the magic in her take hold, like white fire snaking through every nerve. He smiled with the joy of it.

She smiled back, a very dragonlike smile.

His heart sang. It was coming.

And then with the suddenness of a firecracker, Clymenestra, her hot, stuffy cottage, and the stink of her magic — went away.

Chapter Five

ഔ

They were in a meadow of tall, lemony-smelling grass and large blue flowers. Soft blue sky arched overhead. The grass tickled Naida's back, but all she really felt was Arys inside her, stretching her, filling her.

"Naida," he said, his silver eyes glowing at full strength. "Love."

He pumped into her, sending her down into the grass. The friction of his cock in her slippery cunt sent wave after wave of delight crashing through her. He licked her lips, sliding his tongue between them as she laughed.

"Damn, you're beautiful," he said. "And goddess, so tight."

He focused on her, his eyes wild with lovemaking. His shoulders bunched as he braced himself, his hips rising as he fucked and fucked her.

"Fuck," she said out loud. She had come to like the word.

He grinned. "All right, darling. If you insist."

He thrust harder and harder, then suddenly slowed to a near stopping point. She wriggled her hips, wanting more, begging for more.

He laughed and started again, faster and faster. He snaked his hand between them and rubbed her clit.

She screamed. The sensation of him inside her body and his magic inside her mind spiraled waves of joy through her. She came, harder and more crazily than she had in the moonlit pool—having him inside her made all the difference.

"Arys," she said. She hauled him down to her. "I love you."

He groaned aloud, face twisting, as his own climax came. Hot seed burst into her, and sweat dripped from his flushed body.

He crashed on top of her, riding out his climax while she writhed in the hot feeling of it. "I love you," she said again.

He lifted his head, smiling widely, his silver eyes diamond-sharp. "Naida." He laughed and licked her mouth. "I knew you'd free me. I knew you had the magic."

"What happened? Did you bring us here?"

"No, sweetling. You did."

Naida gaped at him. "*I* did?"

"You and your vibrant magic. You are strong, sweetheart. That's why I love you."

She stopped, stunned. "You love me?"

"Of course. I knew you were for me the moment I saw you."

He was still inside her, stretching her tight, her legs wide. "How could you know?" she asked. "I do not understand."

"Your magic nearly knocked me over when I saw you at the window. I knew you had it, magic so strong you could kick Clymenestra's cottage to Hades if you wanted to. I knew if you took me as your mate, you'd free me. And you did. I'm free of her."

"How? How could I have freed you?"

"You said you loved me." He traced her lips with his thumb. "You wanted me, and said you loved me. That's all it took."

"There has to be more to it than that." She paused, still feeling the hot magic inside her mind. "Doesn't there?"

"Well, you are a magical being. That helps."

"Don't laugh at me. I am trying to understand." But his laugh was infectious and she could not help giggling back.

"You are a strong and powerful woman, Naida. I will make you understand what your dreams meant, and what you can do. And if you agree to remain my mate, I will protect you, forever." He lowered his head, caught her nipple in his mouth and suckled. "And I'll do this, too."

"Arys, make love to me."

"That's what I've been doing."

"Again. Please. Make me feel what you did in the woods, and what you did now."

He grinned down at her. "You're a demanding one."

"Teach me how to make you feel good."

"I think I can do that."

He withdrew himself and knelt back, his stem standing out hard from a circle of golden curls. He was so beautiful, bronze skin on hard muscle, silver-blond hair falling to his waist. "Stand up," he said.

She got shakily to her knees, then her feet, unsteady. She felt drained and yet exhilarated, exhausted yet excited.

He did not stand. He leaned forward and licked her pussy from back to front. "I could taste you forever," he murmured.

He licked her again, slowly. He took his tongue across her opening, then began to flicker it a little faster. He tasted her clit, and then her opening again, licking her come, increasing his speed. She clasped her own shoulders, rocking on her heels as he feathered his tongue faster and faster.

He withdrew suddenly, and she nearly moaned in disappointment. Then she gasped as he moved behind her, parted her cheeks, and slid his tongue to her anal star. "*Arys.*"

"Do not move, love," he whispered against her skin, hot breath on her flesh.

He dipped his tongue into the hole, a wet sensation that made her rise on her toes. He went on licking, pleasuring the sensitive opening, from time to time dipping his tongue inside. She squealed, never having experienced anything like it.

Her hands slid down to her clit, massaging the mound while his tongue played in her ass. She came very soon, screaming her joy into the open, quiet air, the large flowers nodding at her.

After that, he showed her how to take his cock in her mouth, closing her lips around it, using her tongue to arouse him like he'd aroused her.

And then he laid her down and entered her again, hard and fast, digging into her with intensity.

"I love you, Naida," he whispered as he climaxed. "Love you."

"I love you." She wrapped her arms around him. "My mate."

"Mmm, I like the sound of that." He smiled lazily, tracing her cheek. "Can we do more mating?"

She laughed, so tired and yet so happy. "As much as you like."

* * * * *

Much later, as they drowsed under the warm afternoon sky, she asked, "I wonder why I came to Clymenestra's cottage tonight of all nights?"

"Fate," Arys said. He was stretched out next to her, his body strong and protective. "Magic." He paused. "Actually, I don't give a damn, I'm just happy you did."

"And I've truly freed you?"

"Yes. I've sensed Clymenestra calling to me while we've been here, but I no longer have to obey." He brushed his fingertip across her nose. "Of course, *you* can call me anytime. I'll come running."

"What was the spell she was trying to do? It had something to do with dragon magic, didn't it?" Naida frowned. "That's why she was happy you'd brought me to her."

"She wouldn't tell me, but when we flashed here, I understood." Arys stretched, a joy to watch. Every sinew and muscle moved in a delightful way, then he relaxed again, rather like a lion in the shade. "She was trying to steal my magic. She thought your blood could help her, since you have strong magic. Silly witch. She helped you free me instead, which enabled you to bring me here."

Naida raised up on her elbows. "What is this place?"

"It's my world."

She swept her gaze across the meadow, to the misty hills in the distance. It was beautiful. "How did I know to come here?"

"Because you were drawn to it. You have dragon in you." He chuckled. "Besides me, I mean."

Naida eyed him in sudden suspicion. "Why aren't you a dragon, if we are in the dragon world?"

He shrugged. "I can be human when I want to be. I wanted you to get to know me like this first."

"When will you be a dragon?" she asked, a little nervously.

"When I'm ready. Let's finish with Clymenestra first."

She looked at him in surprise. "I thought we were finished with her."

"Yes, but we ought to say goodbye."

He flashed her a mischievous grin. He stood up, extended his brawny arm to her, and helped her to her feet.

She looked across the meadow, wondering how they'd get back to Clymenestra's world. As she scanned the clear horizon, she saw a man coming their way.

Strangely, though she was naked, and so was the man walking toward them, she felt no embarrassment. It was as though clothes were of the other world and no longer mattered.

Arys raised his hand in greeting. The approaching man was as large and muscular as Arys and had brown hair and amber eyes.

"Still at it, I see," the man said when he reached them.

"Wouldn't you be?" Arys asked, sounding smug.

"Do you know him?" Naida whispered.

"He's the wolf," Arys said. "Or at least he is in your world."

"Just call me Wolf," he man said. "I don't take human names." He looked sideways at Arys. "Unlike some conceited dragons I know."

It was the wolf, and it wasn't. Naida seemed to see both the man and the feral, powerful wolf-form interposed on each other. And then again, she just saw the man.

"I think I have much to learn," she breathed.

Arys slid his arm around her waist. "Don't worry, I will teach you."

The wolf laughed. "When you're tired of him, come and find me."

Arys ignored this. "We are returning to deal with Clymenestra. Want to watch?"

The wolf snorted. "Not really. I have things to do. Go easy on her, she can't help being stupid."

"True." Arys looked down at Naida. "Ready?"

"I suppose — oh!"

As soon as the words were out of her mouth, the tranquil meadow flowed away and they stood once again in the dark woods before Clymenestra's cottage.

Arys moved away from Naida and faced the cottage. "Come on out," he said, his voice stronger than she'd ever heard it. "Get it over with."

Naida did not think Clymenestra would respond. She was a powerful witch, why should she? But in a few moments, the door opened and Clymenestra walked slowly outside, past the broken flowerbox like she did not notice it. Her hand was clenched, and Naida sensed power in it, a spell of some kind.

Naida moved protectively toward Arys. Clymenestra sneered at her. "You stole him," she said.

"No," Arys interrupted. "You stole *me*. I belong to no one now, except Naida."

"How did you enslave him?" Clymenestra asked Naida, as though Arys wasn't there. "How did you take him away from me?"

"I loved him. Can you understand that?"

"No," she scoffed. "But I suppose it doesn't matter what I understand. Your magic is stronger than mine. Very well, you won. I know better than to fight a more powerful mage."

Her smile was disdainful, and her fist began to glow.

"Arys," Naida said nervously.

Arys shook his head. "Ah, Clymenestra. Foolish to the end."

Clymenestra's lip curled. "I needed you. You would have done the same."

"No. You stole my name, you stole my soul. Now that I have it all back—"

"What? You are going to kill me?"

Arys laughed, not an angry laugh. "No."

Clymenestra lifted her hand. She began to chant, an ugly, thick chant that darkened the air around it.

Arys watched her with a pitying look. "You know what they say, Clymenestra." He held up his clenched fist. Flame and light danced from it, crackling with power. "You should never play with fire."

He sent the spell straight at Clymenestra's cottage. The tiny house exploded into flames. It burned lightning fast, falling to a pile of ash in only a few seconds, as Naida and Clymenestra watched, gaping.

Clymenestra shrieked, and the spell in her hands vanished. "My power—you—" She fell to her knees. "Goddess, help me!"

Arys moved back to Naida and held out his hand. "Ready to go, love?"

Naida gulped, almost as shocked as Clymenestra. "What did you do?"

"The cottage held her power. Her magic is earth magic, as I told you, and she built much of it into the walls of the cottage. She will be too weak to enslave any more magical beings, I think."

"Oh." She stared at Clymenestra, weeping in the mud.

Arys touched Naida's arm, surprisingly gentle in light of the violent spell he'd just cast. "Come, love," he said. "We are finished."

He lifted one hand and sliced through the darkness. A bright rent appeared at his fingertips, and behind it floated the soft smell of meadows.

Arys stepped through the tear, reaching back for Naida. She clasped his hand, letting him pull her into his world again.

As she landed on the bright grass, she saw his body elongate and flash and grow, becoming brilliant silver in the sunshine, liquid light. Huge wings unfolded and mighty legs propelled him from the earth into the blue air. The downdraft of the first flap of his wings poured over her, stirring her hair.

She watched him for a long moment, her mouth open, as he flew and spun and spiraled over the earth. A long stream of flame came from his mouth, spitting fire for the joy of it.

"Come with me, Naida." His voice rang in her head.

Suddenly, she knew just how to do it, knew what all those dreams in the loft of her father's farmhouse had been trying to teach her.

She reached up with her hands and sprang straight into the air. Wide wings unfurled and caught her, and she became *dragon*, gold and white, streaking through the heat-laden sky. She caught up to Arys and dove over him, laughing, rolling and floating as though she were in water.

Arys chortled, his strong voice surrounding her. "Of course, you'd be a golden," he said. "Rarest dragon in the universe. I ought to have known."

About the Author

~~

Allyson James is yet one more name for a woman who has racked up four pseudonyms in the first two years of her career. She often cannot remember what her real name is and has to be tapped on the shoulder when spoken to.

Allyson began writing at age eight (a five-page story that actually contained goal, motivation, and conflict). She learned the trick of standing her math book up on her desk so she could write stories behind it. She wrote love stories before she knew what romances were, dreaming of the day when her books would appear at libraries and bookstores. At age thirty, she decided to stop dreaming and do it for real. She published the first short story she ever submitted in a national print magazine, which gave her the false illusion that getting published was easy.

After a long struggle and inevitable rejections, she at last sold a romance novel, then, to her surprise, sold several mystery novels, more romances, and then Romantica™ to Ellora's Cave. She has been nominated for two Romantic Times Reviewer's Choice awards and has had starred reviews in *Booklist* and Top Pick reviews in *Romantic Times*.

Allyson met her soulmate in fencing class (the kind with swords, not posts-and-rails). She looked down the length of his long, throbbing rapier and fell madly in love.

Allyson welcomes mail from readers. You can write to her c/o Ellora's Cave Publishing at 1056 Home Avenue, Akron OH 44310-3502.

Also by Allyson James

ॐ

Christmas Cowboy
Tales of the Shareem: Maia and Rylan
Tales of the Shareem: Rees

FALLEN FOR YOU

Paige Cuccaro

Dedication

To Jen, a good friend and fresh pair of eyes I can always count on.

Chapter One

೫

"You think they'll try to kill me?"

"Yes." Zade wouldn't look at her. His gaze fixed on the streetlamp across from Isabel's bedroom window. The light's honey glow was a safer sight by far than the little witch drifting toward sleep behind him in the dark.

He was a Watcher, a once-mighty angel, and still this woman could bring him to his knees with a negligent sigh. Zade clenched his jaw, his hand fisting around the Roman coin he always carried in the pocket of his slacks.

Her soft, sleepy voice already had his cock as stiff as a Watcher's sword. And the scent of her sheath was only a wicked tease of how perfectly she'd fit his blade. His dick twitched at the thought, but he pushed the erotic image from his mind.

A rustle of covers, like the sound of a warm body rolling in bed, teased behind him. "Why now?" she said.

"Your skills have grown these past months. All those attuned to the ancient power will have felt your touch. You are a threat to the Oscurità as well as a temptation."

Her small snort was muffled in the pillows. "And here I was only hoping to tempt you."

Zade's nails dug into his palms, every muscle in his body coiling tight. He closed his eyes and reached soul deep for the strength to deny his need. He was here to ensure her safety and train her in the use of the ancient power—nothing more.

Isabel and her kind were the key to destroying the Oscurità, the prideful fallen angels. A mission he and his Watcher brothers had failed to achieve so long ago. For ten thousand years they'd suffered the punishment for their ill-fated complacency. Sentenced to an eternity linked in name and penalty with those they'd been sent to destroy.

She and her witch sisters were the Watcher's second chance and Zade would let nothing distract him this time.

"You can protect me?" she asked.

"Absolutely!" Offense wrenched his chin over his shoulder before he could think better on it. His chest squeezed tight at the sight of her, his cock throbbing hard against the shrinking confines of his slacks.

She lay in all her natural glory like a beguiling nymph worshiping the night. Her oval face turned to the side, eyes fluttering against her body's demand for rest. She smiled, her plump, blush-pink lips parting, sweeping up at the corners, quivering.

Slender arms nestled in the silken fan of caramel hair above her head, pulling and shaping her full breasts. Dark rose nipples puckered to hard ridges, ruthlessly tormenting him in the dim glow from the street light. His mouth watered with want of feeling that hard pebbled flesh on his tongue, suckling the fullness of each breast.

"The daughters of men are a dangerous breed," he said, his voice a soft growl.

"Hmm?" Toasted-almond eyes looked to him for a moment before her small, round chin led her gaze onward toward the opposite wall and the two turret windows behind lacy white curtains. "It's hot…those open?"

With barely a thought, Zade's angelic power threw open both windows. A warm summer breeze rustled the sheer fabric and drew a sensuous moan from the sleepy Isabel.

Zade's heart thundered, his body so stiff and hard he ached from restraint.

His gaze coasted lower along the supple line of her body, her milky skin, flawless over the delicate bones of her hips, and the sweet curve of a deliciously feminine belly. But it was the dark thatch of curls protecting her sex that made his palms itch to touch her.

Zade drew a deep breath through his nose and kept his hands fisted firmly inside his pockets. He would not allow his selfish lust to seduce her with hopes of something that could destroy them both.

"Mmmmm, better...nice breeze," she said. Her sleepy bedroom voice was more of a purr and it vibrated over his body coaxing a hard pulse from his cock. A tiny bead of pre-come squeezed out, wetting his balls, his muscles pulling his sac tight in response.

Isabel rolled to her side, her leg drawing up, pulling smooth skin taut over her round ass. Zade knew he should look away, but like a babe to a mother's teat, his gaze was drawn to the dark bush peeking between her legs. The rich curls brushing along the pink, glistening folds of womanly flesh... He could almost taste their sweetness.

"Shouldn't waste your strength, though," she said, her words muffled in the pillow, eyes shut. "You're weak. I feel it."

"I have strength enough." His voice was too damn low, too raw. Staying so near to her, in this room thick with the cocoa-butter smell of her skin, the earthy musk of her sex, it was madness.

She curled her body toward him, a hand shoving thick waves of hair from her face. She blinked, struggling to keep her eyes open. "I don't mind, ya' know."

"What is that, bella?"

"I don't mind if you want to use me. I know that's what you did the first time. It's been months, though. You must be so cold and weak by now."

Humiliation pinched his heart and Zade couldn't bear to meet her trusting gaze. He turned back to the window, swallowing his self-disgust.

"I meant only to deepen your connection to the ancient power. Your innate skills have strengthened. The power flows through you unrestricted. You do not require the soul-bonding again."

Zade closed his eyes with the warm wash of memories. He'd sent his icy soul into her that first time. Its feathery, ghostlike hand gripped the warmth of hers, drew on the ancient power. He'd increased the natural flow of energy running through her, running through everything above and below — except him.

He'd used his angelic skills to deepen her connection, to lend real power to her magic, like he'd done for a select few witches over the centuries — most of whom were Isabel's own ancestors. Soul-bonding was a deeply intimate act, ten times more erotic than mortal sex and incredibly dangerous to both Watcher and witch.

The heady wash of warmth and power could so easily have a Watcher lost in blissful abandon and have his once selfless soul turn ruthlessly gluttonous. In the beat of a heart a careless Watcher could fall from savior to destroyer, from Watcher to Oscurità.

But always, Zade had been able to remain detached, performing the mechanics while keeping the danger of unpredictable emotions at bay — until Isabel.

He cursed his weakness for her. "Maronn."

"Don't 'Maronn' me," she said. "What is that anyway, some sort of Italian cuss word?"

"Yes."

"Whatever. You're right," she said. "I don't *require* another soul-bonding, but you do. I know about the Watchers' punishment, Zade, how your connection to the ancient power was severed. How your brothers who sent you shun you, say you've fallen."

Another rustle of covers floated through the air and Zade guessed Isabel had sat up in bed. His thumb rubbed the worn face on the coin in his pocket—a nervous habit.

"I know your soul grows colder and your body weaker the longer you go without drawing the ancient power from the only source left to you—mortal souls. I know if you wait too long, you could fall further and become Oscurità."

"I will fall no further," Zade said.

"How long before me had it been since you stole warmth from a mortal soul?"

Zade's gaze fixed once more on the honey glow of the streetlight, his mind fighting to keep guilt and lust from coloring his tone. "Ten years."

"Too long. You need your strength, Zade, especially now. Strength you can only recover by stealing the ancient power pooling naturally in a mortal soul."

He made a sardonic snort. "It is not simply the ancient power I take, but what it provides the mortal—"

"I know."

"Life—a mortal's time on this earth. That is what the power gives to everything it touches, and that is what I steal—"

"I know."

He spun toward her. Angry, disgusted with himself. "You do not *know*, Isabel, or you would not speak so blithely. To trade a moment's respite from my punishment for a mortal's already minuscule lifespan is not just. It is monstrous."

Isabel's whole body flinched and Zade felt her recoil like a punch to his gut. Lord, he was a monster. "I am sorry."

Isabel visibly relaxed with his soft apology. Her knees drawn to her chest, arms wrapped tight around them, she'd tucked the light sheet under each arm so it mercifully covered her naked body.

Her brows bunched, eyes softening. "You are not a monster. The creatures who conceived a punishment in which you must destroy the very thing you love most…they're the monsters. And still, you've never taken it all. You've never ended a mortal life. And you'll never have to—not anymore."

"Isabel…" He knew what she was about to suggest, and the very thought snapped every muscle in his body tight.

"I have the ability to give you all you need. You'll never have to choose between a human soul and your own ever again."

She moved to her knees, the light purple sheet falling to her lap, exposing her flushed chest beneath the feathery ends of her silken caramel hair. Her hands were braced on her knees, arms framing her plump breasts. She tortured his last thread of restraint.

"Listen to me," she said. "I don't know why, but for some reason I'm like a conduit of the ancient power. And it seems a pretty big coincidence this ability is exactly what you need."

"It is possible, as a witch, your natural acuity to the ancient power affords you a unique capacity to replace every bit of power my soul drains from yours instantaneously. But it does not necessarily follow that ability was meant for *my* exploitation."

"Who cares? I…I like how it feels. I want you to do it to me again. Besides, it's my body—my soul—shouldn't I get to choose?"

Her admission nearly buckled his knees. He couldn't breathe without inhaling the musky scent of her arousal. He could hear her heart pounding faster, smell her juices creaming her pussy. She was so ready for him, for what he could do to her, she'd come with one lick.

Zade sucked another deep, calming breath through his nose. Dear God, he was losing his leash on control with each passing second. This was madness!

"No, I am sorry, bella," he said. "You do not get to choose." And then he escaped, vanishing from her sight.

Moving at the speed of thought, too fast for the human mind and eye to follow, Zade reached the lamppost across the street from Isabel's house in an instant.

At three in the morning, on Third Street in Ohio's quaint German Village, the streets were blessedly deserted. Zade leaned a shoulder against the hollow metal light pole and angled his gaze toward Isabel's darkened bedroom window.

Several cleansing breaths had his heart slowing to normal, and his dick only semi-hard. He pulled the ancient Roman coin from his pocket, rolling it mindlessly through his fingers—another nervous habit.

"Maronn! Remember why you are here!" he lectured himself. *Protect her. Train her. Nothing more.* "Easy enough to say."

He'd known Isabel since she was a child and from the moment the girlish blush of her cheeks turned to the ruddiness of womanly need, he'd wanted her.

Denying his hunger for her was easy back then. Like most humans, Isabel scarcely noticed his existence. Humans use such a small portion of their brain, they're easily overtaxed by the simple normalcy of life. Rarely do any of them notice the extraordinary creatures who dwell so near. Except for the witches.

When Isabel passed her twenty-fifth birthday several months ago, she'd come into her power. Her attunement to all things above and below heightened, and she'd suddenly noticed him.

Zade could still feel the impact of her brown-sugar gaze deep in his core. She'd melted his heart in that instant, reminded him of all he'd forsaken in the passing of ten thousand years—the joy of laughter, the beauty of a sunset, the simple pleasure of a summer day. When was the last time he'd relished the feel of human touch, a woman's skin, a woman's love, a woman…

Zade straightened, shaking the warm, tempting memories from his brain. What good were such thoughts? He'd gone too long with the single-minded obsession to aid the witches in defeating the Oscurità. He didn't know how to consider anything else. He didn't know if his resolve was strong enough to withstand all that Isabel threatened to stir within him.

What if his love, his desire, his monstrous angelic need overwhelmed him and in his fall, he destroyed her?

Zade could never take that chance.

Chapter Two

ഔ

"Did you need any incense, crystals or oils today?" Isabel's standard last-minute sales pitch.

She paused from ringing up the teenager's merchandise. Holding the Celtic cross altar candle upside down to see the price tag, her gaze flicked to the young girl dressed head to foot in black.

Her inky, shoulder-length hair, streaked with neon green, shimmered with the shake of her head. Her pierced, mauve lips twitched with a smile. "Unless I need something else for a love spell."

"Try talking to him?"

The girl rolled her pretty blues. "Yeah, right. Whatever."

Isabel let it go. After all, who was she to be giving romantic advice? She'd opened Bell, Book and Candle in the bottom floor of her grandma's old Victorian to make a living in a field she loved. Selling the supplies for witchcraft she was good at, relationships not so much.

Isabel wrapped the candle in tissue and added it to the bag with the rest. "Total's twenty-four seventy-eight."

The brooding teen counted the precise change from the fistful she'd pulled from her pocket and smacked it on the counter next to the bills. Without another word, she grabbed the bag, stomped past Zade, who was perusing the stone and crystal table beneath the front window, and slammed the front door behind her. Zade didn't seem to notice, but Isabel wasn't fooled.

Zade was aware of everything, always, especially where she was concerned. He kept her company and taught her things, things like magic. And he protected her. Even from the klutzy, everyday bumps and bruises. Sometimes she wondered if he realized he was doing it. He just seemed to know what she needed — even before she did.

Despite his ever-present scowl and somber, warrior mentality, Isabel knew there was a softer side to Zade. A side that was warm and caring…that made her heart race and her belly flutter. A side he seemed determined to bury and she was just as determined to unleash.

Isabel went back to restocking the aromatherapy display next to the register. In the past months she and Zade had discussed everything from religion to the shelf life of Twinkies. He knew her and she knew him, as well as he'd allow. They were easy together — teacher and student, protector and witch. But tonight, she'd change everything. Tonight, they'd become more. Tonight, they'd become lovers.

The summer's eve ritual was exactly the kind of opportunity she'd been waiting for. A way to seduce Zade into accepting what Isabel already knew — they were meant for each other.

No other man had made her feel the way he did. No other man had made her feel so…normal. Something she hadn't felt since college four years ago when her first and only lover called her an insatiable freak who was destined to stay that way. She'd believed him and sworn off men, terrified of a second, corroborating opinion. And then Zade had appeared.

He'd laid his hands on her shoulders that first time, touching her soul deep, and sent the promise of a mind-blowing orgasm quaking through her body. The flood of power he'd pulled through her was like one long, erotic lick teasing over every erogenous zone on her body. It was the best sex she *hadn't* had in...forever.

But her plan of seduction wasn't completely selfish. Zade was weak. He needed the ancient power to regain his strength and ease the constant pain of a frozen soul. Isabel was the only one in the world, the only one in ten thousand years, who could provide what he needed without danger of him draining her life away. Her plan had to work.

* * * * *

Ten minutes 'til midnight. The back courtyard was ready with her altar and offerings. Isabel pulled the lapels of her fuzzy robe tight over her chest and peeked through the bathroom curtains overlooking the courtyard.

Maybe this wasn't such a good idea. Last night, Zade had taken off like he'd escaped the electric chair. What if pushing harder made him run even faster and farther away? What if he left for good?

Isabel's stomach flopped, her heart quickening. She couldn't lose him. He'd become such a natural part of her life. She hated the loneliness that would surely return if he wasn't there to chase it away. Screw helping her with her growing powers, she needed him to help fill that empty part of her soul.

She glanced in the mirror over the sink, nervously tucking her hair behind her ear. "What if my theory's just a load of crap?"

Except for the erotic nature of soul-bonding, there was almost nothing to indicate that sex would lead to it. Would Zade be able to resist linking souls if he was buried eight inches deep inside her?

Was her theory worth all this?

Dark shadows shifting at the corner of the courtyard caught her eye. She looked just as Zade stepped into the pooling moonlight next to the little altar. His stormy gaze swung up to hers and locked with a palpable impact. Isabel gasped and stumbled back two steps.

"Oh, hell, yeah, it's worth it."

Isabel stepped out of the back door and walked up to the altar, her bare feet chilly against the old, grass-lined red bricks of the courtyard. Zade stood no more than five feet in front of her, the altar between them.

If her eyes had teeth, she'd have eaten him up from the tips of his sexy Italian loafers to the end of his strong, Roman nose. His scent thickened the air with the smell of warm vanilla and simmering opium oil. His long hair curtained his back, spanning from one broad shoulder to the other.

His black leather duster rippled around his calves in a gentle breeze as he watched her. Those dark, stormy eyes, even more ominous peering from the shadows, sent a luscious quiver racing up her spine. No human had eyes like that. She could actually see the thunder clouds rolling through their dark violet depths.

Her smile wavered as her gaze flicked to the shadowy houses looming over the high fence around her backyard. She wouldn't be at all surprised if someone was secretly watching.

Her belly tingled at the thought, exhibitionism sending a rush of adrenaline surging through her body. She shrugged and let her terrycloth robe fall to her feet.

A low, menacing growl vibrated from Zade. "What are you doing?"

"Summer's eve ritual. You'll help—right?"

With his hands parked in the front pockets of his slacks, Zade closed his eyes. "You perform the ritual naked?"

"Skyclad," she corrected. "It's perfectly acceptable." Although not really necessary and a first for Isabel. But she saw no need to mention that.

"And the neighbors?"

Isabel pouted and carelessly shrugged her shoulders. "It's my property. Shield me from human sight, if it bothers you."

"It does." He closed his eyes. A moment later, he said, "Proceed."

"Thanks." She could feel how the effort wore on his already fading strength. Guilt pinched her heart, but she stayed the course. *All the more reason for the soul-bonding. Right? Right.*

With no further fanfare, Isabel cast her magical circle, at once feeling the sensual brush of power pulse through her body into the protective ring. Her breath trembled and she closed her eyes. It was nothing compared to the power Zade could draw through her. But like a bite of bread to a starving man, deprivation made the sensation all the more delicious.

In utter silence, Zade watched her perform the ritual, his gaze as intense as a lion's on his prey. Nothing escaped those dark eyes, and Isabel felt the heat of his stare all the way to her soul. By the time she'd reached the part where the God and Goddess would symbolically unite giving life to the world, Isabel could feel her hot juices tickling down her thighs.

She flicked her gaze to him, peering from beneath her lashes. She made her voice a seductive purr, knowing how her desire would glisten in her eyes. "I'll need your help for this next part."

Zade's handsome face remained a scowling, unreadable mask. Only the subtle shift in the color of his eyes, from midnight purple to sky-blue, gave away the turmoil boiling within him.

"Mind yourself, Isabel." His voice was deep, seductive. "I am not without my limits."

Isabel couldn't help the mischievous smile tugging at one corner of her mouth as she knelt before the altar, her gaze never leaving his. "Blessed be all in the Union of the God and Goddess."

She'd heard other coven sisters talk about ritual sex, how orgasms heightened the intensity of the drawn energy. It was considered an offering to nature, but tonight Isabel would make the offering to and for Zade alone.

Catching her bottom lip between her teeth for a moment, she stretched her arms above her head. "I open my higher consciousness to the God and Goddess for illumination." She lowered her hands to her eyes. "My mind to perceive more clearly." She dropped her hands to her chest. "My heart for the essence of purity."

She opened her arms. "My body and soul in the blessed power of unity."

"Isabel…" There was a warning growl in his voice that bristled the fine hairs at the back of her neck. But if Zade was true to his word, there to aid her in all things magic, he would not, could not, refuse her.

"I am in need of my Watcher, Zade," she said, ignoring instinctive wariness. "I've offered my body and soul in unity. Would you prefer I pick a stranger off the street?"

In the single beat of her heart, Zade's eyes paled from sky-blue to winter gray, a faint red band ringing each iris. His inky pupils constricted, and somehow his very presence intensified. He seemed larger, more frighteningly powerful, fairly crowding out all sound and air.

In a soul-quaking voice of biblical proportions, he said, "Ready thyself woman, for you know not what you tempt."

Chapter Three

ဆ

It began as a warm glow centered in the pit of her belly. Isabel's hands cradled the spot instinctively. As the heat spread up her chest and down toward her legs, she looked to Zade.

He watched her, his lips a harsh slash, his dark brows knotted above intense, dove gray eyes. One hand stowed in the front pocket of his slacks, the other twirling an old coin through his fingers. A breeze swirled around the edges of the courtyard, fanning through the long silky strands of his hair.

His essence was inside her, his angelic powers awakening every nerve ending in her body.

"I am your Watcher, Isabel." His low, velvet voice brushed her mind, its sensuous caress cascading through her body like ripples in a pond. *"It is my duty to aid you in your magical workings. In this no other man will do."*

The warmth continued to spread, growing hotter and thicker, producing a palpable weight so it felt like large masculine hands stroked over her body. Her flesh tingled along the path they took from her belly, over her ribs to her breasts. She trembled, feeling a wide palm scoop up one heavy breast, then the other, rough fingers kneading her flesh.

Wet heat, hot as a mouth, enveloped her left nipple, clamping down on the sensitive skin—suctioning. When she looked, her left breast tented out from her body, the nipple flat as though suckled in her lover's mouth. But there was no mouth, no lover. Her belly clenched.

Her breath caught just as a small dent formed in the dark rose nub, teeth nipping a moment, before the rough brush of a tongue licked the tiny sting away. Isabel's heart thundered in her ears. Blood surged hot and frantic to swell the slick muscles of her pussy.

Creamy wetness trickled from her cunt with each pulse of her sex, coating the thick curls between her thighs. Zade's pale, manic gaze dropped to her bush, his nostrils flaring as though the warm breeze carried her scent across the courtyard.

He licked his lips. "Mmmm, I can taste your pussy on the air, Isabel. An appetizer. Such a wicked tease."

A new pair of hot, invisible hands spawned from the warmth in her belly and pressed a path down toward her damp curls. Isabel bit her lip on a moan, her own fingers digging into her soft tummy, resisting the urge to guide hands that weren't really there.

"Sweet temptation. Just looking at your pretty tits and pussy makes my cock hard as steel. Maronn... What you do to me, Isabel."

His low, lyrical voice vibrated through her body, stroking places in her mind and soul no mortal man could ever touch. Isabel struggled to keep her breathing steady, her sex muscles clenching and releasing as though his voice could fill her there as well.

She could almost see his thick fingers in her mind, parting her sex, juices glistening like dewdrops among the curls. She could feel his fingers diving between her hot folds, disappearing past knuckles.

Isabel let her head fall back with a quiet moan, her body swaying on her knees. Something soft but solid cupped her back from her head to her thighs, supporting her. She didn't care if there was really something there or not. It didn't matter.

She closed her eyes, losing herself in the feel of his ghostly fingers teasing over her clit and pressing farther into the tight, muscled hole of her sex. Her legs trembled with the delicious pressure of his invasion, a fresh wash of juices coating her thighs.

With her eyes closed all her other senses came alive. Crickets chirped a summer serenade. The breeze sugared her lips with the flavor of honeysuckle and lilac. Opium oil, vanilla beans and the thick aroma of male arousal filled her nose, lined the back of her throat and lungs. She'd never take enough of his delicious scent into her body.

His powerful fingers thrust into her again, pushing between her tight slick muscles. He withdrew, slow, teasing, until only the very tips wiggled at her entrance. She spread her knees, trying to impale herself on the invisible fingers, but no amount of wiggling or adjusting made a difference. The fingers weren't really there.

The heat of his hand still cupped between her legs, his palm pressing against her clit. She could feel his fingers teasing her opening, but there was nothing she could do to force the slow, lazy finger fuck.

Another hard thrust and her muscles clamped down, an electric ripple of pleasure speeding through her body in all directions. He pulled out again, her cream coating his fingers, drenching his palm so it ground her juices against her clit.

"Mmmm, I love how your body responds, bella. So tight and hungry for me. So wet."

He drove into her again, a whip of sensation lashing through her body. No matter how wet she became, how wide her pussy opened for him, the fit was skintight. The invisible fingers grew in length and girth to match the slick walls of her sex — stretching her each time — filling her utterly.

Sultry breath bathed her neck. Lips, petal soft, pressed kisses up to her ear, along her cheek until they took her mouth—stole her breath. The thrusts came harder, deeper, faster into her pussy. Hands still kneaded her breasts, a hot mouth still suckling, teeth nipping, tantalizing her pebble-hard nipples.

Isabel bucked her hips, instinct driving her body into his thrusts, pushing her tits deeper into that sultry mouth, suckling the powerful tongue tangling with hers in her mouth. The barrage of sensations churned inside her, each one spinning the other faster, tightening some feminine spring within her.

The gathering energy sizzled in the air around her. The power generated by her heightening senses fed into her protective circle making it glow with power in the moonlight.

Another invisible hand latched on to her ass, squeezing the soft flesh, driving her body harder, faster, against his ramming fingers. Chest muscles squeezed, her thighs went taut, her hands fisting over her belly. Every muscle in her body screwed tight, held, as he drove into her cunt again and again—slamming between the wet flesh of her thighs and ass.

She teetered on the mind-numbing edge, her body utterly under Zade's seething, angelic control. The invisible hands holding her ass, squeezing her tits, driving into her pussy, worked the quickening rhythm, fucked her all on their own.

"*Let go.*" It was a whisper in her mind. His black-magic voice rumbled soft through her body, tripping an avalanche within her so powerful no force on Earth could stop it.

"That's it, *mio amore*. Come for me. Yes. Come so much your pleasure wets the earth. Yesss…"

"Zade…" Isabel's cry squeezed out of her body, every muscle releasing in rapid succession like dominos, pushing the sound out of her with such force it could've shaken the trees ringing the courtyard.

In a flash of blinding white light the power her heightened senses had gathered to the circle surged inward, swamping over her body. The sex-charged energy filled her up, coursing in waves from the very core of her body out through her head, fingers and toes.

Isabel gasped at the exquisite pleasure, as if every hair on her body vibrated with power. Through her hazy, sex-fogged brain, she looked to Zade.

Quick, labored breaths swelled his chest, his nostrils flaring, jaw clenched tight. A sheen of sweat glistened along his furrowed brow, his body stiff, hands fisted. His gray eyes had paled further, the faint red glow around his irises now a burning, crimson ring. He was weak, tired and battling a powerful need within him. But why, when she'd so clearly offered all she had?

"This isn't what I wanted, Zade," she said, power still zinging through every muscle.

"Your body disagrees," he said, the pain of his need so clear in his voice.

He suffered for no reason, and that single belief solidified Isabel's resolve. Like pushing against a mudslide, she fought to clear her mind and call on every ounce of skill and knowledge Zade had given her over the months.

She focused...collecting the sex-magic still sizzling through her body. It pooled within her, pressing at the seams of her soul, searching for release, for direction and purpose. With an effort of will, she gave the magic its reason, painting Zade as its target in her mind and soul and then released the power.

It gushed out of her, the force arching her back and stealing her breath. In the dim moonlight, she could almost see the air waver between them, following the fast track of magic from her body to his. Small sparks lit off the stream before the power slammed into his chest, glowing white-hot on impact.

The blast of power drove into his muscled torso, knocking his arms out to the sides, thrusting his head back. The booming howl that wrenched out of Zade echoed through the night, his entire body finally glowing in a blue-white halo of power. Behind him, just above his shoulders, the air shimmered, pure-white feathers formed, rustled in the breeze.

Isabel strained to keep her eyes open on the awesome image before her. Raven-black hair fluttered over broad shoulders, his long black duster wavering around his calves. His white shirt, with the top few buttons undone, flapped against the muscled wall of his chest.

Hands fisted at his sides, massive wings stretching ten feet or more behind him, blocking out the moon, Zade radiated a might that had the very trees bowing back in awe. Chin to his chest, eyes glowing red beneath long, ink-black lashes, he focused his piercing gaze on Isabel.

"What have you done?" he said, but the voice was not a voice she knew. It was raw, graveled with an unearthly timber that made her heart shudder.

"Zade—"

"You go too far, *witch*." He closed his flaming, red eyes, took a breath as though struggling for control. "Isabel..." he whispered. "You torment me cruelly." And then he vanished.

Chapter Four

ॐ

Four days he'd hidden from her, struggling against the demonic needs her sex-magic had stirred within him. Warmth, power…sex, the relentless demands clawed at his mind and soul, shredding his restraint.

Seeing her even from a distance had been a battle of sheer will, half of him wanting to spend eternity fucking that soft, sexy body, warming his soul on her font of ancient power, loving her in every way known above and below. But the other half knew he didn't deserve such bliss. He could never forget what he'd become, what he must do to survive, to destroy the Oscurità.

Her abilities were a ruthless temptation, but surely they were not meant for a creature such as him. A woman with the power to appease a punishment ten thousand years in the making? Certainly she was meant for a cause greater than soothing his punished heart.

She affected him too deeply, stirred emotions within him he'd forsaken long ago. And with those banished emotions so, too, went the understanding of how to keep them in check. He couldn't trust those feelings would not consume him—destroy them both. He was a danger to her—to himself. But he could not leave her.

Lord, I am a selfish prick.

Zade swallowed the disgust choking his throat and fell into step ten paces behind Isabel as she emerged from The Coffee Pot, her favorite morning haunt. Newspaper—folded to her favorite comic strips—in one hand, paper coffee cup in the other, she turned down the side alley.

It would be a warm day. The sun had already burned the chill out of the morning air, but the blacktop road and redbrick alley hadn't yet heated to the point he could feel the warmth through the soles of his shoes.

He tried to lose himself in the soft click-clack of her flat leather sandals against the brick. But the gentle sway of her hips hugged by faded, cutoff jeans was a relentless tease to everything male inside him.

"Done stalking me?" Isabel hadn't looked back, hadn't even glanced up from the comics page.

"I was not stalking. I was guarding…from a distance," Zade said, not the least surprised she'd known it was him or that he'd always been near. Her powers were growing stronger by the hour.

"Felt more like stalking," she said.

"That was not my intent."

Thick, towering trees and wooden privacy fences lined either side of the alley. Morning sun filtered through the leaves in brilliant rays. The soft light speckling along the quiet alley shimmered in her caramel hair and made her skin seem all the more luminous.

She'd pulled her thick locks into a ponytail, high on the back of her head. Several strands had already worked free— silken tendrils framing the sides of her face.

Her cotton tunic shirt was light blue accented around the collar with a matching paisley print. Her ragged-edged shorts had psychedelic patches covering worn spots on both ass cheeks.

Toenails, fire-engine-red, brought a quick fantasy flashing through his mind. The two of them naked, her foot on his chest, him painting each pretty nail, then watching as she used those sexy toes to stroke his cock until he came creamy-white between each little toe.

Zade shook the image from his mind and grimaced with his tightening slacks. Maronn, she'd be the end of him.

"So," Isabel said, still staring at the comics page as she walked. He could tell she wasn't reading. "I guess you're expecting an apology?"

"No."

"Good. 'Cause I am."

"Pardon?"

She spun so fast, Zade stumbled back a step. Fiery almond eyes collided with his, and every muscle in his body snapped to attention. Her beauty was a merciless torture.

Her thin brows scrunched above a slender nose, lips pressed to a tight line. "For your information, I could feel how weak you were the other night, and I was just trying to help."

"Help? Nothing more?" He kept his voice calm despite the rapid-fire beat of his heart.

Isabel's brows shot up her forehead. Her luscious mouth opened, then shut. All the fight and indignation drained out as if he'd pulled a plug.

"Forgive me, bella. I did not mean to accuse."

"No, you're right," she said. "I guess I do owe you an apology." Her gaze dropped to her feet, her bottom lip catching between her teeth.

"Helping you wasn't the only reason I asked you to join me," she said. "But when I realized you'd rather suffer the punishment than make love to me, I...I did what was right. I sent you the power you needed."

Her soft, brown eyes grew darker, lips pouting. The hurt he read on her sweet face sliced his heart. Zade turned his gaze to the heavens, scrubbing both hands over his face. In ten thousand years, no one had ever considered his needs. He was Watcher, warrior, protector. It was his duty to care for the souls of mortals, never the other way around.

The leash he held on his wicked desires was tenuous at best. Her tender sacrifice humbled him, but it was quickly becoming a danger to his resolve.

"Bella, denying you was not a reflection on your allure nor my weakness to it. But thrusting the power on me, as you did, was tantamount to attempting a transfusion by submersing the patient in blood."

"No. I felt you strengthen. Your wings...you were glowing with power."

He sighed. *How to explain this?* "It was a brief influx, quickly spent. My body was infused with the power, but not my soul. I could not retain or control it. In the end, your gift only sharpened the punishment. I had no choice but to put distance between us before I lost all control."

A half smile quivered her lips, her toffee-brown eyes sparking in the sunlight. "Really?" she said. "Interesting. You losing control was exactly what I was hoping for."

A spike of anger steeled his shoulders, just as hot blood swelled his cock. "This is not a game, Isabel. It could have cost you your life."

"I'm a witch, Zade. I can take care of myself. And I can take care of you, too, if you'd let me."

"My needs are not your duty."

"No. They're my pleasure," she said. "Don't you get it? The last time we soul-bonded, it felt so...good—real good, and let's face it, you're weaker than ever. What I mean is... Aww, hell, I suck at subtlety."

She shook her head and started again. "Listen, you need the soul-bonding and I need you to fuck me. Any questions?"

"I've got one."

Zade knew that voice. He spun around, instinctively drawing his sword from its invisible sheath at his side. His mind and body were a chaotic mess, but the warrior within never faltered.

"Sariel," he said, recognizing his fallen brother. "I have no desire to do battle this day, Oscurità. Leave now and live to see another dawn."

"I think not." Tawny hair flowing like corn silk brushed the tops of Sariel's broad shoulders. He was tall, with a swimmer's build and had remarked once that he fancied himself Brad Pitt's doppelganger, only with a better sense of style. His billowy pirate shirt, black leather pants and knee-high leather boots argued the opinion. But to Zade, Sariel was Oscurità—nothing else mattered.

Sariel's hand crossed to his opposite hip, fingers gripping air for a split second before the jeweled handle of his sword materialized and he pulled the long, gleaming blade from its invisible sheath.

"Take advantage of my generosity, Oscurità," Zade said. "It is not without limits. Leave or I *will* end you."

Zade was terribly weak, his knees were rubber. But his dick was hard as steel, and Isabel's last words were still ringing in his ears.

Sariel snorted, his sword cocked to his shoulder, his massive wings materializing behind him. "Nice bluff, but I've waited months for this. Did you think no one would feel it—the ripple in the ancient power when you used your pretty witch there to warm yourself? I knew you'd waste it, though. Your ridiculous honor would allow you to grow weak. I, on the other hand, will not waste a moment of the warmth and power she'll provide me."

Zade's heart pinched. So this was his fault. His touch had drawn attention to her gift. He'd brought the gluttony of fallen angels to her.

His grip tightened around his sword. "Then it begins."

A sardonic grin gave a hard edge to Sariel's angelic lips.

"Zade!" Isabel's shriek jerked him around just in time to take a melon-sized ball of fire to his chest. The flaming orb—launched by a withered old woman, Sariel's mindless compatriot—exploded, burning through shirt, skin, and muscle.

"Brimstone," he said, his teeth clenched.

The smoke filled his nose, crept through his body, sickening him and weighting his limbs. Only an angelic sword—forged in the fires of heaven—or the rank odor of brimstone could harm his kind. The last time he'd inhaled the foul stench, it had trapped him and his Watcher brothers within the earth for seventy generations, beginning their punishment.

"She's got another one," Isabel said, positioning herself between him and the hag.

"Isabel, run!" Zade commanded his weakening legs to hold steady. The smoke and searing burn on his chest were quickly draining him of what little strength he had left.

"Like hell. I'm not leaving you. I can take her."

"No!"

"She's an old woman."

"She's younger than you. She's his slave, Isabel—a witch—a hag. They are soul-bonded. He is raping her soul of power and life as we speak. She's under his thrall. She has no mind of her own, no remorse, and she will not stop until she is dead."

"The hag will outlive you," Sariel hissed.

Pain ripped through Zade's back. His gaze dropped to his shoulder where the point of Sariel's sword stabbed straight through from back to front. An instant later, it vanished as Sariel withdrew his blade from Zade's body.

Zade stumbled, slowly wheeling to face him. Sariel cocked his sword, this time readying a final blow that would separate Zade's head from his neck.

"Stupid Watcher," Sariel said. "A font of power right under your nose, and you let your doubts and fears keep you weak. She wanted you. I can smell her hot little pussy even now, and you turned her away. Fool, you could've saved her."

In a blur of glimmering steel, Sariel's blade whipped toward him. Zade reached deep, using his guilt, his protective instinct — his love — to swing his sword and deflect the deadly strike.

Behind him Isabel mumbled an ancient incantation. He felt the snap of power when the spell took hold and knew instantly the invisible wall she'd cast would withstand hurricane-force winds. An instant later a second flaming brimstone orb slammed into the shield and ricocheted off, spiraling back toward the hag.

Her mind lost, her body and soul near death, the hag had no hope of survival.

"Oh God."

Isabel's sob nearly ended Zade, her grief and regret cutting him deeper than any sword. But he couldn't console her, couldn't permit the distraction. Sariel was already whirling toward him, aiming his blade for Zade's throat. And this time, Zade hadn't the strength to stay the blow. Only one option remained.

Faster than the speed of thought, Zade's frozen soul reached for Isabel's. The bond was instantaneous, natural, Zade's deep draw on the ancient power like a drowning man's first gulp of air.

His body hummed with a strength and vitality he hadn't felt in ten thousand years. The ancient energy pulsed within him like the sun, filling him from head to toe and out his fingertips. He was alive, connected to everything above and below, but it was Isabel he was connected to most of all.

He could feel her body warm, go soft and pliant with the erotic rush of power his soul pulled through hers. He could feel her pussy clenching and releasing, her tight walls slick, ready for him. The sweet, earthy aroma of her sex made his thigh muscles quake and his balls tighten.

Zade wasn't sure which was the greater torment, the temptation of Isabel or the unearthly power of his lust now that he'd succumbed to that temptation. Either way, if he didn't find the will to rein in his need quickly, it'd be the end of them both.

Chapter Five

ɛꙩ

With no small effort, Zade pushed the distracting call of Isabel's luscious body from his mind. Seconds passed like hours, and by the time Sariel's sword reached the apex of its swing, Zade was at his full Watcher strength. Like a crack of thunder, angelic blades clashed, then sparked as they zinged apart.

Sariel's eyes stretched wide as understanding crept through his mind. "You…you've tasted her. She's feeding your soul now," he said, his voice hushed and accusing.

"It is a good day to end, Sariel," Zade said, unwilling to discuss anything so intimate as his soul-bond.

"But you wouldn't… No. No. She's mine. I've been waiting." With each statement, Sariel's voice grew louder, his breaths heaving his chest and shoulders, his gleaming, white teeth bared, his soft, boyish face twisting with rage.

"You do not deserve such a —"

"No. You don't deserve her, Watcher."

"Yes," Zade said. "I know."

Seething with fury, his sword high over his shoulder, Sariel charged.

Nothing of Zade moved. Like a mountain unfazed by time and emotion, he stood firm, his blade ready. "Your end has come, Sariel. Blessed be."

With blinding speed, Zade whirled, his long leather duster fanning around him, his sword slicing the air and Sariel's neck in one fluid motion.

A brilliant flash of light, energy and matter escaping like a million fireflies from a jelly jar, and the once-mighty angel, Sariel, was no more.

Pain sliced through Zade's body as though *he'd* been the one to lose his head. The constant flood of ancient power from his soul-bond with Isabel had healed his wounds instantly. But the pain ripping through his body now had nothing to do with physical injury.

Zade leaned on the pommel of his sword, the blade stabbing a seam of grass between the red bricks of the alleyway. He closed his eyes, his jaw clenched, his hand fisted over his chest. Another excruciating wave of pain, like wild animals chewing on his gut, ripped through him.

Isabel's hand parted his curtain of hair, her warm silken palm soothing against his cheek, but Zade pulled back. The pain was too sharp—and his alone to endure.

"What is it?"

"The quelling," he said. "Death without the relief of it." Slowly the pain began to ease, and he straightened.

Sucking a deep breath through his nose, he ran a hand through his hair, raking the long strands from his face. He would not have her pity. He didn't deserve it.

"Even in the fall, there survives a bone-deep link between our kind," he said. "To kill means to suffer the agony of your brother's death. It is called the quelling and it is already passing."

For the first time, Isabel could feel Zade's iron will, his uncompromising pride. Their soul-bond connected them in a way most humans would never experience. They were one, and Isabel knew she'd never be the same.

His powerful chest swelled with a deep breath, and another scintillating flood of energy swamped through her body and soul into his. It was like a thousand fingers pattering over her skin, tingling along her breasts and stroking between her thighs. It was all she could do to keep from moaning out loud.

Isabel leaned against him, her knees weak, her breaths ragged as she fought to turn from the edge of a public orgasm. "Please tell me you feel that."

"I do." His tone was sharp, his words clipped. "I am trying to lessen my draw, but…it is an addictive sensation. I want…more."

Isabel snapped her gaze to his. "So take it."

The thought no sooner left her mouth than he was on her. His steel-corded arm cinched around her waist, cementing their bodies together.

"Hold on," he said. The scene around them wavered like heat vapors and then changed completely.

Gone were the red brick alleyway, the high, wooden privacy fences, and the thick canopy of maple trees. Lush tropical gardens surrounded them now and spilled into the sea. Seagulls squawked overhead while glistening waves lapped at the shore and tickled their toes. Some five hundred yards behind them on a small hill stood a mammoth villa of granite and marble. Its tall Romanic columns and archways framed ivory terraces, shaded with blooming bougainvillea vines. It looked ancient, solid and sinfully romantic.

Palm trees and citrus groves lent shade in spots as far as she could see and added to the sweet fragrance of a warm ocean breeze ruffling her hair.

"Where are we?"

"My…home," he said. "A small island off the coast of Sorrento, Italy. We will not be disturbed here. In three thousand years, you are the first mortal to step foot on these grounds."

Zade smoothed his hand from her neck down her chest, and it was only then she realized their nudity. He was a powerful angel now, able to alter the material world on a whim, and yet he touched her with a gentle reverence that nearly made her weep.

"Of all the daughters of men—through time unending— you are a temptation I can no longer resist," he said, his hot breath warming her neck before satin-soft lips pressed a kiss to her thrumming pulse at her throat.

A tremble goose-bumped her skin and Zade lifted his head, gifting her with the stark beauty of his smile. His soul still held hers, drawing a small but steady flow of ancient power. She'd grow used to it, she knew, the warm trickle of energy throbbing through her body would eventually become almost imperceptible. But for now the sensation was too new, too erotic to ignore.

The warm caress of power stroked through her, wetting her pussy, convulsing the muscles as surely as a physical touch. Her thighs were slick with the hot juice, and she shifted her weight trying to find some modicum of relief.

"Maybe…" She could barely speak, her voice low and husky between shallow breaths. "Maybe you weren't supposed to resist…" Her head lolled back as he kissed and licked and nibbled his way down her neck.

His thumb rasped over the sensitive nub of her nipple, the full weight of one breast cupped easily in a manly palm. His gaze flicked to her, his stormy eyes lighter now despite the thick roll of winter-gray clouds rumbling in their depths.

"Sariel was right. I do not deserve you. But…" His gaze dropped to the breast he massaged in his hand. "Such beauty… Of all that's above and below I want…"

He closed his eyes, his whole body stiffening. When he looked at her again, the color had nearly vanished. His eyes were the palest of blues, almost white, the irises ringed in glowing red.

His hand squeezed hard over her breast, powerful fingers pressing into her flesh. "I want to suck your tits, Isabel, feel the puckered flesh of your nipples on my tongue, between my teeth. I want to taste the juice I smell creaming your pussy. I want to feel your cunt squeezing my cock while I fuck you hard and deep."

The muscles in his other arm bulged, tightening his grip around her waist, pulling her flush to his naked chest. Her breasts crushed against him, tender nipples searing against his hot skin. His knee shoved between her thighs, sliding his muscled leg against the swollen lips of her sex.

"God, you're so wet, my leg's already drenched. You like that? You like stroking your hot little clit against my leg?"

He was a different person, as though something inside him had let go. He was wilder, filled with a primal lust he'd kept too long under control.

"Is this what you want, Isabel?" His voice was pure magic, licking flames over her skin, swirling hot and wicked in her belly, between her thighs. "Think well on your answer. This is what comes from not resisting. This is what I've been protecting you from."

Instinct screamed for her to fight, to get away before his angelic passion overwhelmed her. But this was Zade, gentle, protective, loving. She couldn't run away from what she'd started.

She had tempted an angel. Her wild desires always too much for mortal lovers, she'd set her sights on her angel teacher. Now here he was, pushed beyond his control. He needed her. This was no time for doubt. They were meant for each other—they had to be.

Isabel caught her bottom lip between her teeth and shored her resolve. She slinked her arms over Zade's muscled shoulders, looping them around his neck. Her fingers tangled in the long, silky strands of his hair, her hips beginning a slow, sexy grind against his leg. The wet folds of her pussy stroked against him, creaming the coarse hairs on his leg and sending ripples of electric pleasure tingling through her body.

She trailed a hand down the hard swells of his chest, over the rippled muscles of his abs to the nest of dark curls at the base of his rock-solid cock. Thick as a baseball bat, her fingers gripped around its base while her lips found his mouth and stole his gasp. Ten thousand years of punishment would finally come to an end.

Chapter Six

ℰ

Zade's mind was a chaotic jumble of thoughts, worries and desires. Dear God, what was she doing to him? His demon roared for release and with each passing second, with each delicious stroke of her hand on his cock, the demon gained ground over his soul.

Her tongue teased hot and sweet inside his mouth, her teeth nipping his lip, coaxing his response. Zade's hold on his desire loosened, his fingers digging into the soft flesh of her hips, driving her slow, erotic grind — faster — harder.

Her small, sexy whimpers only stirred his frenzied brain. Her little hand, so hot and tight around his cock, stroked up and down the length of him until he found himself pumping against her, quickening the pace.

But then she pushed away. Faster than his frantic brain could follow, she dropped to her knees, her hands grabbing his ass, jerking his hips and stiff cock toward her open mouth.

"Isa...bel...n—"

It was too late. Moist heat surrounded his dick. Luscious suction pulled and released, pulled and released. Her devilish tongue flicked over the head of his cock, her teeth scraping the ultrasensitive flesh. Every muscle in his body coiled slow and steady, building toward an explosion ten thousand years in the making.

Reason left him. Guilt, doubt, care — all melted away in the heat of his unchecked lust. The demon was free. Zade clamped his hands on either side of Isabel's head and held her steady. His hips bucked as he fucked her mouth, pumping his cock past her lips, his balls slapping against her chin.

She didn't cry out, didn't resist, but rather took his lead, his frenzied lust somehow feeding hers. She sucked him harder, taking more of his cock down her throat, her fingernails biting into his ass sending another layer of pain and pleasure sparking through his body.

His thighs trembled, fighting against the delicious pressure building inside him. But when she brought a hand from his ass to his balls, massaging them through her fingers, he couldn't stop the spurt of come that coated her mouth and trickled down her throat.

"Enough!" he said, disengaging her from his dick. She stared at his still-hard, swollen cock like a woman starved and the sight almost had him thrusting into that sweet, fuckable mouth again.

No. He wanted more. He wanted her pussy. The erotic musky scent had been teasing him for years, and he was long past denying himself.

Snagging her under the arms he lifted her. She weighed nothing to him and, with the steady feed of ancient power pulsing from her to him, he'd never grow tired.

Isabel's sexy, brown-sugar eyes gazed at him, utter trust making them all the more sultry. He gathered her to him, her slender arms looping around his neck. He took her mouth in a devastating kiss, his come salty on her lips. She wrapped her legs around his waist, wiggling against him, her hot pussy teasing his cock, dribbling juices over the sensitive head.

He leaned her back so her arms were nearly straight, her hands hooked on his shoulders. He supported her full weight, lifting her, positioning her so the tip of his penis pressed against her velvet folds.

Frustration puckered the soft skin between her brows, and she moaned, writhing against his hold, struggling to take him in. Male satisfaction curled a smile across his lips. "You want it, bella? No, wait. How did you put it? You want me to *fuck* you?"

"Yes!" She squirmed again, nearly succeeding against his best effort to hold her still. Her wanton gyrations made his cock twitch. Maronn, teasing her like this demanded more control than remained to him.

With no further warning, he drove his hard shaft deep inside her. Her hungry muscles latched on to him, pulsed and milked his cock, drawing a moan from his very soul. He lifted her, bringing her cunt to the very tip of his penis then slammed her down his shaft again, pelvis and balls smacking pussy lips and thighs.

Within seconds, a rhythm was set, his cock driving hard, his belly and thighs glistening with her cream. Muscles trembled with that delectable tension again, his gut tightening more and more with each thrust. But there was more to be had from this beautiful, wanton siren, and Zade had lost all ability to deny his need.

Like taking a deep breath, his soul drew long and hard on hers, pulling a tidal wave of power through her body. Isabel shuddered with the magically erotic stroke, her pussy muscles clamping tight around his penis weakening his knees. The faster they fucked, the faster the power flowed through them. It filled him to overflowing until it spilled out, surrounding them both in a shimmering nimbus of light.

Instinct took over, his thrusts becoming manic, the excess power flooding into his wings unbidden so they solidified behind him.

Isabel's eyes opened wide and then softened. She saw him for what he was — not what he believed he'd become, but what he'd always been—and loved him for it, because of it and despite it. His heart skipped, then melted.

Her head fell back, long caramel curls bouncing over her shoulders, swaying down her back. "Zade…Zade…"

He could feel her body tightening, her muscles squeezing around him. And then…

"I love you," she cried out as her release exploded through her body. Hot come washed down his shaft as she rode her orgasm, impaling herself on his cock all the harder, all the faster, driving him toward the ragged edge.

Zade couldn't hold back, angelic come shooting into her again and again. His roar shook the very foundation of the ancient villa behind them and rippled along the crashing waves of the sea.

For one single, shining-clear moment, the world stood still and Zade saw the past, present and future laid out before him. Like a map, all that had been, all that was, and all that was yet to be stretched before his eyes and he was given a glimpse of how he and Isabel fit within the fabric of time.

An instant later, the vision was gone and he felt the solid beat of Isabel's heart as he gathered her close in his arms. She clung to him, her body quivering with blissful aftershocks, her head nestled on his shoulder. Not until he'd laid her gently on a bed of clover and soft ferns at the edge of the sea did he withdraw his semi-hard cock from her body.

His semen, silvery in the afternoon sun, trickled from between the pink folds of her pussy and down her thigh. It was then he realized he hadn't held back. She'd taken all of him, his lustful, ravenous demon, his wounded heart and frozen soul.

No other above or below could've withstood such an assault. And yet, even as he lay next to her, brushing wayward strands from her sleepy face, he could sense her body awakening. Hot liquid flooded her pretty little pussy, its thick cream scenting the air. Her nipples pebbled before his eyes, making his dick twitch at the sight.

She was his match—meant for him. He knew that now, even without the vision. She'd restored his strength, his heart, his soul, and he would need it all to protect her from the trials the future held for them both. But together they were stronger than either could ever have been alone, and suddenly ten thousand years of punishment seemed a fair price to pay to have her at his side.

Her soft hand smoothing along his jaw brought him from his thoughts. She peered at him from beneath long lashes and heavy lids, smiling, the corners of her mouth quivering.

"This is how we were meant to be. Everything in our lives before this was just to get us here...together," she said. "I was born for you."

Zade welcomed the joy blooming deep in his soul, the smile spreading fast across his lips. He kissed her and said, "And I must have fallen for you."

About the Author

හ

Paige is a multipublished award-winning author. She's a member of Romance Writers of America and two RWA chapters—Central Ohio Fiction Writers and Futuristic, Fantasy & Paranormal. Paige has been writing since the birth of her oldest daughter fourteen years ago. But it wasn't until she moved from Pennsylvania to Ohio that she began taking her writing interest seriously.

Paige has been happily married for fifteen years and is the mother of three beautiful young girls. Her love of reading, a vivid imagination and the countless characters peopling her mind have left her no choice but to—in the words of Natalie Goldberg—finally shut up, sit down and write.

Paige welcomes mail from readers. You can write to her c/o Ellora's Cave Publishing at 1056 Home Avenue, Akron OH 44310-3502.

THE JOINING

Jory Strong

For Martha Punches, unsung heroine.
Your behind-the-scenes efforts are much appreciated.

Chapter One

🔊

"Do you open it, or do I?" Jett du'Zehren asked as he turned from the doorway with a sealed parchment envelope in his hand and looked at his partner, his lover for the last five years, the man he would soon share a woman with—if their Petition for Joining had been approved.

Mozaiic du'Zehren rose from the richly textured cushions they'd brought back from their last trading expedition away from Adjara and moved to stand next to Jett, resting a hand on the other man's shoulder, lightly stroking it with his thumb, his heart swelling with love, his cock swelling with lust. They'd been best friends from the first day they met as boys, the summer in which their two tribes had settled and camped together in the desert, waiting for their allocated time to harvest the gems in the mountains. They'd been almost inseparable since then. So much so, that no one who knew them was surprised when they declared for each other as soon as they were of an age to do so.

They were alike in so many ways, and yet different enough to complement each other. "We have only just reached the minimum time of pairing," Mozaiic reminded Jett. "It's not unheard of for pairs to remain so for ten or more years before being allowed to add a female to the joining. And it's not as though we don't find great pleasure with each other."

Jett turned to look at Mozaiic, a man whose dark looks were similar to his own, except that Mozaiic's eyes were emerald green where his own where the color of onyx. He ran his hand along his partner's bare side, smiling when he noticed Mozaiic's erection, the twin to his own. Five years together and they still coupled like honeymooners. Jett laughed softly. "Yes, even when we were just friends, we found great pleasure in each other's company, and now that we're bound—" His eyes shifted to the parchment envelope in his hand. "Do you open it, or do I?"

Mozaiic took a deep breath and reached for the envelope, taking it from Jett's unresisting fingers and opening it, neither of them able to do more than stare as they reread the contents of the missive over and over again. *Petition for Joining hereby granted for Mozaiic and Jett du'Zehren. Female assigned: Siria Chaton. Location of female: Planet, Qumaar. City, Remeus. Female's Value: Water diviner.*

"A water diviner," Jett said, his voice holding both awe and suspicion. "Why hasn't she already been assigned and claimed?"

Mozaiic looked up from the missive, his eyes taking in their own accommodations in the mobile tent city that constituted their home, except during the periods of time when their tribe claimed the mountains. Outside, the desert winds were already building for a sandstorm, a daily occurrence during this season, so they'd have to move quickly if they intended to leave before it struck. Still, his own thoughts echoed Jett's, and yet— With a shrug, he said, "Perhaps those in charge of locating females who will add value to our tribe only just found her. And besides, why question the match? Have you known any to end up with an unsuitable female?"

"No." Jett also shrugged. "No. You're right." He cocked his head, also listening to the wind, the impending storm usually a signal to wander through the enclosed tent city and visit, or to strip out of their loin coverings and take their pleasure while it was too dangerous to venture outside. "Leave now or wait?"

Mozaiic laughed, reaching over and stroking Jett's erection. "What do you desire?"

Jett grinned, turning, his hand sliding down Mozaiic's arm, gliding over the colorful tribal tattoos that told the tale of his partner's lineage and accomplishments. "You know what I desire, but who's to say we can't enjoy that while we're searching for our third. The sooner we leave, the sooner we will find her and know what it's like to couple with a woman, to claim one for our own."

* * * * *

Siria Chaton plopped down on her bed, battling both exhaustion and fear. *Water, water everywhere and not a drop to drink.*

If only it were true!

Her eyes teared up as the saying from childhood sang through her mind, along with her mother's soft prediction of a day when Siria would be valued for her talent.

If only it were true. But how could it ever happen? Especially here?

Qumaar was a water world and what land there was constituted only a small part of it, densely packed islands surrounded by an endless and dangerous sea. Generations ago the nature of the planet had made it seem like the ideal prison world. A place where both criminals and "undesirables" from other places could be dumped, left to fend for themselves—a task they were well suited for, having survived by brute strength, wit, or supernatural ability on their home worlds.

Just who—and what—was "undesirable" could vary greatly, and did. Which had made Qumaar a very dangerous place, especially after dark, even now when it was no longer a prison planet—though warships still guarded it, keeping the inhabitants, the progeny of those first inmates, trapped on the planet. The experiment of turning Qumaar into a penal world had been abandoned when those on it quickly took over, the prison officials no match for the combined psi abilities they'd inadvertently thrown together.

Within a generation, those with psi abilities ruled while those without, or those with lesser supernatural talents, were relegated to menial duties, an underclass with few rights. During the day, martial law survived to keep it safe, but even the powers that be had given up trying to rule in the night.

Siria's heart jerked just thinking about what it would be like if she lost the tiny living space that had always been home—a safe, happy place in an urban jungle where the weak preyed on the strong just as often as the strong preyed on the weak.

The credits she'd been left when her mother, her best friend, her protector, had died were just about to run out despite skimping and getting by on the bare minimum as she'd tried job after job in an attempt to find something she could do, only to be met with failure.

Water—her curse, her talent.

To be trapped in an office building for long hours, surrounded by pipes carrying it through the walls, was pure torture. A steady hum that grew louder and louder until she couldn't think, couldn't concentrate.

Outside was little better. Even now, as an adult, she could only tolerate being away from home for several hours at a time. In truth, she was far more a prisoner of her talent than of the warships that kept her on Qumaar.

The only place she had any respite was in her tiny apartment, a space her mother had found ways to insulate from the constant call of water. But there was no hope of an employer offering something similar, not when she was considered little better than one with no psi talent at all.

Siria rubbed her head, feeling some of the tension and pounding start to leave now that she was home. Surrounded by protected walls and comforting memory.

She'd even gone so far as to consult an "exorcist" who claimed he could get rid of unwanted talents. But in the final analysis, she couldn't go through with it. Her mother's face had haunted her, making even the thought of getting rid of her ability to locate water seem like a repudiation of both herself and her mother's gift of prophecy.

"Oh Mom," Siria whispered, "I miss you so much. When you were alive it was so much easier to believe everything was going to turn out all right."

She shivered, her thoughts returning to her limited options. For a price, transport off Qumaar could be arranged. But even for the wealthy it was risky. The individuals who made their trade in smuggling things and people might just as easily kill their passengers or sell them into slavery as deliver them to a new life safely.

Siria shifted, rolling onto her back, her hands going to her breasts, feeling the weight of them before toying with the nipples. On another world, she would probably be viewed as desirable with her dark hair and dark eyes, her small frame and generous breasts. But on Qumaar...her looks were not in vogue among the ruling psi class, and even if they had been, her talent would have labeled her less in their eyes, good enough to fuck, but not to marry.

She could probably find a husband within the "undesirable" class, a man who would consider her a trophy while at the same time resent her for having supernatural ability, especially one so useless. And then what? A lifetime of scraping, of barely getting by, of producing child after child while her husband dreamed that one of their children would turn out to be a true talent and be their ticket out of poverty.

It would almost be better to take her chances with a smuggler, to trade a certain number of her years for a chance at something better. She shivered, knowing that no matter how frightened she was of being turned out on the streets, if she couldn't gain enough credits to keep her apartment, she would never go to a smuggler.

Rumors abounded of women not only being taken to brothels or sold as slaves, but of ending up on the nearby planet of Adjara, where the men formed marriages with each other, and needed a woman only long enough to produce a child for them.

Siria shivered. Little was known about Adjara. It was primarily a desert planet, harsh, unforgiving, closed to outsiders. Few in their right mind would attempt to go there, though the dream of gaining riches beyond measure by exploring the small range of mountains for rich deposits of precious stone had lured many to their deaths.

Her mother had been fascinated by Adjara, making it a game in the evenings to search though whatever news reports could be captured using their ancient computer. Telling Siria that her ability to locate water would make her a princess in such a place.

Once her mother had even found a rare picture of an Adjaran without the trademark robes and face covering they wore even when they weren't in the desert. He'd been stripped to the waist, his body bronzed by the sun, lean and fit from life on a planet where the weak didn't survive, one arm covered from shoulder to hand with exotic tattoos. Siria closed her eyes, remembering that day.

"Here's a prince to your princess," her mother teased.

"And what about the rumors of women being used to produce a child and then being disposed of?"

"I'm not so quick to believe them," her mother answered with a shrug. *"Look at the rumors that abound on Qumaar!"*

"You win. Of course, what makes the rumors about Qumaar so frightening is that the truth is often more horrifying!"

"True. Now admit he's handsome at least," her mother pressed, running her finger over the computer screen.

Siria knew when she was beat. "I'll admit it. He's handsome."

"And if rumor is true, he comes with a second man."

"Mother!" Siria yipped, her face flaming, only to realize by the play of expressions on her mother's face that she hadn't intended it to be a sexual comment. But once she did realize how her comment had been interpreted, her mother's laughter filled the room, contagious and fun, irresistible, and they'd both ended up in tears, holding sides that ached from their amusement.

"Still," Siria said, when they finally stopped. *"No one has ever heard of a woman going to Adjara and leaving again."*

Her mother shrugged. *"The same could be said, except in reverse, for Qumaar. No one who leaves here is ever heard from again."*

"Oh Mom, I wish you were here," Siria whispered, feeling her heart sink further when the monitor on the inside of the door hummed, announcing a message—no doubt from the landlord, who'd been harassing her since her mother's death. She rose from the bed and answered the summons. Staring in disbelief at the message she found there.

It seemed almost too good to be true. An absolute miracle. Which made Siria suspicious as she looked at the message flashing on the screen.

Her psi talent had been registered with the government agency charged with keeping track of such things since it had first manifested. And yet until this very moment, no one had ever contacted her with the prospect of a paying job.

She rubbed her arms, a chill moving up her spine and making her heart lurch. *See, you've got a little bit of my talent after all*, her mother used to say. The trouble was, unlike her mother's ability, the precog dance along Siria's backbone wasn't marketable and could just as easily be attributed to fear or nerves.

Indecision held her in place as she glanced through the small window. She could make it to the meeting place her potential employer suggested—a café not too far away—and back again before dark. If she hurried.

Even for the chance of a job and a good meal, she wouldn't willingly risk being caught outside when the sun set. Still she hesitated for only a second longer, wishing she did have a touch of her mother's precognitive ability, but finally yielding to the inevitable and tapping a response into the communicator before opening the door. What choice did she really have? In two days she would have nowhere to go, save the alleyways and ancient buildings that had once housed those long-dead men and women who were to run Qumaar as a prison planet. She shivered, remembering childhood horror tales repeated in the dark about those places and the creatures that haunted them.

Chapter Two

෨

Anything could be had for a price—especially when Adjaran gems were involved. It was a lesson every trader learned early on, and Mozaiic was no exception. It had been much more difficult to find a safe hiding place for their small craft than it had been to breach the airspace of Qumaar. It had been even simpler to locate Siria and gather all the information her government knew about her before persuading an official to send a job interview invitation to her.

Mozaiic shifted in his seat, his cock, usually in a state of readiness for Jett, now aching with an additional need. To know a woman for the first time.

By the sands of Adjara, if the picture the government official had provided them with was accurate, then the female assigned to them was exquisite. Her dark coloring a perfect match to their own, her body—beautiful, desirable. Her breasts alone were enough to make a man come just looking at them. And he could envision hour after hour suckling them.

He closed his eyes and gritted his teeth, trying to imagine what her nipples looked like as he surreptitiously reached under the table to reposition his cock. How men endured tight trousers day after day was a mystery to him, but both he and Jett knew better than to come to this planet dressed in their desert robes.

Mozaiic heard the sound of someone entering the tiny café and opened his eyes to take in the sight of their woman. The picture didn't do her justice. She was beyond compare.

Lush and yet feminine. Soft in a world that was in many ways harsher than his own. He stood, giving a brief wave of his hand to indicate his presence, a courtesy since he was the only one in the building save for the owner who was also the chef.

She was suspicious, wary, and so he forced his own eagerness deep within himself — and hoped that Jett was successful in gaining access to her apartment. There was no time to return to their ship tonight, and yet neither of them planned to let her out of their sight until she'd fully joined with them and considered herself their third.

In a planet full of males, in a society that produced only male children, a female not in a committed relationship was a disrupting influence and a danger to their way of life. If he and Jett couldn't trust her, then even to gain a third, a woman who could aid all of them by finding water, they would have to leave her here.

A Petition of Joining was a serious matter, not just for the men involved, but for the entire tribe. While it was true that granting of a petition was a means of providing males with the opportunity to breed and share a female, the female had to be of value to the tribe in her own right. None were brought to Adjara *only* to produce children.

"I have taken the liberty of ordering a meal for us," Mozaiic said, making no move to touch her when she drew near to the table.

Given the psychic nature of the people on Qumaar, he couldn't risk that she had another talent, one not reported to the authorities. One that would allow her access to his thoughts and intentions.

Alarm bells chimed in Siria's head at the sight of the man in front of her. Mozaiic. He hadn't provided a second or third name in his message.

For a moment she could barely breathe. It was almost as though the long-ago image of the handsome male Adjaran her mother had found was overlaid onto the man now standing in front of her.

Siria shook her head, forcing the thought away, telling herself that desperation was also making her paranoid. Still, she couldn't keep her gaze from dropping to his hands. They were gloved.

She didn't know whether to be relieved or not. Many on Qumaar wore gloves because their psi talents made it uncomfortable to touch people and objects directly. But... She nibbled her lip, wondering if he would bother to cover both hands if he were merely trying to hide the tattoo marks on one. Then again, she'd been registered for years, how likely was it that just as she was on the verge of losing her place to live, someone from Adjara would seek her out?

"Shall we sit?" he asked, his expression relaxed, calm, setting her at ease as he nodded toward the chair in front of her, adding, "I had hoped we could share a meal as we discussed your ability to find water."

As if on cue, the only other person in the café appeared, placing a steaming rice dish in the middle of the table. Siria's stomach growled and her mouth watered. The sight and smell of the food very nearly reduced her to tears. It had been almost a year since she'd indulged in a meal like the one in front of her.

She sat. Her initial answers to Mozaiic's questions held to one- or two-word answers as she ate. Filling herself as if to ward off possible starvation in the future.

Mozaiic watched her, already wanting to take her in his arms and tell her that she need not worry about the future anymore. The official at the government agency where they'd gone to learn more about her had been quick to wink and say, "Whatever you want from her, you'll get her cheap.

She's only days away from losing her housing and the landlord has already informed us that he intends to evict and settle some of his relatives into the space if she can't come up with enough credits to pay the rent."

Siria's cheeks heated with embarrassment as she pushed her plate back. "I'm sorry," she mumbled, "the food here is delicious."

His smile was gentle, a bit unnerving, as though he understood the true reasons for her ravenous appetite — reasons that had as much to do with the body as with the soul. "It was a good meal," he agreed, glancing at the window and frowning.

Siria followed his gaze and her chest tightened with dismay when she noticed how much darker it was outside. "Can we meet again first thing in the morning?" she asked, fear prickling along her spine as she grew angry at herself for concentrating on the food rather than discussing what he wanted of her. What questions he had posed had been so general they gave no hint as to what job he needed done.

"We can continue our conversation," he said, standing, the meal apparently already paid for as the owner made no move to stop them when they left.

When they were outside the café, Siria grew worried, hating to part from him. What if he didn't call? What if the job opportunity disappeared before it had even been presented? What if —

"I'll walk you home," Mozaiic said, interrupting her worries, something in his voice making her womb flutter and her breasts grow heavy, making her gaze drop to his erection before jerking upward again. This time catching heated desire in his eyes.

For a heartbeat it thrilled her that a man who looked like Mozaiic would want her, but just as quickly, her spirits plummeted as she wondered if he was really in the market for a mistress and not a water diviner. Could she sell herself to keep a roof over her head? To keep herself from having to live on the streets? Millions of women throughout history and the galaxy had made just that choice.

Tears formed and hope flickered, threatening to die in her chest. "You're not really interested in my talent are you?" she asked, hating how thin and lost her own voice sounded.

Pain ricocheted through Mozaiic's chest. Surprising him with its intensity. For all he and Jett had dreamed and schemed about gaining a third, that female had been a creature of their fantasies and not a real woman with feelings and needs, strengths and vulnerabilities.

Despite his intention not to touch her until they were in a secluded place, Mozaiic reached out and cupped her face, forcing her to meet his gaze. "Your talent is one I am both awed by and value greatly. One that—" he forced himself to stop before he revealed too much. Instead he said, "If you'd prefer to travel home alone, then I will honor your wish."

Some of Siria's tension eased. "You won't have time to get to shelter if you see me home." Her eyebrows drew together in worry as it suddenly occurred to her that he probably wasn't a resident of Remeus. "Did you arrange for lodging?"

He shrugged. "I thought I would see to it after I met with you."

Alarm moved through Siria. With only a few minutes to spare before true dark arrived, he'd be lucky to find a boarding house with an available room—much less one with an owner willing to open the door to a stranger. For a moment she stilled, concentrating on the masculine hand which remained on her cheek, trying to summon what small measure of empathic ability she did have in order to determine if he was dangerous to her.

She gasped, her cheeks flaming when she was immediately drenched in lust, a lust her own body responded to with a wild rush. He jerked his hand away, as though sensing what she was doing, but rather than embarrassment, his expression grew worried. "You should hurry home," he said, expanding the distance between them, his body language telling her that he did so reluctantly.

Siria brushed her hair back from her face in an attempt to busy a suddenly shaky hand. She'd never invited a man home before, especially one like Mozaiic—one she could imagine herself— She blocked the thought. Her situation was so dire that she couldn't let the needs of her body interfere with her future safety. "You won't find lodging, not this late," she told him. "You'd better come with me. I have a couch you can sleep on."

Her offer stunned Mozaiic. And shamed him. He'd fully intended to stay in her apartment. Even now, Jett was no doubt lounging on her couch, waiting for her to return, with him close behind. Their plan to trap and contain her until she agreed to go with them an unworthy one now that he'd met her.

They hadn't thought beyond their own needs, their own desires. And now it was too late to change the course of events to come. There was no way to contact Jett and tell him to get out of her living quarters.

"Thank you," Mozaiic said, wishing he could take her hand in his, but not daring to now that he knew she had some ability to read him.

They hurried through the already abandoned streets. Mozaiic silently cursing himself and Jett. In their haste to get to Qumaar and claim their third, they'd forgotten to take into consideration that Qumaar darkened earlier than their own planet. And even though they were seasoned travelers, the Qumaarian nighttime was no place to venture out in.

It was full dark when they stepped into her apartment and found Jett pacing shirtless in the small confines of the room. Siria jerked to a stop in front of Mozaiic and though he was no empath, he could sense her immediate fear.

"You're Adjaran," Siria whispered, shock and fear rushing through her at the sight of the man in front of her, the tattoos along one of his arms making it easy to identify him.

"We mean you no harm," Mozaiic spoke from behind her, his voice a reminder that there was no escape route— even if she'd been desperate enough to rush out into the night.

"You're here to take me to your planet," Siria said. Not needing any psi talent at all to know their intentions.

"Of course," Jett said, striding over to stand in front of her. His proximity making Siria step back quickly and end up against Mozaiic.

Mozaiic's lust touched her senses again, this time tempered with concern and…chastisement? She calmed, picking through what she read from him. Wishing her ability was stronger, and yet it was strong enough for her to know that Mozaiic spoke the truth when he said they meant her no harm.

Mozaiic stood perfectly still, willing Jett to do the same. The tension easing from his body as it eased from Siria's. When he thought it was safe to speak, Mozaiic said, "This is my partner Jett du'Zehren."

"You need me to find water," Siria said, wishing she could savor this first time when her talent was truly valuable, but her heart was pounding too hard, her mind racing, wondering if that was the only reason they'd sought her out. Her body reacting to the nearness of the man in front of her. "You'll take me whether I'm willing or not."

Jett's nostrils flared and he exchanged a glance with Mozaiic. Mozaiic said, "No, we will not take you if you are not willing."

Surprise moved through Siria, but she believed him. They were still touching. And despite the fact that he'd guessed she could read him, Mozaiic had made no effort to move away from her. "No woman ever leaves your planet alive," Siria said starkly and he grimaced, knowing she was testing him.

"True," Jett said, "What of it? As far as I know, none wish to leave—especially after they have given birth." His dark eyes moved over Siria, his thoughts as obvious as the erection pressing against his trousers—making a groan escape from Mozaiic, one that had nothing to do with pleasure for a change.

What was Jett thinking!

Mozaiic sighed, the desires of his own cock making itself heard. What was Jett thinking, indeed? He'd had little else on his mind but exploring her body since the first glimpse of her.

"The rumors of women used only for breeding purposes and then destroyed after they have served that purpose are false," Mozaiic said. "Our women are respected, valued members of our tribe. If you choose to return to Adjara with us as our third, you would be treated the same."

"I have a choice?" Siria asked and Jett took a step backward, as though her question offended him.

"We have no desire to take an unwilling woman," he said, his voice gruff.

"Perhaps we can sit and talk," Mozaiic suggested. "Our world and culture are closed to outsiders, so there is much we can't reveal, but if you allow us to, Siria, we will tell you what we can so you can decide whether or not to return with us as our third."

Chapter Three

ୱ

Siria stared at the ceiling above the couch, trying to concentrate on what they'd told her, to analyze it and come to a decision. She failed miserably.

It was impossible to ignore the sound of clothing being shed, to keep from imagining what the two men looked like naked — what they looked like together, lying in each other's arms in her bed. It was all too easy to picture their hardened bodies, all too easy to imagine them touching each other's cocks, kissing —

She tried to squelch the images, shock coursing through her at how arousing she found them. Unable to stop herself, her hand tunneled into her own panties. She was swollen, wet, her clit erect, her body primed in a way it seldom got.

You've been under a lot of stress during the last year, there hasn't been a lot of emotional room left for getting horny, she tried to tell herself, but she knew it was a lie.

The bed squeaked slightly as first one body climbed onto it, and then the next. A male sigh escaped and Siria closed her eyes, hearing in that sound the pleasure of skin touching skin, the peace of being in a lover's arms at the end of the day.

They kissed. Not the sounds of ravenous hunger, but of love, companionship, a welcoming. When it ended they began speaking, and despite the low murmur of their voices, Siria could still hear their conversation and envision what was taking place on the bed.

Jett rested on his side next to Mozaiic, his leg thrown over his partner's, his cock trapped against Mozaiic's hip while his hand slid down Mozaiic's chest. The path familiar though no less erotic from having been traveled so frequently.

"We shouldn't," Mozaiic whispered despite the way his cock jerked and pulsed against Jett's hand.

"Why not?" Jett asked, forestalling the answer by pressing his lips to Mozaiic's and teasing him into opening his mouth, the kiss slow, thorough, allowing plenty of time for Jett's hand to move up and down along Mozaiic's shaft, for his thumb to brush repeatedly against the wet head, the tip of his own cock beading with arousal.

Mozaiic groaned, hardly able to think under Jett's onslaught. The desire they felt for one another always hovered around the edges of their day-to-day responsibilities, ready to flow in when time and opportunity presented itself. He'd thought to push the need aside until they could join with Siria, had resisted the urge to reach for Jett first, to take the role of the aggressor, the dominant partner in their next coupling. But apparently Jett had no such reservations.

"We shouldn't," Mozaiic repeated when the kiss ended, though his body arched and a pant escaped as Jett's hand cupped his testicles, his fingers lightly skimming over the pucker of Mozaiic's anus.

"Why not?"

"Siria—"

Jett once again covered Mozaiic's mouth with his, the kiss more aggressive this time, more commanding. And Mozaiic jerked, reading Jett's intentions in the way his partner's body tensed, became purposeful, Jett's grip on Mozaiic's penis tightening before it began stroking up and down and sending sweet sensation and hot desire along Mozaiic's spine.

They'd been together so long that they knew each other's bodies as well as they knew their own, knew which touches excited, which teased, and which left the other helpless. Mozaiic could do nothing but give in, his body yielding to Jett's desire, rushing toward a release that left him quivering, shaking, his seed spewed across his abdomen.

Jett took only a second to use the edge of the sheet to wipe away the evidence of Mozaiic's orgasm before covering his partner's body with his, his legs on either side of Mozaiic's, content for the moment to trap their cocks in between them. To savor the heated touch of hard flesh against hard flesh. "What's the use of denying our own pleasure," Jett whispered, returning to their earlier conversation. "Even to know the pleasure of a female's body, I'm not willing to give this up, to give you up. Isn't it better to know right now if she's repulsed by our coupling, by us?"

Mozaiic laughed softly, his heart filling with love, his cock filling with need. Usually he was the more logical of the two, and Jett the more impulsive, but he couldn't argue with Jett's conclusion. For Siria to be their third, she needed to accept not only their feelings for her, but their feelings for one another. "You're right," he said, trailing the fingers of one hand down Jett's spine while the fingers of the other speared through Jett's hair, pulling him down for a kiss so carnal that within seconds Jett's legs were forcing Mozaiic's apart, his hand reaching for the lubricant they always carried with them.

Siria's fingers plunged in and out of her own channel, keeping time with the squeaking of her ancient bedsprings. She was burning up, so hot that the blanket had been tossed to the floor along with her own clothing.

A whimper escaped and she bit her lip, not wanting them to know how turned on she was by their lovemaking.

The image of Jett's taut body covering Mozaiic's, thrusting in and out, was forever burned in her mind. She hadn't been able to resist looking and it had taken every ounce of willpower she possessed to lie back down on the couch, its back shielding her eyes from what was taking place on the bed, but not shielding her ears.

She pressed her palm to her clit, feeling the touch all the way up to her nipples and wishing it was a man's mouth latched on to her areola, tugging and pulling, instead of the fingers of her own hand. Another whimper escaped as she struggled to find even a fraction of the pleasure Jett and Mozaiic were experiencing, their murmurs having long since given way to moans and grunts, the sound of flesh slapping against flesh, as the air filled with the scent of sex.

With a shout, Mozaiic came. Followed almost immediately by Jett and Siria stilled, her fingers still deep in her own cunt, frustration raging throughout her. Her body tense, unsatisfied.

For a long moment Jett and Mozaiic lay on the bed, their breathing ragged, their hearts pounding. It was Jett who finally spoke, his mouth only inches away from Mozaiic's ear. "You'll check on her reaction while I take a shower?"

Mozaiic laughed softly. Tenderness flooding his heart. The sudden memory of Jett standing in the doorway earlier in the day with the sealed parchment envelope in his hand, making him smile. For all of Jett's boldness, he hated bad news. Always preferring for Mozaiic to experience it first and break it to him second.

"I'll check on her," Mozaiic said, hugging Jett before letting him make a hasty escape to the bathroom.

Siria scrambled to cover herself with the blanket when she heard someone rise from the bed. It would have been pointless to try and get her clothing back on, just as it was probably pointless to pretend she'd managed to go to sleep while they were making love only a few feet away from where she lay. But she tried it anyway, desperately pressing her eyelids tightly together when she heard the bathroom door close and the remaining man get to his feet and move in her direction.

Joy rushed through Mozaiic as he looked down at Siria's flushed face, as the scent of her arousal reached his nose, different than what he was used to, feminine and heady rather than masculine and musky—but no less intoxicating. He knelt down next to her, smiling inwardly as he leaned over, his face inches above hers, thinking perhaps she was more like Jett when it came to facing things—especially matters of an emotional nature. Preferring that someone else tackle the conversation, and require only a yes or no response, and only then if a head nod wasn't sufficient.

"Neither of us has been with a woman before," he whispered, unable to withhold his smile when her eyelids popped open in response to his admission.

"Why not?" she asked and his heart sang when she made no move to put distance between them, when he saw curiosity in her eyes and not fear or disgust.

"Jett and I have known each other since childhood. When we became adults we became a couple. We were each other's first lover. We wanted to offer the same to our third, to the female who would complete our joining. We wanted her to know there had been no others before her, just as there would be no others after her." He dared to lower his head and capture her lips with his, reveling in the way she tasted different, felt different than Jett did.

Siria whimpered, unable to stop him when his hand pulled the blanket out of her unresisting hands. She was so aroused it was painful, the small amount of psi talent for empathy that she did possess was more than enough to load his hunger and desire onto her own, making it pointless to try and fight.

"Beautiful," he whispered when he lifted his head and looked down her body. And she shivered, knowing he meant it, feeling it deep inside her. When his hand reached out, reverently cupping her breast, she made no protest. When his lips followed, his tongue licking over the tight nipple before he began sucking, she arched into him, unable to stop her fingers from threading through his hair and holding him to her body.

It felt so good. To be held. To be desired. To know that he had never been with another woman. It was heady temptation and she couldn't resist, didn't resist, but opened her legs instead when his hand smoothed over her stomach, making her womb flutter and her pussy clench, sending a wash of arousal to coat already swollen cunt lips and drenched inner thighs.

His fingers found her clit and latched onto it, exploring it, playing with it as though it was a miniature penis. She cried out, arching into him as white-hot pleasure lashed through her body. "Put your mouth on me," she urged, sure she'd prefer that torture than the one he was exacting on her.

He groaned, his reluctance to stop suckling at her breast sending a wash of feminine satisfaction through her. And even though she'd ordered him between her legs, she still whimpered when he released her nipple.

Mozaiic felt fevered, barely able to function. The sight of her full breasts and large, dark nipples had nearly undone him. The dark hair between her legs equally arousing. Her body was a wonderland he could spend a lifetime exploring. The textures and scents were so different from what he was used to, the sounds she made softer and yet no less beguiling.

He was panting by the time he kissed his way down to her mound, torn between looking at her cunt and tasting it.

Unable to stop himself from burying his face between her thighs and inhaling deeply before rubbing his nose and cheeks against her soft pubic hair.

She was beautiful. Perfect. Incredible.

He'd seen whores before on some of the planets he and Jett traded on, women who stood naked in windows, positioned so their hole was exposed—and he'd looked. What man wouldn't? But he'd never wanted to sink himself into one of them. Never been as fascinated, as enthralled as he was with the sight before him now. With Siria.

Her clit fascinated him and he licked over it, jerking when she jerked in response, then latching onto it and sucking when he realized her reaction was one of extreme pleasure, her thrashing an indication of how sensitive the tiny knob was.

His own cock pulsed and screamed for the feel of soft lips. Hers. Jett's. It didn't matter. But Mozaiic forced his own needs aside and concentrated on Siria.

Within seconds she was writhing underneath him. Whimpering and pleading. Making his cock swell further and his balls pull more tightly against his body.

Masculine pride roared through him, along with the need to shove himself into her channel and spew his seed. But he held off, the taste and feel and smell of her wet mound too heady to give up so soon.

She screamed as she came, making his own cock throb in warning. He reached down, taking himself in hand, holding himself in order to delay release. He still wasn't ready to leave his cradle between her legs, not until he'd explored her channel with his tongue and lapped at her juices.

With one last suck her released her clit and moved lower, stopping for a moment to look at her swollen woman's flesh, open, dewy, enticing, an exotic flower meant to draw a male to it so that he'd leave his sperm, so that the next generation would be born.

"Beautiful," he whispered, his voice hoarse, nearly reverent.

With a quick flick of his tongue he explored her slit, the heat of her nearly burning his tongue, the taste of her making him ravenous. He groaned, plunging in when only seconds before he'd intended to linger, to savor, and when she widened her legs, arching into his tongue, he was completely lost. He could do nothing but yield to her silent command, fucking in and out of her with his tongue until she cried out once again in release and lay limp beneath him, not protesting when he lingered, licking her clean.

Mozaiic was rock-hard, hurting, his heart pounding as wildly as it had the first time he and Jett had made love. "Take me into you," he whispered, repositioning himself so that his face was above hers, his body above hers.

Siria's heart melted as she read the fear of rejection in his eyes. "Mozaiic," she whispered, putting her hand on his chest, unable to resist brushing her fingers over the tight male nipple.

He jerked in response, closing his eyes, whispering, "Please," and she knew he was too close to release to tease.

She trailed her hand down his tight abdomen and took his cock in her hand, reveling in its size and hardness, in the way his buttocks clenched and he pumped into her closed fist, the action and the small sound torn from him making her feel as though he belonged to her, as though she was in control of his pleasure.

Siria guided him to her entrance, smiling when he opened his eyes and immediately looked down, as though fascinated by the sight of entering her body. She was already so wet, so well prepared that despite his size, it was easy for him to slide into her, the expression of ecstasy on his face forever burned into her memory.

For a long moment he held steady, his eyes once again closing, as though he wanted to savor the moment, to memorize it. But when she wrapped her legs around his waist he was lost.

"Siria," he groaned, his first thrusts jerky, uncontrolled, torn between staying still and moving, but then he gave up the fight. His mouth covered hers, his hands went to her wrists, holding them against the couch as though he suddenly feared she would try to escape—or perhaps he feared her touch would hasten his own release. His thrusts become more aggressive, more dominant, silently demanding that she come for him again as he shifted, finding the spot where his body could strike her clit. And she responded, cresting with a scream, her inner muscles clamping down on his penis and making him come in a hot, fierce rush.

Only then did she realize Jett was in the room with them, watching, his cock in hand, his expression carnal, unpredictable, as though the sight of Mozaiic fucking her wasn't entirely pleasant to him. A look passed between the two men, and then Mozaiic rose from the couch, giving Siria a kiss before moving away and leaving her for Jett.

Chapter Four

ঞ

She started to protest, unsure whether she was ready to accept a second lover, but before she could even open her mouth, Jett was on her, pinning her down as Mozaiic had done, covering her lips with his, kissing her roughly, but making no move to impale her with his shaft.

Siria tried to fight her own out of control lust. But the battle was lost before it even began.

"Yield," he growled, his dark, dark eyes boring into hers so that she could read the desperate need in him, to have her just as Mozaiic had her, to know what it felt like to sink into a woman, to know he wouldn't be left out.

She yielded, going soft underneath him, submissive, telling him without words that he could fuck her, could have her as Mozaiic had. He groaned and covered her mouth with his, positioning himself so that he could bathe his cock in her juices, coating himself with her arousal.

Siria opened her legs wider, providing him easy access and expecting him to plunge into her, to rut wildly. But instead he growled, forcing her body down so he wouldn't be tempted by her wet sheath while he ate at her mouth.

Emotion surged through Jett, wild and unpredictable. Conflicting needs and desires assailed him. And yet the longer his body lay on Siria's soft one, the more in control he felt.

By the sands of Adjara, her body was a feast he wanted to devour! Her soft body and unfamiliar curves a miracle to embrace.

He forced himself away from her mouth and onto her breasts. The sight of them sent waves of lust through him, made him want to hold them in place and fuck his cock between them.

One day... But not today. Not this first time with a woman.

His cock was screaming, desperate to feel her wet heat. To know a woman's channel for the first time. And yet he wouldn't deny himself what Mozaiic had already experienced. Jett latched onto a nipple, his cock pulsing in time to his suckling.

Siria whimpered and writhed underneath Jett, aroused by his mouth on her breast, by the sight of Mozaiic watching them, by the thought of having both men together. She nearly beckoned Mozaiic over and, as if sensing her attention was on another man, Jett clamped down on her nipple, a sharp bite of warning followed by a gentle wash of his tongue when her eyes met his. She shivered, overwhelmed by the feelings they brought out in her, the desires she possessed but had never explored before.

Jett reluctantly pulled himself off her breast, drawn by her cunt, by her clit. He laved and sucked, fucked her with his tongue until she came, and came again, going limp underneath him.

But rather than take her the same way Mozaiic had, Jet guided her off the couch, positioning her on her hands and knees on the floor. Spreading her for his view, for his pleasure, and leaving her there, exposed, submissive, while he hovered behind her with his cock in his hands.

Every cell in Jett's body screamed for him to mount her, to take her, and yet he held off, drawing out the pleasure, the anticipation. Enjoying the dual sensation of Mozaiic's eyes on him and Siria's building tension.

He hadn't liked seeing Mozaiic on her—hadn't really expected to find them fucking when he emerged from the bathroom.

The expression of ecstasy on Mozaiic's face had been like a lance through his heart. And yet…the sight of them coupling had become more acceptable, more arousing the longer he'd watched. And once he'd touched her body, tasted her, experienced a small measure of the pleasure that a female had to offer—he couldn't begrudge Mozaiic for enjoying it, for wanting to repeat it again and again. Just as he would.

And now…he read the same mixed feelings in Mozaiic's face, saw him realize what adding a third would mean… Their eyes met, their lust for one another growing stronger because of Siria, not weaker.

Jett's nostrils flared as his attention returned to her woman's flesh, plump and glistening, beckoning, a siren's song he couldn't resist any longer. He nuzzled her, laving her with his tongue, spearing her with it, relishing the way she quivered and pushed against him, silently begging for him to take her.

She was a beautiful, exquisite. Theirs. To fuck together. To fuck alone. Theirs.

No wonder women weren't allowed on Adjara unless they were joined to a proven pair!

With a groan, he mounted her. Guiding himself to her opening and tightening his grip to keep himself from thrusting wildly. He wanted to savor this moment. This first. Just as he'd savored the first time he'd been the dominant partner with Mozaiic.

"Please," Siria whimpered, pressing against his hand, begging him for more than just the tip of his penis.

He panted in response, his cock jerking in protest of his restriction.

"Please," she begged again, her arousal washing over the head of his cock, making his hand as wet and slippery as the inside of her channel. Making it impossible to hold back any longer.

Jett surged into her, crying out in pleasure as the tight fist of her sheath quickly gripped him, pulling him in and trying to hold him there. Claiming him.

Nature took over. A male's need to thrust in and out, to rut, to mate and reproduce in a hot spew of seed. And yet Jett made sure Siria found pleasure too. His hand going around to her clit, treating it as a smaller version of Mozaiic's penis, his fingers well used to making a partner come while in this position.

Siria was weak, completely sated, barely aware of her body or her surroundings when Jett gently placed her on the couch, covering her with a blanket before moving to the bed.

Mozaiic paused long enough to kiss her before joining Jett. The sounds of their pleasure now music to Siria's ears, forcing her to sit up, to watch this time, fresh arousal flooding her system when Mozaiic positioned Jett on his hands and knees, just as Jett had done to her, both of them aware of her presence, of her watching as Mozaiic coated his penis with lubricant and then slowly prepared Jett before pressing into him, fucking him until they were both shouting in release.

Sleep settled over the men shortly after they took showers, but didn't touch Siria. She lay awake for hours. Restless. Confused. Uncertain. Reeling from what they'd told her, what they'd done to her and shown her about herself as well as their love for each other.

They'd swamped her senses, given her pleasure she never could have imagined feeling, pushed her limits to where none existed when it came to the three of them. They'd made her feel things she'd never felt before, want things she hadn't dared to hope for, especially during the last year.

But did she dare trust them with her life? Did she want to bind her life to theirs? She shivered, wondering if desperation was making her consider a course she would have once considered insane—allowing herself to be taken to Adjara.

"No woman ever leaves your planet alive," she'd said.

"True," Jett had replied. "What of it? As far as I know, none wish to leave—especially after they have given birth."

And she'd grown wet at the way his dark eyes moved over her, his thoughts as obvious as the erection pressing against his trousers.

Would it be so different to be trapped on Adjara as opposed to Qumaar? At least there she would be surrounded by desert, valued for her ability to locate water.

Siria finally gave up any attempt at sleeping, rising from the couch and casting a quick glance in their direction as she dressed, not surprised to see them soundly sleeping. She'd never traveled between planets, but she imagined it was tedious, and then there'd been the sex… She smiled, wanting to linger on those thoughts but forcing herself to move through the apartment instead, to gather the card that not only identified her but allowed her access to her credits.

With a look backward she made sure they were still sleeping, then slipped out of her apartment and into the early dawn—not to escape, but to allow herself time and opportunity to think without their presence influencing her. To ponder if this was the future her mother had seen for her so many years ago, but had masked under an interest in Adjara, leaving her daughter more informed than many, perhaps more accepting, and yet free of choice as to whether or not to embrace a different way of life, a different culture, a different and unknown world.

Mozaiic sighed, shifting to his back, counting the seconds before Jett exploded off the bed and paced over to the door, putting his hand on it before turning back and snarling, "So that's it? We let her escape?"

"And what would you have us do?"

Jett's expression mirrored the range of his emotions, finally turning mulish in an attempt to hide his fear and insecurity. "You're right, let's go. If we leave soon we should be back home with plenty of time to get things done before the wind drives us back inside."

Mozaiic's eyebrows lifted but he was careful not to let the corner of his mouth follow. "Fucking a woman was a disappointment? You found Siria unappealing? Not a good third for us?"

Jett prowled around the tiny apartment, making three loops before returning to the bed and sitting, his scowl deepening when Mozaiic rose and put an arm around his shoulder, though he didn't shake the touch off. "I hate waiting," he said.

"You have always hated waiting." This time Mozaiic did laugh. "You even hurried for your birth, kicking and pounding inside your mother's womb, your antics so obnoxious that neither of your fathers protested when she kicked you out early and named you Jett."

Jett chuckled. "Well, to hear them tell it, my sudden and rapid appearance interrupted a private moment they'd been looking forward to all day."

Mozaiic's free hand moved to Jett's chest, stroking, comforting, teasing over his tiny, hard nipple. "Let's wait a reasonable time for her to return. And if she doesn't, then we will find lodging and consider what to do next."

Jett's hand covered Mozaiic's, holding it in position over his heart. "I could love her if she'd allow me the chance."

"As could I."

Chapter Five

ℰ

Siria approached the door to her apartment with her heart in her throat. Would they still be there? Or would they have fled in fear of her reporting their presence on Qumaar?

Her hands were actually shaking when she swiped her identification card in the slot that would unlock her door.

They were there, dressed, Jett on the chair, Mozaiic on the sofa. Their expressions torn between relief and concern.

"I needed some time to think," she said, her hand waving in the direction of the bed. "Without anything distracting me." She licked her lips, nervous now, but no less committed to her decision than she had been when she'd made it while walking around, taking a last look at Qumaar, a place with so much water that she'd been forced to spend much of her life inside the apartment. "What will it mean if I go back with you?" They'd told her some of it the previous night, but she needed to ask it again, to make herself feel more confident about her choice.

Both Jett and Mozaiic came to her, surrounding her with their warmth and masculine scent, though neither touched her. "If you go back with us," Mozaiic said, "you will be our third. The mother of our children. Our partner. You will be a respected member of our tribe, but you will also be expected to accept our way of life completely. It's hard at times, and yet simple compared to many worlds. But our rules are strictly enforced and the punishment for breaking them often harsh."

She searched his face, looking for some clue as to what he might be warning her against, but finally gave up and asked. "Is there some rule you're worried about in particular?"

Jett shoved his hands into his pockets, his shoulders hunching slightly as he blurted out an answer. "You were selected for us when we requested a third. Matched to us by some process we know nothing about." He cut a sideways glance at Mozaiic before mumbling, "We could both come to love you as much as we love each other. We want you as our third. But once a joining takes place it is difficult to undo it…" He stumbled to a halt.

Mozaiic said, "To break an oath as serious as a commitment vow is to be cast out of the tribe, left in the desert to live or die as the sands will it."

"A woman's punishment only?" Siria asked, her outrage quelled before it could build when Mozaiic quickly shook his head and said, "No. Our laws do not favor men over women."

She relaxed, thinking about what they were saying, accepting it. She could love them, too. She wouldn't have been able to give herself to them if she couldn't. And she'd witnessed their caring, even longed to be cared for in the same way.

"Okay, I can live with that," she said.

They both reached for her, pulling her into a loose embrace. "We can allow you time to get to know us better before we return to Adjara," Mozaiic said.

"Because once I'm on Adjara, then I can't leave."

Mozaiic shrugged. "There are exceptions. But our women are too few, too valuable, so it is rare for them to leave."

"Your mothers?"

Both men laughed. "Very much alive and no doubt wondering where we're off to," Jett answered. "When we got word that our Petition for Joining had been granted we left so quickly neither of us thought to send word to our families until we were nearly here."

Siria smiled in response to their obvious respect and love for their mothers, their families. Joining. She liked the sound of that. She was also touched by their willingness to stay on Qumaar, despite the danger it held for them. "There's not much point in staying here now that I've decided to go home with you," she said, her emotion swelling when she saw how happy her words made them.

"You'll be our third?" Mozaiic asked, both of them taking one of her hands and placing it over their hearts so she could feel the wild beat of hope.

"I'll be your third."

"We leave now?" Jett asked.

Siria looked around her apartment with the knowledge that most of what she treasured already lived in her memory. A small smile played over her lips as she realized she'd like to add one more memory before she left. She kissed Jett and then Mozaiic before whispering, "Not right away. I want you both at the same time before we leave." Their surprised expressions made her laugh out loud and the hands holding hers against their hearts were unresisting when she pulled away to stroke over their erections and add, "My bed's not big enough for the three of us, pull the blankets off and get the extra ones out of the closet. You two can prepare a place for us while I take a shower."

She took a long shower, letting their anticipation build, knowing they'd wait and not start without her. And when she finally emerged from the bathroom, they were just as she'd pictured they'd be, naked, stretched out on their sides with just enough space between them for her. It was definitely a sight she could enjoy seeing often.

Siria joined them, going to her knees and gently pushing them to their backs, trailing her hands over their chests, teasing the tiny nipples, so much smaller than her own, then trailing lower, cupping their testicles, weighing them, before circling their penises, both of them content to let her explore their bodies this time, though she could already see which one of them would break first. With a small feminine smile, she leaned over, kissing Mozaiic then Jett. Laving and sucking Mozaiic's nipple, then Jett's. Slowly moving down their bodies and feeling them tense under her attention, waiting for the moment when her lips touched their cocks.

With a groan, Jett jerked upright as her tongue swirled around his navel, his hands fisting in her hair, forcing her into position over his straining, wet penis. "Now," he groaned, impatience and need resonating in the single word and she laughed softly, her earlier guess confirmed, then took him in her mouth, tormenting him with the swirl of her tongue and the suction of her mouth until he was hunched, his hands cupping and playing with her nipples while he pressed hungry kisses along her spine.

The sight of Siria pleasuring Jett with her mouth was almost more than Mozaiic could stand, the sounds they were making and the image of her breasts being fondled by Jett as they hung heavy and full from her slight frame were enough to make Mozaiic take his own cock in hand in order to avoid orgasm.

For several long minutes he just watched, but then the need to participate became overwhelming. The need to see her swollen folds, to run his tongue through her slit and taste her arousal consumed him.

Mozaiic moved behind Siria, glorying in the sight of her taut buttocks, unable to resist the urge to rub his cheeks against them and gently nip, the gesture making her spread her legs and give him a glimpse of her wet cunt.

With a groan, Mozaiic pressed his hand between her thighs, forcing them to open wider so that he could gain access to her erect clit and slick channel. She jerked as his fingers circled the tiny knob, its hood already pulled back to expose the sensitive head. And he found pleasure in tormenting her clit just as ruthlessly as she was tormenting Jett's cock, Mozaiic's own lust growing as he watched Jett's face tighten, his body shake as he grew closer and closer to release. With a groan, Mozaiic also leaned over Siria, his fingers plunging into her sheath, fucking her roughly as his lips moved along her spine toward Jett, only lifting from Siria's back and meeting Jett's mouth when he felt the first deep tremors of release as her inner muscles tightened on his fingers.

Jett was overwhelmed by sensation and emotion unlike any he had known before, or imagined. With a series of jerks he came, his release washing down Siria's throat as he cried his pleasure into Mozaiic's mouth. And even then he lingered for long moments afterward, not wanting to lose the feel of their lips against him.

It was Mozaiic who pulled away first, his mouth leaving Jett's and going to Siria's shoulders, kissing her as his hands forced Jett's away from her breasts so that he could cup and play with them.

Siria laughed, straightening, her hands covering Mozaiic's as she leaned forward and kissed Jett before turning and pushing Mozaiic onto his back. But rather than follow him over, she moved around, straddling him, presenting him with a sight that she already knew fascinated him.

He groaned in response and plunged his tongue into her slit, lapping and eating hungrily at her as she lay along his body, taking his cock in her mouth.

The sight of Mozaiic and Siria pleasuring each other orally had Jett's penis engorged within seconds, and made him desperate to explore one of her tight openings with his cock.

She'd said that she wanted to have them both at the same time and now he couldn't get the thought out of his mind. Of taking her as Mozaiic took her. Both of them in her body, their cocks rubbing against each other in her wet heat, separated by such a thin barrier that it would be almost nonexistent, making it seem as though they were together, joined intimately and deeply, a trio instead of a pair.

Jett found the lubricant and positioned himself next to them, his cock pulsing when Mozaiic's hands spread her buttocks, presenting the tiny rosette so that Jett could begin working first the lubricant and then his fingers into her back entrance.

Within minutes Siria was shaking with need, the assault on both her ass and cunt making her suck harder, more hungrily on Mozaiic's penis, as though she could pull her own release through it. Her actions driving his, until they were both writhing, pressing, bucking against each other.

She didn't resist when they rolled her to her back, Jett moving between her legs, latching onto her clit with his mouth while his fingers continued to prepare her anus, Mozaiic moving to her breasts, suckling there until his own penis was hard and full again.

By then the tears streamed down Siria's cheeks, her body so aroused, so needy that she thought she'd die if they didn't put their cocks in her. "Oh yes," she cried in relief when Mozaiic pulled her on top of him, impaling her with one sure thrust as his hands once again spread her buttocks for Jett.

Only instead of fingers, this time it was Jett's cock that slid into her anus. One slow inch at a time. His presence making her feel so full, so complete, so well loved that Siria knew she'd never want to do without this. "Oh, yes," she whispered again, her fingers spearing through Mozaiic's hair, her own desire building when she read the hungry need in his, the joy he found in the tightness of her channel and the presence of Jett's penis so close to his own.

Sweat glistened on Jett's body, his breathing little more than a series of shallow pants by the time he was fully seated in her anus. For a moment he was overcome, not only by the exquisite sensation of being in her body like this, but by Siria herself. By her trust. Her generosity. Her openness and willingness to accept not only what they needed from her, but what they needed from each other.

He pressed a kiss to her shoulder in gratitude, knowing that he would never be able to come up with the right words, but promising himself that he would always try to come up with the right actions to show her how much he valued her as their third. And then Mozaiic moved, the feel of his penis against Jett's leaving no room for thought. No room for anything but thrust and counterthrust, for touching and caressing, for kisses and hungry bites as they raced out of control toward a peak higher than any they'd ever known before, toward ecstasy.

A homecoming.

A joining.

About the Author

෨

Jory has been writing since childhood and has never outgrown being a daydreamer. When she's not hunched over her computer, lost in the muse and conjuring up new heroes and heroines, she can usually be found reading, riding her horses, or hiking with her dogs.

Jory welcomes mail from readers. You can write to her c/o Ellora's Cave Publishing at 1056 Home Avenue, Akron, OH 44310-3502.

Also by Jory Strong

෨

Carnival Tarot 1: Sarael's Reading
Carnival Tarot 2: Kiziah's Reading
Carnival Tarot 3: Dakotah's Reading
Crime Tells 1: Lyric's Cop
Crime Tells 2: Cady's Cowboy
Crime Tells 3: Calista's Men
Fallon Mates 1: Binding Krista
Fallon Mates 2: Zeraac's Miracle
Supernatural Bonds 1: Trace's Psychic
Supernatural Bonds 2: Storm's Faeries
The Angelini 1: Skye's Trail
The Angelini 2: Syndelle's Possession

Why an electronic book?

We live in the Information Age—an exciting time in the history of human civilization in which technology rules supreme and continues to progress in leaps and bounds every minute of every hour of every day. For a multitude of reasons, more and more avid literary fans are opting to purchase e-books instead of paperbacks. The question to those not yet initiated to the world of electronic reading is simply: *why?*

1. *Price.* An electronic title at Ellora's Cave Publishing and Cerridwen Press runs anywhere from 40-75% less than the cover price of the <u>exact same title</u> in paperback format. Why? Cold mathematics. It is less expensive to publish an e-book than it is to publish a paperback, so the savings are passed along to the consumer.

2. *Space.* Running out of room to house your paperback books? That is one worry you will never have with electronic novels. For a low one-time cost, you can purchase a handheld computer designed specifically for e-reading purposes. Many e-readers are larger than the average handheld, giving you plenty of screen room. Better yet, hundreds of titles can be stored within your new library—a single microchip. (Please note that Ellora's Cave and Cerridwen Press does not endorse any specific brands. You can check our website at www.ellorascave.com or

www.cerridwenpress.com for customer recommendations we make available to new consumers.)

3. *Mobility.* Because your new library now consists of only a microchip, your entire cache of books can be taken with you wherever you go.

4. *Personal preferences are accounted for.* Are the words you are currently reading too small? Too large? Too...**ANNOYING**? Paperback books cannot be modified according to personal preferences, but e-books can.

5. *Instant gratification.* Is it the middle of the night and all the bookstores are closed? Are you tired of waiting days — sometimes weeks — for online and offline bookstores to ship the novels you bought? Ellora's Cave Publishing sells instantaneous downloads 24 hours a day, 7 days a week, 365 days a year. Our e-book delivery system is 100% automated, meaning your order is filled as soon as you pay for it.

Those are a few of the top reasons why electronic novels are displacing paperbacks for many an avid reader. As always, Ellora's Cave and Cerridwen Press welcomes your questions and comments. We invite you to email us at service@ellorascave.com, service@cerridwenpress.com or write to us directly at: 1056 Home Ave. Akron OH 44310-3502.

THE
☥ ELLORA'S CAVE ☥
LIBRARY

Stay up to date with Ellora's Cave Titles in
Print with our Quarterly Catalog.

To receive a catalog,
send an email with your name
and mailing address to:

CATALOG@ELLORASCAVE.COM

or send a letter or postcard
with your mailing address to:

Catalog Request
c/o Ellora's Cave Publishing, Inc.
1056 Home Avenue
Akron, Ohio 44310-3502

erridwen, the Celtic Goddess of wisdom, was the muse who brought inspiration to story-tellers and those in the creative arts. Cerridwen Press encompasses the best and most innovative stories in all genres of today's fiction. Visit our site and discover the newest titles by talented authors who still get inspired - much like the ancient storytellers did, once upon a time.

Cerridwen Press

www.cerridwenpress.com

ELLORA'S CAVEMEN: *LEGENDARY TAILS IV*

ဢ

Orgasm Fairy
By Ashleigh Raine

~

For Orgasm Fairy Cammie Witherspoon, frustration is a way of life. She helps people deal with their sexual frustration every day, but nothing and no one can help ease her own. You see, Orgasm Fairies can't orgasm. It's part of their curse.

Crystal-eyed, dark haired, and all-over hottie Neal Fallon is determined to seduce Cammie. And even though nothing can "come" of it, she knows Neal will make her feel more than she's felt in a very long time.

Boy oh boy, is she in for a wicked good surprise.

Overcome
By Marly Chance

~

"Have you ever been ravished?" The question uttered in that sexy masculine voice sent Ansley reeling. Held captive on a hostile planet and scheduled for interrogation, agent Ansley Morgan is shocked when her former partner appears. She is even more surprised to discover that he is supposed to be her Enraptor, paid by the enemy to forcibly seduce her into revealing information. Is he there to help her or betray her?

Secrets We Keep
By Mandy M. Roth

~

Trisha hasn't been able to keep a lasting relationship to save her life. When one of the string of losers she dates asks her to marry him, she says yes, thinking it beats being alone. Besides, the man of her dreams doesn't view her as anything more than friend.

Dane can't get his best friend Trisha out of his head. She consumes his every thought. He's wanted her for seven years but mating with a human is forbidden. It's not every day a human learns of their existence and it's not every day a lycan gives himself over to someone unconditionally.

A Love Eternal
By N.J. Walters

~

Sitting alone on a bridge late one night, Genevieve Alexander laments her safe, boring life. But when she attracts the attention of a dangerous, mysterious stranger known only as Seth, her entire world changes.

Accompanying him on his nocturnal journey through the dark streets and into the throbbing nightlife of the city, he introduces her to a world of sensual desires unlike anything she's ever experienced. But Seth has a terrifying secret. Will she be able to throw off the shackles of her past and accept the risks that come with being with this sexy, compelling man?

Keeper of Tomorrows
By Ravyn Wilde

~

Raine opened her door late one night to a tall, dark haired man. A man from another dimension who swears he's waited centuries just for her. Will a passionate night of show and tell convince Raine of her destiny?

Talon needs his Keeper to accept him as the man he truly is. Their worlds, *all worlds*, need a matched Guardian pair to save mankind from untold evil. This may be his last chance to persuade her of what a life together might be like. He can offer her adventure, love, and his body for eternity. Will it be enough?

Seeds of Yesterday
By Jaid Black

~

The wealthy and influential Hunter family never thought much of Trina Pittman. Born on the wrong side of the tracks, Trina wasn't considered a worthy choice of a friend for their daughter, Amy. Being disliked by Amy's parents had been tough on Trina while growing up, but putting up with Amy's older brother, Daniel, had been brutal. Those dark, brooding eyes of his had followed her around high school - judging her, reminding her she'd never be good enough for them. It was almost a relief when Amy was shipped off to boarding school, permanently forcing the two girls apart. Fifteen years later, Amy's tragic death reunites Trina with her past...and with Daniel.

COMING TO A BOOKSTORE NEAR YOU!

ELLORA'S CAVE

Bestselling Authors Tour

UPDATES AVAILABLE AT

WWW.ELLORASCAVE.COM

Discover for yourself why readers can't get enough of the multiple award-winning publisher

Ellora's Cave.

Whether you prefer e-books or paperbacks,

be sure to visit EC on the web at
www.ellorascave.com

for an erotic reading experience that will leave you breathless.